SECRETS IN THE TALLGRASS

SECRETS IN THE TALLGRASS

by **Jeza Belle**

RESOURCE *Publications* · Eugene, Oregon

SECRETS IN THE TALLGRASS

Resource Publications
An Imprint of Wipf and Stock Publishers
199 W. 8th Ave., Suite 3
Eugene, OR 97401

www.wipfandstock.com

PAPERBACK ISBN: 979-8-3852-7715-5
HARDCOVER ISBN: 979-8-3852-7716-2
EBOOK ISBN: 979-8-3852-7717-9

VERSION NUMBER 040126

To my readers, my friends, my fellow LGBTQIA+ community members, and our many supportive allies, all of whom are struggling immensely during these troubling times.

Living free *is* rebellion. Keep being.
Existing *is* a threat. Keep breathing.
Loving *is* universal. Keep sharing your heart.
Divine love *is* given to us all. Keep basking in the glow of God's love.
Earthly sunlight *always* returns in the morning, but heavenly sunshine reigns eternal.

"They are not two, yet the form is twofold."

Ovid, Metamorphoses

Contents

Acknowledgements

My Husband- for always being there.

Dylan Garity- for another great job as editor.

Wipf and Stock / Resource Publications- for allowing me to see The Presence Collection come to life. I will never forget the incredible team of people at this organization who are full of warmth and kindness of spirit.

Prologue

Newton, Kansas

June 18, 1866

Steady rain fell onto the sea of swaying buffalo grass. Alongside a dirt road, a single hickory tree stood above several wooden crosses, which sat atop a couple of dozen oval mounds. Some of the graves were heaped high with fresh dirt, while others had settled over time and grown over with Berlandier's Flax, the yellow-orange flowers now drinking up the storm water.

Standing over one of the newest burial sites, a priest recited prayers. The woman next to him, dressed in all black, held an umbrella over her head with one hand. With the other, she clutched a large silver cross that dangled around her neck. The tears that flowed down her cheeks were indistinguishable from the ones God was spitting out from the heavens above on this moody afternoon.

Off in the near distance stood a gruff and unkempt figure. The man wore a rain-soaked poncho that hung over his lumbering frame. His head was gently bent down in reverence, causing the water to rush off the brim of his hat, past his stubbled chin, and into a pool of pity alongside his boots.

As the priest finished and made the sign of the cross, the man lifted his unshaven face, and as he did so, he caught the woman's eyes, causing her to stop herself in the middle of a sob.

"You savage!" she screamed at him over a chorus of thunder.

For a moment, he held her gaze as if he were Ares and she Athena, both gods of their realms and siblings. Yet each was committed to war, though he was motivated by outright fury and she cold calculation.

At last, the man was broken by the moment, turning to walk to the horse that was standing nearby. He mounted his steed quickly, then rode it hard across the vast plains toward his barely visible homestead, which was but a lone and distant dot of civilization on an endless landscape.

"I'll never forgive you for killing my sister . . ." the woman's voice receded into the wind.

Chiverie

New Orleans

May 1, 1866

"Alone at last," Remy declared in a husky French accent, closing the hotel room door behind him.

Phreddie backed up against the wall as he moved toward her, 175 pounds of newly minted husband. Remy might as well have been a team of wild horses pulling a wagon of lead downhill the way he roared forward.

"And now," he declared as his lips closed in on her neck, "you cannot deny me what I have wanted all of these long weeks of betrothal . . . Mrs. Delaroux."

The streetlamp flickered outside the window, but all the fiery gas in New Orleans was nothing compared to what burned in Phreddie's belly at Remy's touch. She could not help but get lost in the kisses that made their way over to her lips, and she let out a moan half made up of desire and half fear.

"God, I love you," she said through labored breath.

"No more protests of chastity. We are wed now," Remy said as he moved in. "We have a few short hours alone, and then we must catch the first of our ships to the continent and my waiting father."

His forceful tongue pinned her head against the bedroom wall, and his hands freely roamed her bosom. They plunged into the top of Phreddie's bridal dress until they released her breasts, which encouraged Remy's mouth to move down toward the erect, ripe nipples that sat atop those soft mounds.

"Remy," Phreddie called out in between her cries of ecstasy. Never before had a man touched her so intimately. Had she known the power of passion, and had she not been so afraid, she might have let herself slip into his grasp sooner.

Their lightning-speed romance had been a surprise to those around them, but most of all to Phreddie. Only six weeks had passed since Remy and she met at the Guidry Mansion over on St. Charles Avenue. Phreddie had worked there as a laundress for the past two years since she aged out of the orphanage.

Just out from under the ever-watchful eyes of the Catholic home's strict nuns, Phreddie had adapted easily to Mrs. Guidry's nonnegotiable rule that her household staff be like the famous New Orleans spirits. Ghosts drifted between moments the way maids and laundresses were expected to pass between the rooms of the house: unseen and unheard, unless their betters chose to notice them. And in the rare air of life at the Guidry, there was little expectation that family members or guests would behave as coarse mediums and call forth to the cold souls of that world's somber spirits.

That was why, when Phreddie tripped on a rug with a basket full of clean linens right in front of the visiting Delaroux son, who had just concluded his business luncheon with the elder Guidry, she lost her position instantly. However, much to the disappointment of Mrs. Guidry, who believed in clear lines of class demarcation, Phreddie gained the interest of the young man whose handsome features had caused her to trip in the first place.

"And your name is?" Remy had asked as he helped her back onto her feet. She could not stop herself from getting lost in his eyes. They were like the fine blue porcelain teacups in which Mrs. Guidry served all of her visitors steaming Earl Grey. Yet hot water over dried leaves and bergamot would have seemed as cool as a fall evening compared to the warmth Phreddie felt in her loins when she looked at Remy's deep eyes and those full, long, dark eyelashes. She caught herself staring and bit her lower lip to calm her nerves.

When he stooped down beside her and handed her the corner of a fallen bedsheet, his hand brushed up against her own, and a small moan escaped her. "Phreddie," she released in answer to his question, though she was not sure if she had actually spoken or only mouthed it, because she had now caught sight of his beautiful lips.

By the time Remy had helped her refold all of the sheets, Mrs. Guidry's ire had been invoked beyond repair, and the unstoppable passions of two young lovers from different worlds had been ignited.

"I will make love to you, my wife," he whispered to her now in their hotel room.

While the urgency of his words filled her with unimaginable fire, the truth gnawed at her insides.

Why didn't I tell him weeks ago? she wondered to herself as the seconds grew more heated. Love was so heady that it pulled her downstream, as if she had been caught in a flash flood, and that one moment in which she'd sought to lay herself bare had never quite presented itself. It was too late now, as she had already been swept away and over the falls.

At last, though his caresses made her head spin, just as his words and deeds had during these last six weeks, she knew that she must declare herself, as the hour to do so had long passed.

"Do you really love me?" she blurted out frantically.

"*Oui*," he answered into her breasts.

"Is it unconditional, the same way I love you?"

"Of course, *mon amour*." He sighed as he made his way back up to her mouth and plunged his tongue inside.

She pushed him out and pressed, "No matter what?" Her voice trembled from something between terror and ecstasy.

He moved his mouth toward her ear, and his hot breath tickled her lobe. "*Oui*, Phreddie. Yes," he declared. "There is nothing you can do or say to change my love for you."

She was on the verge of completely losing herself once more, but she regained her composure just long enough to lift her own lips up to his lobe this time. Her jaw clenched before she sucked in a breath and released a soft and tentative whisper into his ear.

Suddenly Remy's kisses ceased, and his arms grew stiff. Then, he reached down, his hands disappearing beneath Phreddie's ivory hemline.

"*Quoi*?" he asked, confusion spreading across his face.

"I wanted to tell you sooner," she blurted out in a panicked shrill, but it was too late.

Her husband's eyes widened.

"I couldn't b-b-bring myself to . . ." she started to stutter. "I was afraid to . . ."

"To do what, you *chienne*?" he asked, venom in his voice. "To tell me the truth?"

Phreddie's lips quivered as she watched Remy's beautiful face begin to twist with rage.

"I expected one thing from you, Phreddie," he spat. "Honesty."

The word hung in the air like smoke exhaled from the lips of a cheating parlor room card player.

"My love *is* honest," she began, but the words fell to the floor in bereavement, just like his smile had done seconds ago. Remy and she had only just declared their love as husband and wife in front of a minister hours ago, and here it seemed to be dead before it had lived legally for even an afternoon.

"My father warned me that Americans were greedy." Remy started to pace. "He told me that they would stop at nothing to get their hands on our fortune, but this? I thought you were different. A quiet little field mouse that I plucked out of the gutter, who would make the perfect mother to my children."

Phreddie watched him put his head between his hands, and they both stood there in silence for a moment, until his frame began to shake.

"I picked you!" Spittle flew out with his words. "You were nothing to begin with but a set of meek tits and fertile loins to unassumingly bear me Delaroux babies, and again, to nothing you will return!"

"Remy—" she started, but he held up his palm to silence her.

"How could you have kept this a secret for so long? How could I not have known? And why in *merde's* sake did you not tell me rather than let me go to the altar in God's presence?"

"You have no idea how many times I tr—" Phreddie started to cry, but Remy's fist found her mouth before she could finish her answer.

Blood drooled out from between her lips and spilled onto her white dress.

"Thief," he said as he lifted his hands once more. "You will not get a silver penny from me for this charade." His right fist jabbed into the air.

"Remy, please! I don't care about your money," she sobbed as she threw herself out of his line of fire. On the bed, she picked up her veil and pressed its lace against her mouth. "I just cared about your love."

"*Je vais te tuer, putain*," he screamed, more violently than before.

Remy turned around and lifted up the wooden chair that had been placed in the corner of their well-appointed hotel room. He hoisted it into the air, then slammed it down onto the floor, where it shattered into pieces. He tore off one of the legs, now attached only by shards of broken timber, and lifted its jagged knifelike point.

"Did you think that I would accept your duplicity?" He fumed as he stepped over to her. "You will not make an *imbécile* out of me."

Phreddie tried to back away further, but there was no place left to go. "But if you love me . . ." Her heart hurt worse than her jaw.

"*Amour*?" he roared. "I might have loved, had it been born in truth. Had I been given the chance to decide. But I cannot love a falsifier. And I cannot be wedded to a . . . a . . ."

Phreddie cried as Remy lunged for her with the spike. Letting out a small yelp, she nervously leapt aside, which caused Remy to miss and slam hard into the wall.

"You are a *connasse*," he yelled. Then he stood up and began to laugh at his own words. "A cunt?" He chuckled to himself. "If only."

At first, his laugh was ironic, then it became maniacal, and Phreddie knew now that she had only seconds to escape the room before her worst nightmare came to pass. The one she feared more than anything in the world. The horrible dream she knew would become her reality. She would die at the hands of the first man who bedded her.

It was too late to escape, though. Remy was already halfway across the room, and she would have no time to open the door, let alone turn her body around in acres of bridal dress and get out of his way. So she closed her eyes and braced herself for death's impact, but it never came.

Instead, there was a loud crash.

When Phreddie opened her eyes, she looked down and found Remy on the floor, his ankle caught on the edge of the bed. His body was stretched out, and the wooden stake he'd pulled from the chair was lodged in his throat.

The only thing Phreddie could think was that, in his flight toward her death, Remy must have tripped and impaled himself on the wooden blade.

"Oh, Remy," she screamed. She threw herself onto the floor in an attempt to save her new husband.

"Let me pull this out," she said frantically, but he shook his head no, all while his throat gurgled with blood and his body convulsed.

Thinking removing the makeshift blade would save his life, Phreddie ignored him, and with a quick tug of her rapidly shaking hands, she yanked it from his body. Blood began spurting out in rhythmic beats, until Remy's pulsing heart pumped no more and the flow slowed, then stilled.

Phreddie stood up and moved away from her husband's body until she had backed up against the door. With her eyes as dead as her love, she slid down onto her backside. There, in shades of white meant to signify eternal commitment mixed with the blood of her "till death do us part," Phreddie held up the bloodied wooden shaft and cried uncontrollably.

•

Phreddie did not know how long she had been slumped against that hotel room wall. It might have been seconds, or it could have been days. But when the stupor lifted from her clouded head, she realized that if she stayed there any longer, if she did not get up off that floor and make a plan, she would be as dead as Remy.

Any woman found with Remy's blood all over her dress and a makeshift spike in her hands would be headed for the noose for his murder—or worse, if his family were the judge and jury. It would not matter that Phreddie had not killed him. It would not matter that she was more frightened wallflower than criminal and that it had been an accidental death. She hadn't even known or employed any form of self-defense against her enraged husband, though her split lip and the torn-up room might imply otherwise. No one would believe her, especially once the full story came to light.

One simply did not harm anyone in the Delaroux family, for it was a powerful clan both in Europe and in New Orleans. During their courtship, Remy had told Phreddie about his father, Aloïs Delaroux, one of the wealthiest men in Occitanie. He'd made his first fortune on the backs of slaves at a series of sugarcane plantations his family owned on the Caribbean island of Martinique.

He'd found his second, even bigger, pot of gold when he founded a manufacturing and distribution empire in New Orleans that saw the cane's fine, crystalized grains rolled out by cheap labor and sent all over the world. The war had impacted many of the sugar refineries in the lower confederacy, but due to Aloïs's ruthless business sense, his was one of only a handful of plants that managed to keep lucrative contracts on both sides of the conflict. After all, whether they supported the gray or blue, no one liked their coffee bitter. The profitable powder might as well have been diamonds, as people from far and wide craved it with an addictive passion that meant the Delaroux's riches knew no end.

When Aloïs had recently returned to his home town of Toulouse to attend to family matters, Remy and his older brother, Oscar, were left to see to their father's interests in the Crescent City. With money came potency, and sugar had given the Delaroux men the force to control many aspects of life in their city.

Over candlelit dinners, Remy explained to Phreddie how he spent most of his time filling orders and outsmarting competitors, ensuring that the Delaroux financial engine flowed unhindered at any cost. During these heady champagne evenings of conversation and courtship, the couple, both dressed in their finest, shared as much of their souls as either was willing to offer prior to entering into *I dos*, when warts and character flaws tended to reveal themselves.

And while handsome women, single and married alike, batted lashes and heaved their bosoms toward Remy wherever he and Phreddie went, and though he described himself as somewhat ruthless at business, Remy had given Phreddie nothing less than his undivided and gentle attention. So much so that for a time she had even forgotten that she was different from most other women. Remy had loved her, and when he got down on one knee, her difference left her mind completely. In its place was the thrill of acceptance and even adoration.

The thought of their romance made her foot begin to go numb, so Phreddie shook it to wake it up. She begged it to fold up under her body and propel her legs to push her up off the now sticky floor. But instead, her foot and the rest of her body lay lifeless, her toes stinging with pins and needles. The tingle caused Phreddie to remember the first time she had met Remy's brother, Oscar.

It was the night he had taken her to see Jules Massenet's *Le roi de Lahore* at the Théâtre de l'Opéra. Her head had still been filled with visions of Sita and Alim in the Temple of Indra, and Remy was walking her toward her modest lodgings when they came upon a fight between two men.

Up until this point, Remy had said little about his older brother beyond mentioning his insatiable interest in women and his enjoyment in pulling the heads off bugs. Phreddie had laughed at this description of Oscar, as she'd believed that her fiancé was merely referring to a childhood remembrance of a rough-and-tumble brother. After all, all men had once lived their youth as boys somewhere between lustful hormones and an interest in creepy things that crawled in the dirt.

However, as they turned the corner onto Esplanade Avenue, near where Phreddie let a room in a nearby boarding house, Remy's eyes widened. "*Merde*," he shouted, unhooking his arm from Phreddie's and running the few paces down the block to the scene of the altercation.

When Phreddie approached, she saw a man with his boot on the face of another man, who was quivering on the ground. The attacker looked similar to Remy—his hair was a mess of blond curls instead of brunette, but his eyes were the same pools of azure.

"Please, Mr. Delaroux," a man called from between cement and a leather sole in an Italian accent, "I meant no insult."

"Just do it already," shouted a woman who was standing nearby with hands on her hips. She was wearing a tight fitted corset, and her bare ankles advertised her position. "I told you he reached out and slapped my bum when we passed by."

Remy put his hand on this man's shoulder to steady him, but it was too little, too late. Oscar's foot lifted slightly, then fell hard onto the crying man's European peasant features. There was a crack, and Phreddie cringed as blood shot out from under Oscar's shoe. The street woman laughed crudely, and Oscar looked up and smiled at her before he joyfully walked over and introduced himself to a trembling Phreddie, wiping his boot on the sidewalk as he spoke.

"At last, *la femme qui a le cœur de mon frère*. I can see why you have captured my brother's heart," he cooed, as if he had not just gravely harmed a man on a public street.

The casualness of the assault terrified Phreddie. She thought about breaking things off with Remy right then because of that fear. Oscar's boot might be a welcome response in comparison to what he'd do when Phreddie's own offense was uncovered. But her feelings for her lover were too strong, and she convinced herself all would be well if she just trusted those feelings.

Phreddie had never been in love before, and so she'd believed that Remy would protect her from the world. Only in the end, he had proven as reliably unreliable as all men, and as a result, his kindness had melted into hot fury. Now he lay as motionless as that Italian man on the street, and Phreddie would not escape blame.

So, she finally lifted herself off the floor with great effort, then changed out of her wedding clothes. Once she had on one of the fresh, blood-free dresses she had packed for the honeymoon trip they had been set to embark on later that evening, she bent down over the body and lifted Remy's wallet out of his breast pocket. Phreddie took all the money and the tickets her dead husband had on him. She folded them up and placed them into her small handbag before she made her way out of the room and down into the lobby, where she smiled and nodded nervously at the staff who extended their congratulations to her on her marriage.

Once she made it outside, she realized she had been holding her breath since she left the hotel room, and so she gulped and heaved to take in some air. Then she made her way down the streets. Occasionally she would glance suspiciously at the handful of Union troops who remained behind to guard the city even after the great capitulation at Appomattox last year. But mostly she kept her head down and pressed her feet onward, until at last she reached the Port of New Orleans.

Her hands shook as she forced a smile and handed the docked ship's attendant the papers she had taken from Remy's breast pocket.

"Ah." He smiled widely as he led her up the gangway. "Congratulations, Mrs. Delaroux, but we were expecting both you and your mister on this passage."

Phreddie handed the man a dollar bill. "Mr. Delaroux had important business come up unexpectedly and urged me to go ahead of him, as he now plans to take the train to meet me when we port in several days."

"And your bags?" the attendant asked.

"Coming soon by servants," she replied coolly.

The man clasped his hand around the tip and shrugged. "Not a bad life, marrying one of the richest men in New Orleans, then?" he joked. "You get a stateroom on the newest steam engine all to yourself. That's a holiday no woman, including my own wife, would say no to."

Phreddie feigned a giggle, then turned and boarded the ship. She walked to the top deck, where she leaned on the rail and looked out at the city.

You will die alone, Phreddie, she heard the harsh voice of Sister Adrienne echo in her mind. *Not even your parents wanted you.* Though the memory saddened Phreddie, the nun's prediction looked to be coming true.

"What was I thinking?" she asked herself.

Chaton, the gulf wind purred, and she recalled how Remy had often whispered this term to her. She *had been* his kitten from their very first moment together. Remy was warm and inviting, so unlike the sisters and the other children at the orphanage with their cruel taunts and fists. Phreddie had melted at the affection Remy had supplied and the gentle words with which he would caress her heart as if they were rose oil. But those soft words were gone in a hurricane of blood, and now all that she could do was wait for the storm surge to subside and calmer weather to return. Phreddie decided that she would start over in a new location, but this time, she would not allow herself to dream. She would never trust a man, and more importantly, she would under no circumstances ever allow herself to fall in love again.

•

Oscar Delaroux was enjoying himself in Hermance Marie Broussard's establishment on Delphine Street. This particular house was known only to well-heeled customers, such as the local *politique*, former Union generals, and visiting businessmen who were in the city for dealings with important tradesmen like Oscar's father, Aloïs. Hermance's brothel was better known to locals as Melancon Manor, bearing the moniker of the proprietor's husband, who had mysteriously disappeared almost a decade before Hermance refashioned their stately home into a house of pleasure.

Oscar lay in bed on the second floor. Hermance kept this room open at all times in case he showed up looking for a payout of some sort or another. On this night, Oscar preferred the company of Mahogany Montigny, Delphine Street's most sought-after woman. Few, though, had access to her, and even fewer the kind of access that Oscar did.

Having spent himself more than once, Oscar lay naked between Mahogany's Creole breasts, which resembled local, fleshy Misbelief fruit that had turned from yellow to caramel and were ready to be juiced like apricots. When there was a knock on the door, his first instinct was to reach under the pillow and pull out his Colt Single Action Army revolver, otherwise known as the "Peacemaker," and train it on the door.

One thing Oscar had learned on his journey from sugarman's son to well-known privileged prick was that there was always someone waiting around the corner for you. Most anger toward him stemmed from jealousy of his station and not his reputation for being an irreparable *connard*, or so Oscar thought. Fortunately for him, his daddy's Morgan dollars meant he had a large contingent of paid protectors inside every bar and brothel near and far, who kept their pockets heavy and their bellies full with the beer and whiskey that his Delaroux gold bought them.

Oscar looked at Mahogany, then nodded toward the door. She slipped out of bed with a sheet wrapped around her and cracked it open.

"Yes?" she said softly.

"Is Mr. Delaroux still there?" a man's voice asked.

Mahogany opened her mouth to answer, but Oscar called out, "It's just Luke. Let him in."

Two men in their late twenties entered. Luke had a brown mustache that matched his suit. He was followed by Landy, a thin man with hair as white as snow and a permanent scowl. While Luke had a strong jaw and green eyes like lily pads on a still pond, Landy looked as if all of the color of life had drained out through the tips of his follicles and somehow rendered him speechless. Landy was, in fact, a mute.

"What is so important that you need to interrupt Miss Mahogany's magic?" Oscar teased, placing the barrel of his pistol down over his nakedness to shield it from view.

"I think it's best you get dressed," Luke said with concern in his voice.

"Did Landy try to choke another of Hermance's girls?" Oscar asked him before turning to Landy. "You have got to stop being so rough with *les filles*," he admonished, then got out of bed and began to slip on his pants. "I'll go down and sort it out, but *bon sang*, this better be the last time!"

"It's not that," Luke said, lowering his eyes. "It's Remy."

"Remy?" Oscar buttoned his shirt. "Remy is fucking his way to heaven right now in *chiverie* with his matronly wife *avec les gros seins*," he said, laughing and cupping his hands in the air as if handling a set of large breasts. "What could possibly be wrong with him?"

"One of the maids found footprints outside the hotel room door," Luke said.

Oscar sat back down on the bed and pulled his shoes on, then began to lace them up. "Footprints? What kind of footprints?"

"Bloody footprints," he replied.

Oscar rose to his feet, and his smile faded to annoyance. "*Qu'est-ce qui se passe, bordel*? Cut the shit and tell me what you are trying to say already," he barked.

Luke looked up at him and said softly, "Remy is dead."

"Very funny." Oscar laughed at Luke's joke. "Bad enough you ruined my own time in the *le lit* with this bad humor, but let's leave Remy's conjugal bed *sacre*."

"It's no joke, Mr. Delaroux," Luke replied. "Remy is dead and his bride is missing."

Oscar's eyes narrowed. He felt a slow rumble in the pit of his stomach as he searched his mind for who would murder Remy and steal his bride on the day of their wedding.

"Let's go to the hotel immediately," he commanded. "I need to figure out who has done this, and we need to rescue Phreddie from them if she is still alive. Whoever they are, they will pay—heavily." He stormed out the door, and Luke and Landy followed.

Oscar's chest was puffing hard by the time he entered the lobby, having bridged the blocks between the brothel and the hotel in minutes. Once he got to the room, he studied it carefully.

"Bring that maid to me at once," he demanded when he spotted Phreddie's blood-soaked dress, which had been crumpled up and dumped in the corner. He lifted the garment and was studying it closely when an older woman entered.

"Here is the maid," Luke informed his leader.

Without taking his eyes off the dress, Oscar addressed her. "I saw the footprints," he began. "You did well by reporting your findings, but now"—he folded the dress and put it back on the floor—"I must ask you, since there was only one set of prints, did anyone see Mrs. Delaroux leave the hotel?"

"Yes, sir," the woman said in a thick Louisiana accent. "I saw the missus come down the stairs and wave goodbye, but she was all by herself. It wasn't till later that I saw the bloody prints on the floor, and I let myself inside—after knocking several times, of course."

Oscar's head began to hurt, so he rubbed it as he looked down at his brother's body. "You are telling me that woman left completely on her own?" he asked forcefully.

"Yes, sir," the maid answered.

"Then that can only mean one thing," he said, this time to himself.

He felt his head begin to clear. The facts started to connect as much as they also became more confused. Rubbing his jawline, he reviewed what he knew: His brother was dead. The room looked as if a storm had ripped through it. Phreddie's dress was covered in as much blood as his brother's body. And to put an exclamation mark on it all, the girl was gone of her own free will.

Oscar asked himself, *What do I really know about Phreddie?* Frankly, he'd just been happy Remy had found a girl to settle down with, because it left him free to spill his own seed recklessly across New Orleans. Remy claimed to have handpicked a chaste and sheepish maiden to wed and bed for heirs. It was part brag, but also part accusation, as Oscar had failed to procreate and their father had made his desire for *petite enfants* to carry on the business undoubtedly known.

And so his brother was going to responsibly ensure that the dynastical line of Delaroux continued through Phreddie. But Oscar had never even thought to ask about her background, or even how they had met. For all he knew, Phreddie could have been the daughter of one of their biggest competitors in the sugar business, sent in to lure Remy in *son le cul* and faux purity while Aloïs was away. It would have been the perfect time to snuff out one the Delaroux and take a step closer to cornering the market.

A silent assassin? he asked himself.

The answers he needed would not be found standing around in front of Remy's murdered carcass.

"I want you to find out where this Phreddie lived up until the wedding." He pointed to Luke, who nodded.

Then he looked at Landy. "And I want you to start walking around to the whore houses and gathering information. Give a note to each madame with a list of questions. If anyone knows the whereabouts or doings of a lone *chienne*, it will be one of the *putains* or their *mères*."

Luke and Landy left on command, which left Oscar to think.

"Where would I go if I had killed my husband on our wedding day? I would want to leave this city," he said aloud as he rubbed his temples again. Then he slapped his forehead. "Ah, yes!"

He stormed toward the door. Stopping and turning back one last time to look down at his brother, his eyes narrowed. "I'll get that bitch, Remy," Oscar declared. "And I will make her wish for *la mort*, but it will not come until she has suffered many days, or weeks, or even months of terror at my hands."

Then, with a sign of the cross, he left Remy's soul to God.

•

It was almost three o'clock when Oscar made his way down Canal Street. He had already checked the train station, where no trains were scheduled to depart to exotic destinations until the next day. That meant there were only two ways Phreddie could have left the city. One was by coach, which would likely mean she'd found a local hideaway, perhaps someplace he could reach within an hour once he had learned more about his brother's wife. The other was where he was headed now, his footsteps heavy with revenge.

"Of course," he chastised himself loudly. "It was my own gift, *pour l'amour du Christ*!"

Oscar pushed past some people who were ahead of him at the docks. As he stepped toward the harbor, he scanned the crowd for any evidence of the woman he so desperately sought.

It was then that he spotted Phreddie, in between the bodies milling on and off the various boats and vessels. She was leaning against the rail of *L'Ange*, a schooner retrofitted into a hybrid steamship for its transatlantic passage. The tickets had been Oscar's gift to the wedded couple.

What kind of salope diabolique can kill my brother and sail away on their lune de miel?

Oscar remembered how excited his brother had been to receive this wedding gift. He knew how much Remy missed their father, and so an opportunity to go home, even if just for a few short weeks, seemed like the perfect present. Not to mention the endless hours that he and Phreddie would spend rocking on rough seas in the marital bedroom.

Oscar had wanted everything about this trip to be perfect, so he'd booked every aspect of it himself instead of relying on the usual cadre of lackeys whose friendships he purchased. From this very harbor, Remy and his wife were to depart New Orleans and head through the Caribbean and up the East Coast of the United States. Once in New York, the ship would be restocked for its voyage to the Old World, which would take them to Burgundy. There, they would disembark and make the rest of their journey to Occitanie on horseback.

A lump formed in Oscar's throat at the thought of Aloïs waiting for his beloved son for the rest of his life.

A bell sounded, and the ship pitched forward.

"*Merde*, it is leaving," he yelled, and Phreddie looked up. Oscar locked eyes with his brother's wife.

"*Il y a cette méchante femme*," he hissed to those around him at the sight of the evil woman. Then he threw his body forward with the force of a prized stallion and began to run across the docks toward the vessel.

But the ship's engines hissed back. Oscar and *L'Ange* each picked up speed, but the schooner at a quicker pace. When he realized there was no way he would catch the boat, he stopped short, his hands on his knees and his lungs burning as he heaved in air. He lifted his head and glared, watching as Phreddie turned her face away from the rail and disappeared into the ship.

Then Oscar threw his head back and let out a primal scream that could be heard across the ocean and as far as Toulouse.

Betrothed Then Butchered

"Mr. Bronson will see you now," Phreddie said quietly as she escorted a group of suited men through the First National Bank of New York and into an office.

"Thank you, Miss Smith," Mr. Bronson said through a warm smile. "Why don't you go enjoy some luncheon." He nodded toward her. "We will be here for a while."

Phreddie nodded back and closed the door behind her. In a few steps, she was by the row of desks where she and the two other secretaries tended to the bank managers' tasks and visitors.

"I'm going to lunch now," she called weakly over the ferocious click-clack of fingers against the Caligraph typewriters. Neither of the other ladies acknowledged her existence, so she lowered her head, grabbed a small coin purse from the pocket of her coat, which she'd hung along the wall, and headed toward the door.

Outside, the streets of New York City bustled with activity. Lone mounted horses, covered carriages, and men, women, and children on foot flitted in every direction. Phreddie Delaroux tiptoed out into the crowd and just barely avoided being run down by a group of children. "Watch out, lady," a guttersnipe in torn shorts yelled out as the others laughed.

Phreddie continued down the sidewalk until she reached a lunch cart with a sign that read *Hot Vienna Waffles*. The smell of batter frying hit her nostrils, and she smiled. The waffles were a favorite of hers; she must have eaten them at least fifteen times during her first few weeks of employment in the part of town known as Union Square. As had become her routine, she paid the vendor two pennies, then took her food across the dusty road over to a small park.

It wasn't easy to situate oneself on a stiff park bench while wearing an enormous bustle, but she had gotten used to New York fashion. It was not quite as free-flowing as the dresses she'd worn in New Orleans. There it had been all about swooping necklines, which had always revealed too much flesh for her comfort, but the somber navy fabric she was wearing now choked all the way up to her neck and gripped her arms tightly from shoulders to wrists. Even worse was the hard-boned corset that seemed to press the breath out of her very lungs. Together, the ensemble acted as part modesty enforcer and part prison. The clothes tamed her womanhood and her fuller form, and as such, she was not immune to their shape-hiding advantages. Bustles, corsets, and the like were masters of illusion, and she loved anything that made her true self less conspicuous.

Phreddie, who'd returned once more to the last name of Smith that had been given to her at the orphanage, sat back and began to nibble on her waffle. For a quick moment, she had considered retaining the Delaroux name earned through her short marriage to Remy, but in the end, she reverted to the one she had always known. Now she sat back and recalled the long journey from New Orleans to this park bench.

While on board *L'Ange*, Phreddie had done her best to stay in her cabin, even requesting that her meals be brought to her. It had been a difficult passage, and nausea plagued her from port to port, though she was unsure if it was from the rolling waters or the memory of blood pouring out of Remy's neck that haunted her thoughts. Either way, all she'd wanted for most of the trip was to take in some fresh air. But fresh air meant interacting with others, and Phreddie sought to avoid all questions about Remy and his whereabouts for fear that her guilty face might convict her. Instead, she'd kept to her room, where her stomach rollicked like the seas until *L'Ange* entered the New York Harbor Estuary.

When Mrs. Delaroux disembarked *L'Ange*, nearly eight days had passed since her May morning nuptials. Phreddie had told the captain that she would be meeting her husband in a hotel near Beekman for two nights, rather than berth on the ship while it was resupplied for the next leg of its journey. Though the captain protested, Phreddie insisted she needed to do some shopping of her own and that Remy and she would most definitely rejoin *L'Ange* at slip number twenty-three, right in between the Morrisania and Mallory transport lines, in less than forty-eight hours.

Instead, within moments of planting her feet on terra firma, Phreddie had disappeared into the ether. Now, nearly eight weeks on, she felt confident that both the captain and Oscar Delaroux, whose eyes she could still see staring up at her from the dock when the ship left the harbor, had long forgotten about her.

In her new life, Phreddie told folks that she was just a single woman whose mother had recently died from yellow fever. On her deathbed, she had implored her daughter to go up North to find her cousins. Here Phreddie was, she would say, halfway across the country and happily alone but longing to one day reunite with her kin.

A chewy morsel caused Phreddie to reach up and loosen her collar. Each time she felt the dress choke her, she was thankful it was not a hangman's noose. Instead, she was free to sit here and eat waffles while on a short break from her gainful employment.

Phreddie smiled, thinking Sister Adrienne would have taken sick comfort knowing that all of those rulers she'd applied across Phreddie's teenage knuckles when she had been forced to learn the Pitman's shorthand system had actually paid dividends. Though the sister had insisted Phreddie would never do anything useful but stay hidden below stairs to iron and stir boiled undergarments for the wealthy, she'd allowed the girl to learn the phonography. It provided another excuse for Sister Adrienne to abuse Phreddie for her failings.

Now, however, she was free from Sister Adrienne, free from Mrs. Guidry's basement, and free from charges of murder. In fact, everything about New York was refreshing and new. For Phreddie, new meant no more scalded hands at last, as she was determined to never wash another person's dainties. She might not have love, but at least she would finally be left alone, free from servitude and outright abuse.

A woman's coquettish laughter brought Phreddie back to the moment. Without thinking, she chewed her lower lip when a man took hold of the giggling woman's hand and kissed her as they passed by. It reminded her of her first date with Remy.

They had agreed to meet at St. Anthony's gardens behind the large white cathedral that was at the center of the French District. There they'd sat on a clean sheet and shared a fresh hollowed-out French loaf stuffed full of fried oysters while they lounged next to rows of pink camellias and antique red roses.

"*Je pense que j'ai trouvé mon amour,*" he had whispered when he plucked at the stray petal the breeze had carried into her hair.

Phreddie did not understand French any more than she'd understood the flush of warmth that rushed through her body at his smell when he got close. It was a cross between soapy citrus and earth, and she was as intoxicated by it as she was by the sips of gin fizz tossed about by the shaker boy Remy had hired from the Roosevelt Hotel to serve them that day.

She thought she could hear the ice being tossed against the tumbler again, but it was just the sound of bells on a pair of horses that had pulled a milk cart into the park, summoning buyers to its wares. The echoing peels reminded Phreddie that loneliness had felt like a life sentence until Remy came along. Alas, he had ultimately failed her, and Phreddie learned her lesson hard.

From her bench, she glared at the lovers as they walked away and cursed the bells until they stopped their singing, vowing to herself that she would never make the same mistake again. Love might be the destiny of other women, such as the park-walking giggler, but Phreddie was not like her or any other woman she knew. It was simply not realistic to hope for affection and intimacy, and she'd resigned herself to it. Instead, she would return forever to living the kind of quiet, unassuming life she'd had before Remy swept her up in romance and made her believe that she could possess something more.

Her lunch over, Phreddie licked the last of the cinnamon sugar from her lips and made her way back toward the bank. As she got closer, she saw a small group of men approaching the building from the opposite direction. At first she didn't believe her eyes, but her heart thumped as if she had just sprinted uphill. It squeezed hard enough for her to know that what she was seeing was true.

Phreddie froze in place and watched as Oscar Delaroux approached the door of the First National Bank of New York with two men in suits and a police officer alongside him. She pulled the brim of her hat down over her face in case Oscar looked over in her direction, but he didn't. Instead, he and the others disappeared into the building in a flash.

How could he have found me? she wondered frantically. But there was no time for pointless questions. Rather than search for an answer, Phreddie lifted her hand in the air and waved it rapidly until she flagged down a carriage.

"To Twenty-Third Street and Sixth Avenue—quickly," she called to the cab driver as she hopped into and closed the door behind her. She tried to sit back gently as the wagon bumped along the cobbled streets at the same frenetic pace as her nerves.

Thankfully I never told anyone where I live, she thought as she raced through her mind trying to determine what might have led Oscar to her workplace. *Then again, I never told anyone where I work either*. She'd thought she could get lost in the anonymity of New York's population. Now she shivered thinking that, even here, Remy's brother had managed to find her.

"Oh, what do I do now?" she fretted aloud.

At last the carriage drew to a stop.

"Thank you," she said softly. She pulled her last coin from her purse and reluctantly handed it to the driver, who was now parked in front of her brownstone.

The exchange over, Phreddie ran up the stoop and entered the boarding house, where an old, unkempt woman with an open palm greeted her in the foyer. "Where is it, Miss Smith?" she asked in a thick Irish accent.

"Tomorrow, Miss Post, I promise," Phreddie assuaged as she looked back out the front door to see if she had been followed.

"You promised me as much yesterday," Miss Post growled.

Convinced Oscar was not behind her, Phreddie returned her gaze to her landlady. "We go through this every Thursday, Miss Post. The bank pays its employees on Fridays, and that is tomorrow."

"There may not be a tomorra for ya," the woman said plainly before turning around to limp into her apartment, where she slammed the door behind her.

Phreddie shook it off and ran upstairs to her shared room. By the time she reached the top floor, she was practically crawling. "This never gets easier," she gasped aloud as she looked down over the edge of the stairwell to the lobby six floors below.

She turned and opened the middle of the three bedroom doors. "Blam-jam," she muttered aloud once inside, but she wasn't alone. A young woman, dressed only in a pair of white cotton-and-lace drawers, greeted her with a look of disdain.

"What's the matter, honey?" her roommate, Clara, asked unamused. "You look like you've seen a ghost."

"Or its brother," Phreddie whispered under her breath as the young lady threw a light bathrobe around her body and sat down on her bed with a newspaper.

Phreddie took off her hat and sat down at a small table by the window, propping her elbows on it. "Bobbing apples," she whimpered, then dropped her face into her hands and rubbed her temples.

"Say what?" Clara asked, but Phreddie ignored her.

Instead, she fretted over what to do next. *If New York isn't safe, where is? Boston? England? The Orient?*

"Oh, hot fires," she finally groaned, which caused Clara to let out a howl of laughter.

"Why can't you just say the word *hell* like the rest of us commoners?" she chastised.

"Because I don't believe in it," Phreddie replied softly.

Clara seemed surprised. "What? Hell? Why not?"

"On account of I don't think there could be anywhere worse than this world most days."

Clara chuckled. "And here I thought you were some kind of puritan or religious nutter. If that's not the case, and you have no fear of hellfire, you might as well let it rip, instead of your silly blam-jams and bobbing apples! A good ole *aw shit* would do you a world of good."

There was silence for a minute before Phreddie pierced it. "Aw . . . sh-sh-ships at sea," she screamed into her hands.

A deep cackle sounded from across the room. "Not quite what I had in mind, but seeing that I haven't so much as seen you in your knickers these past two months, I suppose that's as close to a cuss as you're likely to ever get."

"Yeah, well . . . " Phreddie responded weakly, her head back in her hands. "If you'd grown up with Sister Adrienne ripping to wash your mouth out with lye every chance she got, you might avoid strong words yourself."

Phreddie's mind began to wander before she looked up at her roommate. "Clara, I have a serious question. I know we haven't spoken more than the polite hello and goodbye here and there, but I don't really have many people to talk to."

"Go on then," Clara said, slathering some lavender cream into the back of her hands.

"Say you were being followed by someone you didn't want to find you—" Phreddie began, but Clara interrupted her with another laugh.

"Why, you little hussy," she howled.

"I'm being serious."

"Welcome to the world of men, Phreddie. Why do you think I'm staying at a boarding house with Miss Prison-Matron Post?" Clara said. "I know that even that stalker Charlie Parker couldn't get past her, even if he had a pack of hellhounds in tow."

"No," Phreddie pressed. "Let's say that everywhere you went, they wound up too, and you needed to get away from them forever. Where would you go?"

"Oh." Clara paused and looked up at the ceiling. "Well in that case, I'd go west."

"West? Why west?"

"Who there is to say you are not a baroness or a merchant's daughter? It's a place where everyone is too busy starting from scratch to go looking for backstories or pedigrees."

Phreddie chewed her lip. "That's what I thought about New York."

"Out west, in the great expanse, you can truly disappear," Clara insisted.

They were interrupted by the echo of a loud knock from downstairs. Phreddie ran to the bedroom door and opened it just a crack to listen.

She could hear Miss Post below, interrogating the visitor in her strong brogue. "What do ya want?"

"Is that your Charlie Parker?" Clara teased.

Phreddie hushed her so that she could listen.

"We're looking for a woman who we are told might be sheltering here," an unfamiliar voice said.

Phreddie tiptoed out of the room, wincing as her feet slipped over the creaky floor, and peered over the balcony.

"I have many of those," Miss Post told him. Phreddie could now see it was the police officer who had walked into the bank earlier with Oscar.

As Miss Post swung the door shut, a boot flung out to stop it from closing. Oscar Delaroux stepped forward and pushed his way inside, a wad of paper currency in his hands. Miss Post's eyes drooled at the money, but after a few seconds, she looked up at him and scowled.

"If I was t' sell out all me lasses, I'd have nay but an empty nest, and no one clump of paper could make up fer a reputation of mindin' me business," she said, and she started to push him out again.

However, this time Oscar slammed the door with his entire body, and the woman fell to the ground with a scream. "*Íosa Críost*," she yelled out in Gaelic, but not even Jesus could stop her from being trampled by the small group of men that ran inside.

Phreddie turned quickly. She tried to steady her nervous hands as she closed the bedroom door quietly.

"What is all that commotion?" Clara asked without looking up from the newspaper she'd returned to reading.

Phreddie dashed to the window and threw it open. The gusty wind blew the paper right out of Clara's hands, and she yelled, "It's cold and I'm half-naked, if you don't mind!"

Phreddie didn't bother to respond but instead threw her right leg over the sill just as the bedroom door flung open.

"*Meurtrière*!" Oscar accused with a pointed finger over Clara's colorful protests.

Phreddie's other leg was over the ledge before he reached her. She was halfway across the rooftop when he stuck his head outside. A gunshot rang out, and a chimney pipe near her left ankle exploded.

"I will get you, murderess," he roared at her.

When she looked back over her shoulder, she saw the lanky young man with the white hair push out of the window next to Oscar and follow her. She kept moving, and when she reached the edge of the rooftop, she found herself standing on a precipice. There was an alley eighty or ninety feet below her. In front of her was a gap between the end of this building and the next one's roof.

I'm trapped, she thought, but she had no intention of surrendering just yet. Instead, Phreddie gathered up her skirts, sucked in her breath, closed her eyes, and jumped across the divide.

As her feet hit the landing on the other side with a thud, she opened her eyes wide with surprise and wonder and laughed aloud. There was little time to celebrate though, as the lanky man was closing in swiftly.

With all of the speed she could muster, Phreddie dashed across the lengths of three additional rooftops. Each time she leapt into the air, the white lion closed in on her, inch by inch, until Phreddie knew the kill was upon her.

At last she spotted a thin steel ladder that rose up over the ledge. She reached it just in time and found herself almost free-falling down its rungs until she landed on the metal platform of a fire escape. As the lanky man started to descend the ladder himself, Phreddie again hoisted her dress above her ankles, then ran down the remaining two flights of stairs until at last she was able to shimmy herself to the sidewalk below. Within seconds she managed to disappear into the crowd of people on Twenty-Fourth Street.

She kept looking over her shoulder every few minutes, but the man who had been coming after her was no longer in sight. She finally slipped into a small alley on Seventh Avenue, where she smoothed down her dress and tucked some stray hairs up with a pin.

"What will I do now?" she asked aloud. New York was plenty big for Oscar to have a difficult time finding her, if only she could outlast him a few days. After all, how long could he really be away from New Orleans now that it was his sole responsibility to take care of the sugar business?

A few days was all she needed, she convinced herself. After that, Oscar would be forced to return to his home, and Phreddie could slip back in through the window at Miss Post's to grab some of her belongings. Then she would just have to do what she'd done before: find a new place to live and a new job. Only this time, she had none of Remy's honeymoon money to help her get started.

She shrugged her shoulders and stepped back out into the thinning crowd. It was twilight now, and most people were headed toward their homes and hearths. This was when the city dwellers turned their minds from the moving wheels of industry toward supper and sleep inside of warm homes, if they had them, or shadows and secrecy, if they didn't.

Phreddie had been warned by the other girls when she first arrived at Miss Post's not to make a habit of dawdling on the streets past dusk unless in the company of a suitor, lest she be taken for a woman of the night, either by trade or by force. But the setting sun and cooling temperatures were not enough to agitate that threat in her mind, as Phreddie had bigger worries this evening.

Off she went into the night, unsure of where she was headed but thankful she still had her freedom.

•

Phreddie had wandered the ever-darkening streets for what felt like an eternity, until she finally seated herself on a park bench down by the East River. There, through the open window of a tenement house behind her, she heard the cry of a child in the wind, and it pulled her back in time.

A vague memory of her own wailing voice came to the forefront. She howled as the young couple prepared to hand her off to the nuns at the Sisters of Children and Charity Orphanage. The twisted face of the raven-haired woman who must have been her mother was contorted into a mix of pain and resignation, while the man who was with her angrily tore young Phreddie from the woman's arms and shoved her small body into the forceful grip of Sister Adrienne.

The woman mouthed Phreddie's birth name, but Phreddie could no longer recollect what she had said, so while her mother's mouth opened in her memories, no sound came out. Phreddie instead recalled how she had cried out violently, emptying her small lungs of air, until the nun closed the door on her parents. She remembered how Sister Adrienne had proceeded to slam her small buttocks with a wooden spoon until terror forced her to stop her wails.

"You should be grateful," Sister Adrienne had chastised. "We do not often take aberrant creatures, but your birth parents made a sizable donation—out of guilt and penance more than anything else, I imagine, as a person does not get a devil unless they have been a devil themselves."

The nun dumped Phreddie's little body onto a bed in a cavernous room where more than a hundred sleeping children of all ages lay silent. "Now sleep," she whispered sharply, "for it will be morning soon, and though innocent children are occasionally adopted, wicked children need to be dealt with harshly, and at times even put down. Lucky for you, your former parents made me promise that they could see you were well from the gate every year up until your sixteenth birthday. If they have proof that you are still alive, they will provide similarly large annual donations, absolving them of any guilt for both bringing you into this world and allowing you to remain. So, though I already find you loathsome, you will live at least that long, but I daresay I will see to it that each of your days here are miserable, demon child. And as for your name, what you were once called is forever buried. We will call you Phreddie, for you are in between two worlds—neither one nor the other, but certainly more of hell than of this plane."

There in the cold and drafty room, Phreddie, who could from that moment remember very little of her life before, lay on the bed. She was cold and alone, with only a thin, worn blanket to cover her small shaking body.

A wind swept down the river, and Phreddie shivered back to the present. She didn't know how many hours she had been sitting on the bench, but a couple of drunk men approached her, whistling and hooting as they neared.

"Whatcha say to a silver dollar for me to put my spindle in your honeypot, night flower?" one of them asked as they approached.

"No thank you," Phreddie replied as she stood up, her knees shaking.

The second man laughed. "Ooh, look at this one acting all hoity-toity."

The first one chuckled. "I like when they pretend to be part schoolmarm."

The second took a swig from a bottle. "I wouldn't pay three pennies to touch her quim whiskers anyway." He spat at the ground.

"I wouldn't either, now that you mention it," replied the other. "But I'd sure as shit take it for free." He hiccuped as he reached out to grab ahold of Phreddie.

Only she was too quick for two drunkards who smelled like rum hams that had been soaked for close to a week for the pre-Lenten New Orleans feast they called the Mardi Gras. A few fancy footsteps to the side, and she was on her way back into the streets, leaving the sounds of the cursing, feeble men behind her.

•

At last the sun appeared to be rising, and Phreddie, who had been wandering for hours now, felt a rumble in her stomach. She hadn't even thought about eating in all the commotion, but it had been many hours now since that waffle in the park.

She found herself meandering along outside the bustling Exchange Place depot that she'd walked past on the day she arrived in the New York City harbor. From there, ferries and trains pulled in and out from both land and sea. There were now morning movements everywhere as vendors set up their wares to sell passengers and businessmen of all sorts, who started their days with smiles.

Phreddie's stomach growled loudly when she saw the peanut man pushing his rectangular cart into place between a newspaper stand and a shoeshiner, right alongside the west side of the depot. A small bag of the warm delicacies fell off the cart's great big pile and landed over by the newsstand. Phreddie looked back and forth, then bent down quickly to grab it off of the ground. As she did so, she found herself face-to-face with a sweet, innocent-looking girl, whose dirt smudged cheeks hung sallow from hunger.

The child eyed the goobers with great longing. Phreddie looked down at the nuts and felt the warmth from their shells against her palm, a loud gurgle releasing from her insides. Then she looked back at the young girl.

At last, she relented and handed her the peanuts. A big smile spread across the child's face before she ran off into the streets.

Standing up, Phreddie found herself face-to-face with another person, only this one was far more recognizable. On top of a stack of newspapers, familiar eyes lifted off the front page. It was a drawing of her above the headline *BETROTHED, THEN BUTCHERED BY THIS BRIDE.* She gasped aloud, then grabbed a copy off the top of the pile and began to scan the article.

"Well, blam-jam," she said aloud.

The newsman eyed her and growled, "Hey, either buy the damned thing or don't!" But then his eyes widened, and his arm extended out toward her as he yelled, "That's her . . . it's the butcher bride!"

Phreddie's jaw fell, and she looked around at the crowd that had begun to gather and gawp. There were whispers and pointed fingers.

"How could she kill her husband?" cried one.

"On their wedding night?" said another.

A panic swept through her body when, out of all places in this whole gigantic city that they could have been, Oscar and his wiry ivory-headed helpmate broke through the throng of people and began to run at her. Phreddie's whole body was frozen, except for her eyes, which grew larger. Instinct told her feet to move, but again they failed her.

When the men were only a few paces away, the little girl she had given the peanuts to ran up and grabbed her by the hand. Phreddie looked down at the child in confusion.

"Phreddie!"

Her shoulders jerked at the sound of Oscar's voice. She could almost feel his hands around her throat.

"This way," the street urchin insisted as she tugged.

Phreddie relented. She turned and ran, the little girl at the helm.

As the child led her into the crowd, Phreddie turned back to see how close the men were and saw Oscar frantically looking for her.

"Oh bobbing apples," she whined, but he turned the wrong way and disappeared into the throng.

The girl led her along a shed wall behind the carts and into a small alley, where she released a primal "whoop whoop" holler that seemed to be a passcode to the other street children. Next thing Phreddie knew, a piece of corrugated metal peeled back, and her guide yanked her into the void, where the metal sheet was quickly rolled back.

As her eyes adjusted to the darkness, Phreddie could see a dozen or so children, ranging in age from probably five years old to late teens. They were sitting around on boxes, lying across old torn mattresses, and there was even one sitting on a broken fancy burnt-orange velvet chair with three legs that must have once graced the parlor of a fine family.

"What is this?" Phreddie asked the little girl gently.

A girl in her early teens stood up from the chair. "Our home."

"Your home?" Phreddie looked around at the dirt-smudged faces that greeted her.

"This is where the unwanted go," the teenager explained with some toughness in her voice, as if to say, *If you try us, we will hurt you, lady.* "Here, they become wanted." She stepped closer and glared at Phreddie from just below her chin.

"That's lovely." Phreddie smiled. "Everyone wants to be wanted. I myself grew up in an orphanage."

The girl looked Phreddie up and down. "Then you know what it's like to belong to no one." She turned and went back to her chair. "Well, that's one point for you. The other is Polly"—she nodded to the little girl—"who brought you here. Without her vouching for you, we would have gutted you."

Phreddie let out an uncomfortable giggle, but as she looked around and saw the hardened faces of the other children, she knew this wasn't so much a threat as a warning.

"Well, in that case, I owe Polly my gratitude." She smiled down at the child, who grinned back at her, her red cheeks as plump as ripe peaches. Looking back up at the teenager, she asked, "And you are?"

"Call me Vee," she spat.

"Okay, Vee. I need to find a way out of here," Phreddie explained. "Maybe on a train or something. Any ideas?"

"Like become a stowaway?" The teen perked up.

"I suppose. I do need to get out of town, and fast."

"In that case"—Vee stood back up, and her eyes sparkled—"we can play a game of Knuff and Spell."

"What's that?" Phreddie asked.

All of the children jumped up with excitement. "We haven't done it in a while," lisped a boy.

"You will see soon enough," the leader answered. Her hands were on her hips now, as if she were the captain of a great ship. There were a few whispers and nods, and then within seconds Vee's crew were following their leader out of a small hole in the wall at the back of this abandoned storeroom-come-wayfaring-hotel-for-guttersnipes.

Outside, the children marched in a small band, and Phreddie noticed how the vendors and passersby shook their heads in disapproval at the tattered lot. As they walked, their numbers seemed to swell, until there had to be about twenty boys and girls of various ages, some with hands balled into fists, others carrying clubs and sticks. Those who joined didn't even ask where they were headed but instead fell in line, ready to fight as one no matter the battle that lay ahead.

Phreddie considered the fact that whatever untold circumstances had brought these children to the streets, there was grit in their hardened scowls. Unlike her time at the orphanage, where she'd been taunted by the others or left isolated by Sister Adrienne, this group of children seemed to take care of each other. In fact, they even presented as tough a unified lot as the Reno Brothers Gang that Phreddie had read about in newspapers, and the members of that group were actually related by blood. She would put this pack of disheveled, but loyal, tots up against those bank robbers any day based on intimidating looks alone.

From one street over, Phreddie heard the Frenchman shout out, "*La voilà*!"

"He's found me," she shrieked. "Whatever you have planned needs to happen now, or that man over there will kill me."

Vee stopped and winked at Phreddie. "Then I guess it's time to play," the teen responded.

At that, she let out the same "whoop whoop" Polly had used earlier. The other children broke off in various directions and launched into an impromptu game of street ball known as Knurr and Spell. Several of them released walnuts that they had removed from their pockets into the air. A few of the older children ran up with the sticks, or spells, that they had carried and knocked the walnut knurrs further into the air. The objects flew off hard in various directions, causing mayhem among the people around them.

Shopkeepers cursed aloud as some of the projectiles shattered glass windows, while others peppered the heads of the passengers who were entering or exiting the depot. Screams and shouts ran up and down the area, with vendors rushing to protect their goods and layfolk running to save their noggins. The boys and girls ran between legs and crashed into carts, sending apples and oranges rolling off everywhere. They collected their knurrs and scurried in zigzags to avoid being caught by any adults.

Hidden by the chaos, Vee and Polly led Phreddie along the train shed. Before she'd had time to thank her saviors, Phreddie was rushed to a platform and pushed onto an idling train. Over the heads of the children, she could see Oscar running toward her.

"I got this," Vee yelled out, and threw herself onto the platform at Oscar's feet. She rolled as if to put out a fire, causing both him and the white-haired man to stumble over her body and fall.

The train lurched and moved forward. Phreddie looked at Polly, who was standing in the middle of the fallen bodies and waving goodbye, a big, peachy smile on her little cherubic face. Oscar lifted his head up from the tangle of limbs, a furious scowl on his face as the train pulled away into the unknown.

Phreddie, who had been leaning outside to watch, pulled herself in and threw her head back. *Whoa.* She let out a relieved breath. Though she had no idea where she was going, it didn't matter. With every turn of the wheels, Oscar Delaroux was farther behind her.

Her body was shaking as much from adrenaline and fear as from the jolting of the tracks beneath her. She gripped the bar on the wall of the train and nervously made her way to the first seat she could find. Though tossed about, she managed to angle herself over a bench of plump purple cushions, where she sat down in a heap and sighed.

A man with brown hair and a tidy mustache entered the car from the opposite end. He smiled and tipped his brown hat, which matched his brown suit, at Phreddie, then sat down facing her one row over.

How did I go from an orphanage in New Orleans to this? Phreddie thought, astonished by the great changes in her life over the last few months. She wondered whether she might have been better off had she stayed on as Sister Adrienne's pincushion rather than being forced out into a world she was clearly unprepared for. At last, she settled down, put her head back against the soft headrest, and fitfully dozed off.

•

A few minutes after the train had left the station, the conductor came through and began to ask for tickets. When he reached the woman Oscar had brought Luke along to New York to capture, Luke saw panic in her eyes.

"I don't have one." Her voice quivered, her response more question than explanation, but the attendant's stern face was unmoved, and his empty hand remained extended, palm up.

"Ticket, money, or get the hell off," he stated plainly. "We don't do vagabonds on this line."

"But I don't even have my purse," she begged, attempting to smooth her wrinkled dress.

"Lady, I wouldn't care if Abraham fucking Lincoln came down from heaven to declare you emancipated from the cost of fare. It's ticket, money, or—"

". . . get the heck off," the lady replied with a sigh. Then she stood up to exit at the next station.

"Wait a minute," Luke interjected, leaping to his feet. "Where are you going to, ma'am?" He tipped his hat in her direction.

"Oh." The woman's lip trembled. "Um . . . I need to go west."

She's frail, he thought. *Not exactly what Oscar described.*

"Where out west, ma'am?" he asked again. "I'm traveling that way too."

"Um, let's see. Um . . . well, California is where I'd really like to go." Her face fell to her shoes. "But I have no way to afford my passage. I don't know what I was thinking." There was a certain meekness in her manner, and Luke wondered whether circumstance, rather than bad behavior, had led her to wear the moniker of "wicked."

"Well, it's your lucky day," he said. Then he pulled a wad of bills out of his pocket and handed a few to the conductor. "Two tickets to California," he requested politely.

The man looked at Luke with eyes as big as the moon, then sighed. "That's your $220, my friend, not mine. As far as I'm concerned, ain't no woman, even if it be a pretty one, worth it." Then he looked the lady over, pulled two tickets out of his apron, and moved down the car to the next set of passengers.

"I cannot thank you enough, Mr. . . .?" she gushed, and Luke smiled back calmly.

"Mr. Jones—Luke Jones," he said. "And you are?"

"Ms. Smith." She smiled.

"A pleasure to meet you." He grinned. "Do you have a first name?

She flushed at the question. "I do, only I'd prefer to keep it more formal, if you don't mind." She looked around at the vanishing ticket man and the few other passengers in the car, who were stealing glances at them.

"Lest the conductor, or anyone else here, think I've completely lost all of my morals."

Luke laughed. "Oh no, we wouldn't want that. I can tell you have nothing if not morals."

Seems too soft to be violent, he mused.

He watched as she sat back down, great embarrassment on her cheeks, and closed her eyes. Within minutes, she was gently snoring. Luke decided he might as well close his own eyes, as it would be a long ride to California. A lengthy journey meant plenty of opportunities to earn Ms. Smith's trust.

At least she didn't lie about her last name. Though Smith is hardly one to stand out. Seems like a cold-blooded killer would change their name, though. He shrugged. *No matter.* After all, Oscar did not pay him to think on the whys, but to do the whats when asked. For now, he decided it would be best to dwell on the hows, as in how he was going to handle this whole situation.

If there was a chance along the way to take Phreddie Smith into custody, he would. It would require an opportunity to confine her. If one did not present itself, Luke would make sure she was incredibly comfortable with him over the many miles that potentially lay ahead. He would put her at ease, so much so that he would be able to lead Oscar right to her, even if it had to wait until they arrived in California. By then, Luke knew she would consider them to be close friends. Hell, she wasn't hard to look at. He wouldn't mind it if while they waited for Oscar, they became even more than friends. *I wonder what it's like to fuck a killer?* he teased himself. He wasn't sure if he was more turned on by her modest nature or by the potential bad girl that lay underneath.

Luke imagined he would be able to wire Oscar before the week was over, as they would be in California by then. In no time at all, Remy's killer—who at this moment looked particularly nonthreatening, though something of a morsel—would be on her way back to New Orleans in chains, and Luke salivated more thinking about the size of the reward than her num-nums. Plus, he owed Oscar his loyalty and would pay deference to it before his libido. After all, the two had been friends with for going on ten years now.

The Delaroux brothers had joined Luke's alma mater, the desegregated Fillmore School in New Orleans, fresh off the boat from France. It was one of the first public grammar schools in the region, and the boys' father, Aloïs, had insisted that his children "scrape with the regular people of the city rather than attend a private school with posh prisses and the like."

Luke recalled how when Oscar and his younger brother had first begun their education on Pauger Street, their accents brought them merciless teasing. But those taunts lasted less than one day—long enough for Oscar to corner one of the older bullies in the bathroom and beat the tar out of him while Luke and a few other boys stood by and cheered.

From that point on, Oscar—and by default, his brother Remy—were afforded deference. Wherever the oldest went especially, he had his choice of seat, and the utmost respect was showered on him, but Luke had had relatively little interaction with Oscar beyond sharing a classroom with him until one afternoon in the spring.

Luke had been returning home from Fillmore by way of St. Claude Avenue when a group of Creole boys began to throw rocks at him, shouting "cracker" and "milk face." Luke was one of the only white kids to live in the New Marigny neighborhood where the school was located. He'd tried to run away, knowing that he was no match for the group of six, but he soon found himself with his back up against a fence, and the boys pounced.

One spun him around and pinned his arm behind his back, then proceeded to mash his face into the metal fencing. Luke remembered he'd been staring at the words *Miltenberger & Co.* that had been pressed into the iron when he heard several yelps come from the crowd behind him. The boy suddenly released Luke's arm, and when Luke turned around, he found most of the others doubled over in pain. They were clutching at their stomachs and cupping their bloodied noses. A triumphant Oscar was standing in the middle of the pack, yelling at them in his foreign tongue.

"*Va te faire foutre, bande de corbeaux*," he had shouted, and the boys took their leave as quickly as they could hobble away.

"Thank you," Luke said as he offered his hand, "but why did you help me?"

"Six against one is not fair, but six against two seemed like a fun time," Oscar replied, and they both laughed at his boldness.

From that day on, Luke had been at Oscar's side, whether he was atop Mahogany Montigny or at the *pochen* table, as Oscar liked to call the card game in his native language. Oscar had Luke's back on many more occasions, mostly providing funds and the perks of pleasure that came with wealth. There were too many minor scrabbles and scrapes to remember, but one thing was for certain: whatever Oscar asked of him, Luke would deliver, as he had done countless times before.

He sat back now and let the hum of the engine take him to the same place that Phreddie had already inhabited with her gentle snores, ever closer to their confrontation.

The Asshole of Kansas

"*I'll never forgive you for killing my sister,*" Ms. Ortiz's voice echoed in his mind. Charlie Hodges shook his head hard to try to clear out the sound. Doing so sent the pool of water that had formed along the brim of his hat cascading to his shoulders. He then kicked his horse so hard that she galloped more swiftly than usual toward the town whose gauzy lights lay off in the distance.

The sky had changed from ash to charcoal by the time horse and rider clipped down Newton's Main Street. The road was presently something of a muddy river due to the torrential downpour that had wrapped its heavy clouds around the town's neck.

"Give her a rubdown and feed," Charlie commanded a young man as he dismounted at the nearby stable. He then gave the horse a few taps on the rump and walked back out into the rain and across the street to Miller's Saloon.

As he approached the doors, two laughing drunk men came outside arm in arm. "Two more bits and she said she'd show me her t—" The man stopped midsentence when he found himself face-to-face with Charlie.

The other drunkard quickly stopped his laughter as well. "Flies in the butter," he muttered nervously to himself.

Then they swiftly headed off, all fearful eyes and whispering tongues.

Charlie grunted, then hit the swinging doors with his boot and stepped inside.

A hush swept the room when he entered. Though it was the middle of the day, the bar was full of patrons and dancing girls, all of whom were now staring at him. The bartender, Miller, coughed to get the attention of the pianist, who got the hint and began to play again. Soon, everyone went back to their conversations and rowdy behavior, despite more than one of them casting a side glance at the newcomer and leaning into one another's ears.

Charlie approached the bar, sat down on a stool, and tapped the counter. Miller obliged, throwing down a glass that he poured a couple of ounces of amber liquid into.

After a quick gulp, Charlie gave Miller a nod. "Keep 'em coming. Today's the anniversary of Lily's death, and I damn well aim to get corned."

Miller did as ordered, and the music swelled to drown out shouts of "*Olé*" as well as the hoots and hollers hurled at the girls onstage.

Charlie slung back another and closed his eyes for a second to let the potion calm his nerves. Yet all he could see was water, be it the rain that soaked Lily's grave or the tears that ran down her sister, Ms. Ortiz's, cheeks. Moisture flowed through his mind, and he opened his lids once more and asked for another shot of the fiery kind. *Wash it all away*, he commanded himself with his next sip, then tossed the drink back.

"Gonna be a long night," Miller remarked as he filled the glass back up.

•

Rain pelted the train's windows as it rolled across the plains. It had been four days since Phreddie had left New York City. After that first train pulled into Kansas City, Luke Jones and she had made a quick change at the Missouri line. Now they were on the long final journey that ran straight to the West Coast. Though it was miserable outside, all she could imagine was sunny beaches and smiling faces that played around in shallow waves.

A loud splash against the glass caused Phreddie to jerk upright. In the background, she could see the reflection of the attractive man who was sitting just in front of her with his eyes shut. It was the perfect opportunity to study him. In the gentle quiet, she admired his mirrored image in the window, content that if he were to stir, he would think she was studying the rain-soaked landscape rushing by.

Now here's a man who could make any woman happy, she thought, placing the fingers of her left hand onto her right and twisting the skin. *Ouch!* She had to stop herself from yelling at the pinch, telling herself that she deserved the pain, as that's what men brought her. *Remember Remy?*

While Mr. Jones was a kind stranger—kinder than many and most—he was destined to remain nothing more than a passing acquaintance, as Phreddie refused to let the lessons of New Orleans vacate her mind and leave her vulnerable once again. She had learned his first name at their introduction, and she'd discovered a whole heap about his life as well during the many hours it had taken the first train to travel to Kansas City. While she had initially been hesitant to be too friendly, the man had paid for her tickets, and that alone meant that she was obligated to at least be polite.

By the time they'd arrived in the station, she'd felt almost bonded to him, so much so that she put her arm in his as he accompanied her onto the next train—the Atchison, Topeka, and Santa Fe. It was from there that they began to barrel toward San Francisco.

Over countless hours, the two had spoken about their upbringings. Though Phreddie had left most specific details out, she'd been delighted to hear Luke speak about his large family. He said they had immigrated from England many decades ago, though she could have sworn she heard suppressed hints of a Cajun accent from time to time.

Maybe it was homesickness—not that she'd ever really had a home in New Orleans. True, she had a roof over her head at the orphanage, but she would hardly call it a home. Regardless, she did not linger on the thought, as America was filled with so many crossbreeds of accents and languages, and she had no reason not to take Luke at his word.

Luke shared that he was traveling to California to open a Presbyterian mission on the Pacific Coast, where he would house and feed Filipino and Chinese immigrant children. Thousands of boys and girls were regularly abandoned by their parents, who found seasonal agricultural work and were not allowed to take their children along to the farms. They would be left at churches in the early spring with hopes that they would be cared for by Christian institutions until their parents returned to pick them back up after the harvest.

"That's why I am stacked with dollar bills," he'd told her. Not only was he carrying the money the synod had provided to fund the opening of the mission home, but his family had all chipped in to make sure he had a safe and comfortable journey out west. No immigrant class bench in the back of the train for him.

Phreddie promised to pay back every cent Luke had so generously spent on her, though he insisted that it was nothing more than Christian charity and that the only payment he would accept was "the pleasure of a beautiful woman's company on this long passage to the other side of the world."

It had made Phreddie blush. Maybe Presbyterian were more charitable than Catholic nuns.

They were halfway through the Kansas plains when darkness fell on the saturated land, and she closed her eyes and drifted off to the sound of turning wheels and rain hitting the glass. In minutes, she fell deep into the middle of a terrible nightmare.

As the train rattled along, she could hear Miss Post barking at the police officer who had come with Oscar and his gang to the boarding house to capture her. She was back in the moment when she'd peered over the stairway ledge and watched from above as Oscar forced his way inside the building. Only this time, her brain began to piece together the fuzzy faces of the other men who had accompanied him over the threshold.

First came Oscar, his Delaroux looks reminding Phreddie of her once-beloved Remy, so she emitted a slight yelp as her body rattled along the tracks. The white-haired man followed, the one who'd terrified her with his look of ravenous hunger as he chased her across the roofs. The police officer who had knocked on the door was the third to enter, coming through calmly, without seeming to mind that Oscar had just knocked an old woman to the floor.

Just as Phreddie was about to pull her head back over the landing of her mind and run into the bedroom that she shared with Clara, the image of another man popped into her head. His broad frame moved forward, and his handsome face and brown mustache looked oddly familiar.

The train jerked to a stop, and Phreddie jumped up with a loud gasp. "Oh my god," she screamed.

"What is it?" Luke asked with great concern on his face—the very face that she had just seen in her mind.

Nervously, she straightened her dress. "Oh, nothing." She chuckled. "Just a nightmare." She stepped out into the aisle. "If you'll excuse me," she stammered, "I-I . . . I am going to use the toilet."

"Of course," Luke responded with a smile, then closed his eyes again and began to snore.

Phreddie made her way out of the train car, looking back at Luke one last time. *Keep it together,* she scolded herself.

Assured that he was still resting, she stepped over the feet of another man, which were resting in the aisle, and walked right past the toilet to the coach-class train car. On the right side was an open door that looked out onto the platform. She could see the conductor, who was half inside and half out.

"All aboard," he yelled across the platform.

It is now or never. She threw herself past the man, knocking him to the side, and then right out into the pouring rain that beat down on the uncovered railway platform.

"Miss," the conductor yelled, "I thought you were going to California?"

"Change of plans," Phreddie yelled back, running into the small train station and slamming the door shut behind her, throwing her body against it.

She turned her head nervously to watch through the window as the conductor shrugged and pulled the train door shut. The whistle sang out, and the wheels began to move forward.

Phreddie turned around, closed her eyes, pushed her head back against the door, and let out a loud sigh of relief. *By the time he realizes that I'm gone, he will be halfway to Santa Fe.*

When she opened her eyes, she found herself looking out on a very small and dusty wooden box of a room. "Wait," she wondered aloud. "Where am I?"

At one end, a little window had been cut into the wall where a middle-aged ticket attendant sat. Phreddie approached him with some concern as the reality of her situation began to hit her.

"Um, excuse me." She tapped on the counter.

The man, who was counting money, looked up. "Can I help you?"

"I'm sorry, but where exactly am I?"

"Newton, of course," he replied, then went back to counting.

Phreddie tapped once more. "Um, me again." She smiled. "And where exactly *is* Newton?"

The man's brow furrowed. "Ma'am, no one who comes to Newton doesn't know where Newton is."

"Well, I sure don't," she said, uncharacteristically annoyed.

"The middle of nowhere," he answered plainly. "Or as some people call it, the asshole of Kansas." He then began to pull a piece of plywood over the hole in the wall.

"Wait," Phreddie shouted, and pushed at the wood with a finger.

The man pulled the cover back and arched his brow.

"I seem to have gotten off at the wrong stop," she said sweetly. "Is there anyplace a girl can get some help, as I left my purse on board with all my money?"

"Try the saloon," the attendant told her. "Any woman who comes to this godforsaken town and doesn't have a husband winds up dancing on the tables at Miller's—if they want a roof over their head, that is." He put the wood back over the opening, and Phreddie could hear him laugh and say to himself, "Dancing . . . and a lot more than that."

With a sigh of disgust, she walked to the door over on the sidewall and opened it. There before her was the town, two sides of nothingness on a muddy street. In the flickering, glass-protected lamplight, she saw a post office, a general store, and a hatmaker on one side. On the other, she spied a tack shop alongside a stable, a bank, and a sheriff's station that was boarded over. All the way at the far end stood a large two-story building with a sign that read *Miller's Saloon and Hotel.*

Phreddie lifted her shoulders in the rain-soaked air and let out a squeal as she ran down the station's few wooden steps and splashed her way furiously through muck and mud. By the time she reached the front of Miller's entry, her dress was speckled up to her kneecaps with brown slop.

I've never been inside a place like this before. The thought worried her. There were no other choices, though. It was either go inside or sleep in the rain, so she pushed the doors open and took in the raucous scene.

Music played, women danced, men looked at cards and tossed coins onto tables, and everyone was drinking.

She gasped. "Heck fires."

Through the smoky haze, a woman holding a tray with two empty glasses approached her.

"Um . . ." Phreddie stared at the buxom brunette.

"Can I help you?" the woman asked shortly.

"Miller?" she asked.

The waitress gave her a thorough up and down. "Looks like we got ourselves another dancer." She rolled her eyes, then nodded at the far wall. "He's over there behind the bar, next to that wild buck, Hodges."

"Thanks," Phreddie replied.

She saw a man pouring drinks and the back of Hodges's head, which rested on a huge frame.

"I'm Misty," the waitress said with resignation. "Always room for another."

Phreddie nodded but kept her eyes on Hodges. She knew she should have minded her own business, as she had enough to contend with, but curiosity nipped at her heels, so she asked the waitress, "Why is he a wild buck, then?"

Misty gave a half smile and looked over at Hodges. "Some say he killed his wife—well, *wives*, I should say."

"More than one? Goodness!"

"But I'm not sure," Misty said. "Underneath all of that stubble, looks to me to be a fine-looking man, and that strong, big body of his? He could suffocate me any day or night."

"Thanks for the information," Phreddie mumbled, uncomfortable with Misty's tone. She headed toward Miller, and although he might be serving a real murderer, she was desperate to interrupt. *Fact is, I need a roof over my head, and come heck or high water—and this town appears to have both—I won't find one talking to Misty.*

"Excuse me," she said as she cautiously approached. "Are you Mr. Miller?"

The man eyed her up and down, but his eyes settled on her center parts, the way most men's blinkers seemed to do. "Why, yes I am," he answered her chest rather than her face.

"I seem to be in a bit of a predicament." She smiled meekly, bending down to catch Miller's eye. "You see, I got off at the wrong station, and I need a place to stay for a night or two till I can find some way of purchasing a train ticket to the coast."

"Uh-huh," Miller replied, licking his lips.

"Unfortunately, my bags and all of my money were left on the train, and now I am just plain stuck here and looking for the kindness of strangers to offer me some help."

"Oh, I can help." Miller gave a toothy grin.

Phreddie tapped the bar, and he looked up.

"I can give you room and board. That means food and two drinks of sauce a day."

"Oh my, thank you." Phreddie beamed. "That is so kind of you."

"For a price," he continued.

"A price? But I just said I don't have any money."

"All the girls that eat and sleep under my roof give something to get something," he said smoothly.

Phreddie thought it over. "Well, that seems fair. I can help serve, and change the bedding . . . Oh, and I'm a wiz at cleaning. This bar will look like a fancy establishment once I apply my elbow grease around here for a few days." She put her hands on her hips and looked around the place to see where she would start first.

“I don’t think you understand, Miss. Miss . . . ? What is your name anyways?” he asked.

“Phreddie.” The word shot out of her mouth.

Miller’s face twisted up. “Freddie as in Frederick?”

She was too busy chastising herself for giving him her real name to pay attention to the next question, and answered it just as truthfully as she had the first. “Close to it, but with a *Ph*, not an *F* like men spell it,” she explained, then caught herself.

“Bobbing apples,” she fumed aloud. *How many Phreddies are there in the world? Now if Luke comes back this way, he will know I’ve been here.*

“Aren’t you just the most curious of creatures.” Miller laughed. “That innocent bit might get you some more coins for your bedroom exploits from the whooperups, I do believe.”

“Bedroom exploits?” she asked, but then it hit her. “Oh no.” She shook her head. “I don’t do any bedroom exploits.” She waved her hands in the air in protest.

“Of course you do, sweet thing,” Miller said.

“I really can’t!” she insisted. “I just need to work for a couple of days, and then I’ll be gone, Mr.—”

“That’s what all the raspberry-cream strumpets around here say when they roll in to speak with good ole Miller, but trust me, you seem quite virginal and nervous, and all of that means top dollar. So, I expect you’re gonna be here for a while.” Miller roared with laughter.

Suddenly, a loud crash rang out. Miller choked on his guffaw, and everyone around the room stopped talking. Phreddie stared at the large fist that had slammed against the counter. The veins that throbbed on the back of that balled-up, sun-kissed hand were covered in light brown fur.

“That’s enough,” the murderer, Hodges, growled. Then he threw a few coins down on the countertop and pushed his stool back.

He is menacingly tall. Phreddie gasped to herself as she looked up at the man’s furrowed brow and intense face.

“You can work for me,” he offered plainly, his voice a deep baritone.

“W-w-work for you?” Phreddie stuttered.

“My wife’s dead as Moses, and my place ain’t been cleaned in a year,” he explained.

The crowd gawped at the conversation.

She chewed her lip in confusion, looking at him in disbelief. She didn't know whether Hodges's or Miller's offer was the better one, especially in light of what the waitress had told her about this man earlier. *Two wives*?

He continued, "One week of cleaning and cooking, and I'll pay for your ticket to California, or whatever dog-blasted place you choose."

Phreddie looked at Miller's face, then back to Hodges. At last, her teeth let go of her lip, and she offered a weak smile. "I guess all I can say then is yes, and thank you," she replied tentatively.

Around the room, people gasped and shook their heads in alarm.

"Fool," a man whispered under his breath.

Another moaned and said, "She'll be dead before the week is up."

But when Hodges turned and faced the multitude, everyone went back to their merriment, none brave enough to look directly into his eyes, nevertheless say something to his face.

"Well, let's go then," he commanded, then walked off without waiting for any further reply.

He was through the swinging doors before Phreddie could so much as blink, so she hurried after him. As she passed the waitress, Misty leaned into her and said, "You might have just landed the only eligible bachelor Newton has to offer . . . or you could have just bargained yourself a pine box, depending on who around here you believe."

Phreddie nodded and smiled nervously, though she wanted neither a husband nor death. She would have to take the gamble either way, as spreading her legs for fare was simply out of the question. This was her best chance to get fed, sheltered, and earn some money before she headed off in a new direction. Though with Misty's words in mind, she decided that she would force herself to remain alert, sleep with one eye open even. One week was all it would take, and then she could be on her way to California—or heck, maybe even to Canada. By the time Luke woke up on the train and figured out where she had jumped ship, her week could already be over. Add in the days it would take for him to not only make contact with Oscar but for her brother-in-law to travel all the way from New York to Newton, and she would have already vanished like the morning vapor in the hot sun.

With renewed energy, she lifted up the hem of her muddied dress, raised her head high, pushed through the doors, and stepped outside. There she found Hodges on top of a horse, waiting in front of the saloon's shallow steps. She tentatively stepped forward, but when the horse snorted, she took a step back, a small gasp escaping her lips.

Once again, she tiptoed toward the horse with an extended palm. If she could just encourage her rigid body to move one more step, it would be easy for Hodges to give her a hand up so that she could ride on the saddle behind him, but her body was frozen in place.

Hodges looked her in the eyes, then sighed. At once, he steered the horse away and down the muddied street toward the east.

"Wait," Phreddie called out into the rainy night. "Do you expect me to walk behind you in all of this?" His silent response meant she had no choice but to follow. "Blam-jam," she exclaimed as she stepped out from under Miller's covered porch and right into the watery muck.

•

Their journey went on for what felt like hours, and with each step, Phreddie's shoes filled anew with the soaked earth of the plains. The darkness soon grew pitch-black, and every few minutes, Hodges would turn his head slightly as if to make sure that she hadn't wandered helplessly off into the dismal night.

Phreddie could see why the people at Miller's didn't seem to like this man. In fact, other than that one waitress, they all appeared to be outright terrified of him. However, she was too exhausted to be afraid for long.

Why didn't this philistine let me ride on the horse too? She was fuming, but she reminded herself that walking in the rain beat lying on her back for Miller.

Between the pelting drops, Phreddie was finally able to make out the shape of a house, a barn, and then a corral in the distance. She sighed with relief as she envisioned the warm fire and hot cup of coffee she would enjoy once she was dry and wrapped up in a blanket.

As they approached, Hodges slid off his horse and yelled at her over the driving rain, "Go inside! I need to take the horse to the barn."

Phreddie obeyed, as she did not want to be exposed to the wild Kansas outdoors for one more second. She practically ran onto the little porch, where she threw the door open and stepped inside with a smile of great relief.

She let out a contented sigh. Then, as her eyes began to focus, her relief faded back into her throat. Her elation abated. What remained were her bulging eyes, which stared blankly into the shadows.

Total darkness would have been preferable to what was visible in the faded light that crept out from the smoldering embers in the fireplace. Through the wet, tangled hair that half covered her face, Phreddie surveyed what seemed more like a creature's lair than a man's home. She shook her head to refocus, as if the rain had impaired her vision, but what she saw only got worse.

Standing in an ever-growing puddle of her own making, she glanced around the one-room cabin. She could now make out an old wooden table and two dusty chairs, as well as some long pantry cabinets. The doors hung open, and the shelves inside appeared close to empty. Along the wall by a small window was a rusty old wash basin. As she turned her head back toward the nearly cold fireplace, she spotted a wooden bed frame covered in heaps of crumpled blankets.

A chill ran up her spine. She stepped over and grabbed a poker that she used to stoke the fire, then bent over and picked up a log from the hearth and tossed it inside. It quickly lit up, and so did the room. She then grabbed a stub of candle from the mantle and bent back down so that its wick caught fire. When she stood up this time, she turned around and moved into the center of the room, where the shadows began to crawl back to reveal the true state of the household.

Across the table sat scattered pots, pans, and dishes that looked well used and little cleaned. Random pieces of clothing had been strewn across the floor in every direction. A mouse scurried past Phreddie's cold, wet feet, and she screamed as if the rodent were death itself.

She quietly placed the candle on the table and reached for the old hay broom in the corner. Lifting it into the air, she beat the ground until she chased the mouse out into the rain. Then she slammed the door shut behind it, and as she did so, a large mountain of dust broke free from the ceiling and fell onto her head and face.

•

Hodges stepped inside his home about thirty minutes after he had sent Phreddie inside. Now that he had put the horse away for the night, having brushed, fed, and watered the beast and thrown some dry bedding into the stable, he was ready to deal with his rash decision to house a stranger.

"Silly coot," he muttered under his breath as he made his way toward the door. He had lived alone just fine, and perfectly miserably, for the past twelve months. *What was I thinking, offering this house to a boarder?*

When he stepped over the threshold, he found Phreddie seated at the table, her dusty head bent over, her face laid upon her hands. In front of her sat the stub of a candle, which cast just enough light for him to see that she was a right fright to look at. His stomach grumbled, which drew his attention away from any sympathy he might be feeling for this bedraggled being.

He grunted, then in two bear's paces, he was across the room and in front of the larder, which he tore open. He pulled out half a loaf of stale bread and placed it on the table. Next, he pulled two dirty plates and two cups from above his head and slammed them down next to the bread. "Eat," he commanded.

Charlie lifted the pitcher that sat in the center of the table and poured some water into one of the cups, gulping it down. When he'd finished, he looked down at Phreddie. "Tomorrow I expect you to prepare the meals—three of them."

She turned her dirt-smudged face up to him, then meekly reached for the bread and pulled a piece off with her mouth.

"Breakfast at five, lunch at eleven, and dinner at sunset," he continued as she chewed.

Satisfied with the conversation, Hodges pulled off his pants and shirt right in front of her till he was in nothing but his hole-covered long johns.

"Oh my goodness." She gasped and covered her eyes with her hands.

"What's the matter?" Hodges shrugged. "Ain't never seen a man and his worm before? At least I kept it covered. For now, that is."

"Charming." She groaned, peeking out between her fingers as he walked across the room and set his large frame down on the bed with a thud.

"Where exactly am I supposed to sleep?" she whined.

Hodges pulled a beat-up pillow out from under him and tossed it in her direction. She coughed when it slapped the bread right out of her mouth.

"There's a blanket in the chest."

Charlie watched through half-closed eyes as Phreddie got up from the table and walked over to the chest. She lifted the lid, then pulled a quilt out, her eyes widening in fear. Hodges had forgotten that he kept his guns hidden under that blanket.

"It will be a long day for you tomorrow," he said, as if to close the matter of the guns before any discussion had even started.

Like the conversation, Phreddie shut the lid. Charlie watched as she grabbed the candle stub off the table and used it to lead her way to a corner of the room. She sighed to herself, then lay down on the floor and blew the little light out.

•

Phreddie had been sound asleep, but now a boot pushed against her thigh and nudged her awake.

"What the . . . ?" she sat up on the floor, rubbing her cramped back.

"It's five o'clock," Hodges said plainly.

"What?" she replied, somewhere between an *I have no idea what you are talking about* and a not-so-vague memory of Sister Adrienne waking her in the same manner. She took the blanket and threw it over her head, then lay back down.

This time, the boot struck her more firmly across her backside. Phreddie shot up, terror coursing through her when she remembered where she was and who was kicking her.

"Breakfast is at five," Hodges stated, and walked toward the door. "I'll be back in a few minutes." The door opened and slammed shut.

Phreddie's legs cracked as she stood up. She leaned against a nearby rocking chair to steady herself through a yawn.

In the larder she found a few eggs, so she grabbed the only clean pan she could find and slammed it on top of the fire that Hodges must have stoked to life before he interrupted her slumber.

"If I were grease, where would I be?" she asked aloud, then walked over to a covered bowl and slapped some onto the now-hot pan, which sizzled angrily. "I know how you feel," she said, cracking the eggs open and leaving them to fry while she added some coffee grounds into a pot of water and plopped it next to the pan.

Charlie came back in and sat down at the table and waited. Phreddie tossed the eggs on a dirty plate and pushed it in front of him along with a cup of weak coffee.

He stared at it a moment, then asked, "What's this?"

"You have next to nothing to eat here, so it was the best I could do," she whispered.

Hodges examined it for a minute, then took a sip of the coffee and spit it back out into the mug. He got up from the table. "I'm mending fences today. Won't have time for lunch, but I'll expect a real supper."

"With what, Mister?" Phreddie said, incredulous.

"Figure it out," he responded curtly.

"I'm not Jesus with fish and loaves," she countered. "And even if I was, you don't have so much as a guppy's scale for me to divide, nevertheless a crumb of bread left this morning."

Hodges grunted before he slammed the door behind him.

Phreddie looked around at the woman-forsaken home and sighed. "Goodness, this seems near impossible. I suppose there's no time like the present to begin such a perilous journey," she mumbled. Grabbing a big pot, she headed outside, where she filled it with water from a spout.

"Floors, walls, heck, even the ceiling in this dust ball needs scrubbing," she declared. As she made her way back toward the house, she saw a few scrawny chickens hop out of the barn and start to peck their way through the dust for mites. She made note, then headed back inside, where she spent the morning soaking dishes with hardened food in hot water before she scoured them all to the point that her fingers peeled. "Even the nuns didn't have tasks this demanding," she grunted as she removed a bit of calcified grime from a pan.

Next, she opened the door and swept dust bunnies the size of actual bunnies out of the house. Finally, she turned to tidying up various items and started to make a pile of clothes for washing. When she held up a pair of Hodges's filthy long johns, she nearly fainted from the scent. "Good God, that man is disgusting," she said, scrunching up her nose.

She grabbed a handful of garments from the pile and threw them on the floor. Sitting down next to a large pot of hot water, she dipped each item in and scrubbed it with lye and a large stone. *This is a far cry from Mrs. Guidry's, with her lavender-scented laundry oil.* She groaned as she pummeled the rock onto a rancid sweater.

When Hodges returned, it was after sunset, and Phreddie chuckled at the sight of his wide eyes when he saw that the chaotic pigsty he'd left in the morning was now a respectable home.

"The nuns would beat us mercilessly if we didn't keep the orphanage spotless," she informed him.

"Smells good," he replied with wonder. He sat down and salivated at the sight of the roasted chicken that Phreddie had set on a plate in front of him. As he tucked a cloth napkin into the neck of his shirt, he squinted. "Um, where did you get that?" he asked suspiciously.

"You had three," she replied, cutting him a few slices of white meat.

"Not the white one," he moaned unexpectedly. "Please tell me that this is not the daggum white one."

Phreddie ignored him and sat down beside him to nibble on a wing.

"That was Lily's pet," he said softly.

"Oh my," she cried out.

"It was the only thing she loved," he spat bitterly.

In despair, she responded, "How was I to know that?"

"Tomorrow I'll run you to the mercantile," Hodges announced bitterly. "I need more barbed wire anyway."

Then he stood up without eating a morsel and undressed for bed.

•

Seven days had passed since Phreddie had escaped capture in New York City. Oscar's only comfort was the image in his mind of Luke waving to him from the window of the same train that his brother's murderer had boarded. *It pays to have paid people.*

While Phreddie must think she had gotten away, Oscar knew otherwise. Wherever they wound up, Luke would send word back eventually as to their whereabouts. For now though, Oscar had no choice but to sit back and wait until contact was made. With the continual addition of new rail lines, it would be pointless to make any pursuit, as Oscar might end up traveling in the opposite direction from Phreddie and Luke. Instead, he used these days to pace the floor—and to plan.

There were times he considered abandoning his quest to find his brother's killer. All of these weeks away from New Orleans were not good for business. By now though, his father would have returned home and taken things firmly in hand, and Oscar dared not return to him empty-handed.

It was not just that Remy had been his father's favorite. Oscar found himself almost enjoying the bloodsport of the chase. Granted, every time he pictured Remy's body on the floor of the hotel room, his heart cried out for vengeance. But something else was at play. Oscar never lost, and Phreddie had managed to escape, which both infuriated and aroused him.

It was early evening. He was admiring the fine image of himself in his embroidered magenta waist coat that stared back at him from the looking glass over the wash basin when the knock on his hotel room door finally came. He rushed to open it and asked the young employee, "Arrived?"

"Yes, sir." The boy nodded, and Oscar grabbed his silk top hat off a nearby table and followed him.

The young man led him to the lobby, where a woman dressed in all black was sitting alone with her back to him as she stared out the window.

"Thank you," Oscar said to the boy as he handed him some money, then he approached the figure. "*Sœur* Adrienne?" he asked.

The middle-aged nun turned around and nodded. "Yes."

"So kind of you to have traveled so far, and so quickly."

Her devilish smile reminded Oscar of the look that Mahogany delivered when she wanted a second or third go in a single evening. He shook his head to clear any illicit thoughts of this nun hopping up on his lap with her robes up over her head. Instead, he looked down at her hands and saw the envelope.

"It's in here," she said as she passed it to him.

"Ah, yes." He lifted the flap and peeked inside. "This has definitely earned a sizable donation for the Children and Charity Orphanage in New Orleans," he continued as Sister Adrienne raised an eyebrow with an impish grin. "And of course, its head sister."

"Bless you," Sister Adrienne cooed, and once again Oscar wondered if she wasn't undressing him with her eyes at this very moment.

"The contents will serve us both very well," he concluded.

"I like the thought of that." She pouted her lips as if she wanted him to kiss them.

"If you will forgive me"—Oscar grinned—"I must go now. It is time for my dinner." Though he loved a saucy woman, he wasn't so sure about taking pocket pouch that had pledged itself to the Lord. Besides, this nun's forwardness almost made Oscar uncomfortable, and that was something no other woman had ever done.

At last, he turned and left, but all the while he could feel the nun's eyes running up the backs of his legs and over his wool-suited buttocks.

Cast-Iron Cage

After frying eggs from the two remaining chickens, Phreddie stood in front of a small looking glass and sighed at what stared back at her. Days on the run, dried mud, and working as a hired scullery maid had left her a sore sight. She pulled one of the few pins that remained in her hair out and attempted to use it to capture a wild mass of breakaway strands, but it was futile. She probably looked more savage than she imagined those Indian squaws who lived on the Kansas plains did.

She had heard someone's frightful talk about these people on the train ride, and it singed her mind in a way that she didn't think she could ever forget. The thought of those barbarians, out there in the tall grasses somewhere beyond this prairie homestead, made her shudder.

However, at the moment, her own disheveled image was even more terrifying. She sighed to herself. "I can't go into town like this."

"Under the bed," Hodges rudely interrupted her self-pity.

"What?" Phreddie asked with mild annoyance, then she caught herself. She wasn't sure what it was about Hodges, but she was normally prone to quiet acquiescence. Even though he scared her terribly, he irritated her in equal measure. And with that, she found herself prodding him, trying to get beneath the surface, rather than simply responding with a nod, as any intelligent person who knew about his past or saw his towering frame would do. But his personality was almost as grating as the tracks he left in the drawers she was forced to clean in order to earn her way out of this pit.

"What are you saying?" Her voice sounded agitated.

"Under the bed . . . there's a box with some things," he replied, this time softly.

Curious, Phreddie walked over to the bed and squatted down, spying a large box that she pulled out from underneath it. She lifted the top off and peered inside. There she found a pink hat with a wide yellow ribbon, which she gently placed on the floor beside her. Underneath it was a blue dress with the most delicate pattern of tiny printed daffodils.

"This is beautiful." She pulled it out and held it up to the light. As she admired the dress, she caught sight of the bouquet of dried flowers and wedding certificate that had been hidden underneath. "Oh," she said softly. "Did Lily wear these at your wedding?"

They were silent for a moment.

"It makes no sense to keep them tucked away, as you need a dress and I have a dress," Hodges said at last. He stood up and pushed the chair out from behind him, then walked quickly to the door. "I'll saddle the wagon up, and we'll leave in fifteen minutes," he announced coldly.

"But I couldn't wear your dead wife's wedding dress," Phreddie began to protest, but the sight of her torn, filthy hemline stopped her speech.

"Fifteen minutes," Hodges repeated sternly, closing the door.

It didn't take Phreddie more than a few seconds to slip out of the dress she had been wearing since she went to work on that last New York morning. She had long since removed the corset, but what remained was too tight for Kansas cleaning nonetheless. Now free of it, she breathed deeply as she slipped on the little blue number the way Lily must have done on the day she married Hodges.

Who would choose to actually marry that man? She pursed her lips at the thought, though it seemed curious that a ruffian like Hodges had sentimentally saved the dress of his second wife, especially if he had killed her in cold blood the way the townsfolk believed. Either way, he had the most insufferable personality.

Maybe she begged him to kill her rather than endure endless days with a big, rude, smelly, man-bear, she thought to herself. Regardless, Lily's dress fit perfectly, and Phreddie would only need it for a few days before she was out of Newton forever.

When she came outside, sunlight had broken across the Kansas skies, and for the first time, she got a good look at the expansive and beautiful countryside that surrounded Hodges's homestead. Long prairie grass spread out over flat land and rolling hills, which seemed to stretch on for miles in every direction. Phreddie suddenly felt small in the vastness that surrounded her. One could easily get swallowed up by so much nature running on in infinite green.

The rattling of a wagon grounded her mind, and she turned to find that Hodges had pulled up next to Phreddie. "Hmm," he grunted as he looked down at her, now in his dead wife's dress.

Her hands, which held the hem of Lily's dress to keep it from touching the dusty yard, shook nervously as she quickly stepped around the horses, watching them closely. Once on the other side, she steadied herself against the driver's box floor. She then attempted to pull herself up but fell backward.

When Hodges just sat there looking forward, Phreddie rolled her eyes. "Thanks for the help," she panted as she finally managed to pull herself up into the seat alongside of him on her second try.

Without a word of acknowledgement, he urged the pair of horses forward, and their bodies rattled along across the uneven terrain.

"How did you ever manage to get married, being as charming as you are?" she called out, clinging to the seat with both hands as the wagon wheels dipped in and out of great big ruts that the rain had formed in the ground.

"So help me, Hannah." He sighed.

Phreddie frowned. "Who is Hannah?"

"You're the one who needed the tarnal job," he said over the whining aches and moans of the cart. "I never promised charm, lady, just enough money for your train fare. And with your constant complaints, not to mention what you did to Lily's prized hen, I'm beginning to wonder if you are worth the price."

"Are you always this chivalrous, or are you just trying to atone for something?" Phreddie snapped.

He didn't respond, and they jostled along for what seemed to be ages, Phreddie's lungs rising and falling heavily from their argument, until at last the town of Newton came into view. As they pulled up on Main Street, Phreddie could not help but notice all the townsfolk stop and stare.

When they reached the mercantile, she could have sworn she could see people peering out of windows to catch a glimpse of the duo, but Hodges seemed impervious and just pushed a bag of coins into her hand.

"Two dollars," he informed her curtly.

"But you don't have anything in that house," she muttered, turning to address him.

"I don't plan on coming back here till after harvest, so get me enough till then," he replied as he helped himself down from the wagon.

"When's that?" she asked.

"Two months," he said before he left her.

Two months? She looked at the pitiful coin purse in her lap, opened it up, and dropped the meager contents into her hand.

"This is barely enough for two weeks," she called to the back of his head as it was lost in the crowd of townsfolk.

Sighing, Phreddie shrugged and remembered that this was not her problem. She would be gone from this town many days before two months—or even two weeks—were up, and whether or not Hodges had enough food to eat after that, she didn't really care. This money just had to stretch so that he had enough food to keep him well and happy until he handed her the train fare she had earned. Then he could starve, as far as she was concerned.

When she walked into the mercantile, she spotted an old woman at the counter who was placing a jar of penny candy down. "How can I help you?" the lady sang out sweetly.

"I need the items here on this list for Mr. Charlie Hodges." Phreddie had hardly finished saying his name when the old woman's body tensed.

"You're that girl he's tricked into another marriage?" she asked through a now crinkled-up puss.

"Oh, no." Phreddie giggled. "I'm not marrying him, I'm just—"

"Living in sin, then," the old woman croaked as she yanked the shopping list out of Phreddie's hands. "I'll just as soon grab all of this by myself, and quickly. Best you are in and out of this store before you sully it more than you already have."

She stormed off, muttering to herself, "As if we want the likes of a woman who would live with Charlie Hodges in this . . ."

Phreddie stood there with her jaw open as the woman disappeared into a storeroom. After a minute, she began to eye the jar of penny candy on the counter. *I haven't had one of these in years,* she thought. Sister Adrienne had rarely allowed the other children at the orphanage to have candy, but with Phreddie, she never allowed it. Once, one of the other children had dropped hers, and it broke into a thousand shards of sugar. Sister Adrienne ordered Phreddie to sweep up the mess, and when the crying girl was marched off for a second piece of candy, Phreddie got down on her knees. She lifted a small piece of the confection, blew away some dust, and plucked a hair off the tiny piece of heaven. Then she looked both ways to be sure she was alone before she swiftly plopped it under her tongue.

It tasted like what it must feel like to have a family and a home. To live somewhere you were wanted. It had been that good, and no matter how harshly Sister Adrienne or anyone else abused her the rest of that week, all she had to do was think back on that magic in her mouth and she could get through another minute, no matter how dehumanizing it was.

Now, Phreddie was just about to stick her hand in and grab a candy out of the jar when there was a loud crash behind her.

"Oh my. *Santos Dios!*" exclaimed a woman's voice. Phreddie turned around to find a stranger, dressed in all black, bent down and rushing to pick up a stack of canned tomatoes that she had knocked over.

Phreddie hurried to her side. "Here, let me help," she said as she reached to grab some of the tins.

"Forgive me, but that's my sister's wedding dress," the lady confessed with great surprise as she rose to her feet, cans in both her hands.

"Oh, I'm so sorry," Phreddie said meekly, standing up too. "I don't seem to have much success with wedding dresses," she remarked, mostly to herself.

"I just was shocked to see you in it," the woman explained as she put the cans down and reached out her hand. "I'm a widow, Ms. Hilaria Ortiz, and Lily was my sister. But I've already said that, haven't I?"

"I meant no disrespect by wearing your sister's dress, Ms. Ortiz. It's just that my own dress is filthy, and I had nothing else to wear.

"I see," Ms. Ortiz said, but she looked down over the wire frames that sat on her nose.

"It is beautiful, though," Phreddie remarked as she lifted a piece of the skirt in the air. Catching herself, she lowered it, as well as her eyes. "I am most sorry," she repeated. "I'm not really experienced with having conversations with people."

"You are not the one that needs to apologize, my dear." Ms. Ortiz sighed. "What is your name again?"

"Phreddie," she replied, then put her hand out and shook Ms. Ortiz's. "I'm only staying here shortly with—"

Ms. Ortiz cut her off. "I know who you're staying with, Phreddie. There's no need to say his name. Plus, I know why. You see, nothing that evil man does in this town goes unnoticed."

An awkward silence filled the room. After a few seconds, Phreddie whispered, "I only recently learned how difficult it can be to lose someone you love."

"I thank you for your condolences, but it is your own life that you should be worried about."

Thoughts of Oscar popped up into Phreddie's mind. "Why? Is someone looking for me?" she asked, frightened.

The widow ignored the question and shrugged. "My Lily is already gone. All the same, you are staying with a murderer."

"Oh." Phreddie relaxed.

"You don't seem to be as scared as you should be, young lady," Ms. Ortiz remonstrated her. "I would advise you to flee now, while that man's back is turned. If he let you into town on your own, then you must break away while you can. Take the next train out."

"But I have no money," Phreddie explained. "So you see, Hodges is my only hope at present."

Ms. Ortiz put her hand to her chin. "I could speak to our priest, Father Milfken, about staying at the church."

Images of Sister Adrienne rushed into Phreddie's mind. Then there was the thought of Luke and his made-up Presbyterian ministry. "I've had enough dealings with clergy for one lifetime," she replied with a slight shiver. "Besides, I need money to leave Newton, not just a place to lay my head. That means I'll have to take my chances with Hodges, though it does pain me to say it."

Ms. Ortiz smoothed her dress and stood up straighter. "In that case, maybe the two of you are meant for each other." She turned to go, but Phreddie put her hand on her arm.

"I do not know the circumstances of your sister's death, nor am I completely oblivious to Mr. Hodges's peculiarities, but with him is where I must be until I can earn myself passage."

"Then I will pray for you," Ms. Ortiz said, patting Phreddie's hand. "I once tried to reason with my Lily about that man, but she was as stubborn as our mother. I just hope you come to your senses sooner than my sister did."

Curiosity at last gripped at Phreddie. "If you don't mind my asking, what happened to Lily? People say he killed her, but what actually did happen?"

"That man seems to bedevil the weak," Ms. Ortiz began. "Lily was such a good girl until she up and ran away from our home on the Texas-Mexico border one day. It was as if something had possessed her, for why else would she have turned from her family? We thought she'd been captured by

Indians until she sent back word that she had become engaged to a man all the way in Kansas. Kansas? we asked ourselves. How could she have gone all the way up here? The only thing my family could put it down to was that Satan must have called her on the wind, and as impressionable as Lily was, she just up and answered."

"Isn't the Mexico border very far from here?" Phreddie was confused.

"In the end it didn't matter if she had come from the Amazonas of Brazil. She was lost to us up here in this godforsaken land." Ms. Ortiz's voice became shrill. "I begged my sister to return to us, but she refused. The Bible says that money is the root of all evil, and I came to learn eventually that Lily saw Hodges's vast acreage as a means to move up in the world. But acreage be damned if you're six feet under."

"How exactly did your sister die then, Ms. Ortiz?" Phreddie pressed gently.

"That man shot her," the woman stated plainly. "She must have finally come to her senses. I just know she was going to leave him. Then he shot her." She became incensed. "He did it right in the heart, at that. That miserable man! Why couldn't he have just let my sister go?"

"Blam-jam," Phreddie exclaimed softly. She lifted a hand over her own breast, and her fear of Hodges suddenly grew. *Are all men just one step away from killing their wives?* She asked curiously, "Why wasn't he arrested?"

"Because Newton hasn't had a sheriff since the last one was killed, along with eight others at the big gunfight at Hyde Park. Our jailhouse stands vacant and cobwebbed. Why do you think we're called the wickedest city in the West? There's Satan's blood in this red dirt."

"My word." Phreddie gasped at the imagery

"Exactly. It's on no account of God and his word that I am here." Ms. Ortiz clasped her rosary. "It may be bloody and lawless, but this town has already taken my family, and I have nothing more to give but my duty and my prayers. I have vowed to work alongside Father Milfken to hound the gates of hell until this town, and people like Hodges, turn from their wicked ways, or see to it that they are burned at the stake. Let us hope you are not here long enough to experience either. May you get out before you are corrupted by his ways or wind up dead. Godspeed," she said sharply, then turned on her heels and marched out of the store. The door closed loudly.

The shopkeeper returned to see what the noise was, carrying a large crate of goods to the counter. "Two dollars," she called rudely to Phreddie, who walked back over to her.

"Not much here for two dollars," she worried aloud as she fingered the items in the crate.

The woman put her hand out curtly. "Who cares? Absolutely no one. So just pay and get out."

Phreddie resigned herself to the woman's demands and handed her the bag of coins. She hoisted the crate and went outside to find that Charlie was already there. Handing him the food, she climbed up on the seat and waited for him. She heard the crate slam against the wagon's cart, and then he climbed up next to her and set the horses to moving.

Though they rode back in silence, Phreddie's mind screamed with Ms. Ortiz's words of warning. Images of a woman with a gunshot wound to the heart kept rising to the surface of her mind. Having barely escaped the same fate as Lily, Phreddie was lost in a sea of fear. She could see Remy's wild eyes and the blood that had poured out of her mouth when he struck her. So engrossed was she in the thought that when the wagon pulled to a stop in front of the homestead, she didn't move to get down.

"Hey," Hodges barked, pushing her shoulder.

Phreddie flinched. "Please don't kill me!" she cried, her hand over her heart.

"I was just telling you that we're here." He sneered, then got down from the wagon and stormed into the barn.

"Oh," she said softly. She climbed down at last, went into the house, and closed the door behind her.

•

The door to a long but narrow cage slammed shut.

"This will do perfectly," Luke said to the blacksmith as he handed him some money. "It is exactly the type of transport for a wild beast that Mr. Delaroux is looking for. I'll be back with the boss to get it in the morning once he arrives. With the final modifications, that is."

The blacksmith nodded, and Luke walked out of the shop and headed for a local gun store nearby.

As he crossed the street, he thought back to the Atchison, Topeka, and Santa Fe. *I suppose she isn't as helpless as I thought after all.* He had no idea how long he'd been asleep on the train from the time that Phreddie had gotten up to use the toilet to when he'd awoken to find her missing. Luckily the attendant assured him that, while the train had already passed a number of stops, he distinctly remembered the woman in blue hopping off in the town of Newton.

By the time Luke had doubled back and discovered Phreddie's exact whereabouts, Oscar was on his way to meet him in Kansas City. In fact, Luke himself had only dropped into Newton long enough to learn that the whole community was abuzz about the new girl who had found herself a temporary home with some crazy man just outside town.

A cheap shag and an extra couple of bucks spent at Miller's on a mouthy waitress named Misty let him know that Phreddie planned to be in town for one whole week. This moved him to rapidly send a telegram to New York. He then headed right out of Newton and straight for the Kansas-Missouri line with the list of goods that Oscar had wired, which Luke was to acquire while Oscar traveled west to meet up with him.

In so many words, Oscar informed Luke that once they were reunited, he planned for them to ride the two days from Kansas City to Newton on horseback rather than by train, though with the special contraption he'd been ordered to pay triple for in order to have it quickly made. So long as Oscar kept Luke's billfold filled, Luke didn't care if they swam the mighty Mississippi together out west in the iron box he had made to carry Phreddie.

Luke had dutifully spent the last couple of days working with the blacksmith on the cage, stocking up on firearms and dry goods, and putting together a small band of men that would ride out with Oscar and his boys to hunt down Phreddie and haul her back to justice in New Orleans, Delaroux style.

But now his thoughts ran back to their time on the train together, and Luke wondered how someone who seemed as lovely as Phreddie had during their hours of conversation could possibly have killed Remy in cold blood. The woman seemed more kitten than tiger. Truth be told, over those days he'd begun to understand why Remy had found her attractive beyond her good looks.

He recalled one of their conversations, about motherhood. It started when he commented on the patience of a woman on board the train who was dealing with her especially bratty child. Luke figured he would go whole hog on the identity he had claimed. It seemed natural for someone who was moving to California to start a mission to quote from the Bible, so Luke called on one of the only verses he remembered from his childhood. He considered it to be a particularly fitting way to double down on his pretend position.

He was taken aback, however, when he quoted a proverb about honoring mothers and Phreddie said she didn't believe mothers should be honored any more or less than anyone else. It had both startled and intrigued him, as most women, especially ones that were so demure, seemed to enjoy the topic of motherhood. Yet this woman almost seemed repelled by it.

"Why ever do you not?" Luke pushed. Though the conversation was only intended as part of his performance, he found himself genuinely interested in her response.

"My mother left me as a child. No person should receive any honor simply for giving birth or having a title. Instead, people should be judged by their deeds. In my mother's case, honor is too kind, as only a cruel woman leaves their own child behind to strangers," Phreddie said firmly.

Her face had looked stoic, not from resolve but from the emptiness of a lifetime of disappointment. He could almost feel himself be physically drawn in to this loneliness, because here was a woman who simply needed love.

Alas, Oscar was not paying him to develop sentiments or tend to the feelings of his brother's killer. So Luke repressed his desire and happily played the role of a minister to lost souls. Occasionally, though, he would catch himself looking at her neckline. His gaze would land at the top of her cleavage and run across her neck until he reached her ears, which had the most perfect pearl-shaped lobes.

In any other situation, a little nibble on some flesh would be fine, but the only taste he would be taking of Phreddie would be in his mind. *Unless, of course, sleeping with her would help me gain more trust and keep her close until Oscar arrives,* he'd thought at the time.

But instead he had foolishly napped, and she had slipped away from him. Now, with his ruse exposed, his only course of action was to put her in chains, and any dream of seduction would remain just that.

When Luke walked into the store, he settled in front of a counter and picked up a Missouri toothpick—a large knife with a handle carved out of a buck's antler. He had heard enough dime tales about the plains to know that guns were not enough for safety. He needed a weapon in each boot in case he was ever captured by a band of those redmen, and so he plunked down some coins and pushed the knife deep down into his shoe. Then he headed outside, where he sat down on a bench and waited for Oscar's train to roll into town.

•

Phreddie was nervously cutting into an onion with a long kitchen knife when she heard Hodges come inside the house and close the door behind him.

"Those old wobblin' jaws in town got something to do with what you said back there?" he thundered.

Her back was to him, so he couldn't see that her hands were shaking violently as they sliced through the pungent bulb, sending its vaporous acid up to her already watering eyes. It was as much the onion's enzymes as the trauma that the conversation with Ms. Ortiz had unlocked that caused her tears to fall.

Hearing about Lily's death had forced Phreddie to confront the memory of what had happened with her own spouse, something she had managed to push to the back of her mind since she fled New Orleans. She had never really taken time to deal with it or to stop and freely grieve her loss. But the fear that Lily must have felt when Hodges killed her was her own, and Phreddie wept, half in sorrow and half in terror, thinking about Lily's and her intertwined fates.

She paused to look down at the knife, and the image of Remy's punctured throat stabbed at her. *Why did he have to ruin that we had?* she wondered tearfully.

Hodges stepped up behind her and pulled her around so that the knife she held was all that was between them. "I asked a question," he demanded.

She had not planned to confront Hodges, but she had questions of her own, and his aggressiveness shook them loose from her mouth. After all, she wanted answers from him as much as she did from Remy, but Remy was not there. Hodges was. So with the knife in the air, she nervously cried out, "Why?"

Hodges's face turned red, and his jaw clenched at the question. "Because I don't do gossips and fearmongering," he shot back, his breath hot against her cheeks. Then he released her from his grasp and stormed across the room.

"Not why did you ask me that question," she hissed. "I meant why did you do it? Why did you kill Lily?"

"Jerusalem Crickets," Hodges growled back. "Listen here and listen good, lady. I don't need to explain anything to you, to them, or to Jesus barking-at-the-knife Christ! Lily's dead and buried. That's all you need to know."

Hodges stood over his wooden chest and bent down to open it.

His guns. Phreddie gasped. The image of Remy running at her with the chair leg flashed through her mind, and her hands began to shake with fear that Hodges was going to shoot her.

"Lily may be dead and buried, but I don't plan to join her," she bellowed. Then without thought, she lifted her hand and threw the knife across the room. It sailed through the air and slammed into the top of the wooden chest only a couple of inches away from Hodges's face. His eyes widened as it wobbled back and forth next to him.

"Oh my," Phreddie whispered, greatly surprised by her own actions.

Hodges stared some more at the knife, then he looked back at her. "Argh," he grunted.

Phreddie held her breath and waited for a more serious reply. She could almost feel his bearlike hands closing around her neck already, but instead he lifted the lid from the chest and removed a wooden tobacco pipe. He banged it softly against his palm, then popped it into his mouth.

"I was just going for a smoke," he admonished her softly. Then he slammed the chest shut, stood up, struck a match, and took a great big puff.

"No . . . oh no . . . I'm so sorry." She shook her head back and forth.

Hodges bent over and pulled the knife out of the chest's top and approached Phreddie. She flinched as he slammed its point deep into the table next to the onion.

"Next time, don't miss," he said sternly, then sat down in the rocking chair and began to puff and blow from his pipe as he glided back and forth.

Phreddie's shoulders drooped, and a loud breath released from her lungs. She stood silent for several seconds before smoothing the skirt of her dress with her hands.

"Dinner will be ready in an hour," she said, lifting up the bottom of the apron she had put on earlier and drying her moist eyes with its edges. Then she pulled the knife from the table and went back to chopping the onion in silence.

Womanly Duties

It was pitch-black out, save for the light of the campfire burning low. The moon and stars were hidden by clouds, but Oscar was clear of mind. Tomorrow was the day he would ride into Newton and find Phreddie.

Over the last several weeks, he'd had plenty of time to think about the ways in which he would avenge Remy, and think he did. His mind had become like a clock, running in circles, the hands looping and restarting over and over again. He began in the hotel room and shifted to the port in New Orleans, then to the train pulling away from the platform at Exchange Place.

At first, his movements were predictable, but the more he dwelled, the more erratic his thoughts became, until they jerked unexpectedly backward and forward so that he found himself a capricious visitor to both the half and the quarter hour. With each turn of the dial, new ways to punish Phreddie were born, and each of these ideas made him salivate more than the last.

At first it was a simple noose. That had been back when he'd expected justice to be meted out quickly. *Mon Dieu, I never expected this manhunt to last more than a single day*, he thought.

A person did not simply slip away from New Orleans and the Delaroux. Yet somehow, Phreddie had managed to escape him three times.

"*Vache idiote*," he muttered at the fire, though it was an indictment of two defendants. He had cause for annoyance with both Phreddie and himself, for different reasons. Ultimately though, Oscar was not one to find fault within, so at last his mind settled on the fact that *Phreddie était l'imbécile*. Everything was on her.

When she left New Orleans, she'd had the whole world in which to hide. Had she decided to press on to other parts of America? If she had taken the honeymoon ship across to Europe, the trail would likely have been quickly lost, and Oscar's quest would have been dead-ended.

But Phreddie was just woman enough to be as stupid as Oscar thought that all women were. Lazy as well, as she disembarked *L'Ange* at the ship's first port and stopped there. New York City had a lot of people to hide among, but so did New Orleans, and while the accents were different, at heart, the people were the same.

It had taken Oscar no time at all to grease the right palms. A shopkeeper only a block away from slip number twenty-three informed him that a young woman had asked for advice a few weeks back about where a single female might find appropriate boarding. The man's distant cousin happened to be an Irish landlady. A few more pennies in discerning pockets, and Oscar knew not only where she lived, but where she worked as well.

Yes, she was definitely the fool for making that part of the pursuit so easy.

"Silly woman," he whispered.

He imagined that Phreddie must have been drawn in by New York's tall buildings and fresh immigrant voices, which sounded nothing like the Creole from back home. Then there were the intoxicating smells of the city's many different foreign foods, such as bee sting cake, with its crumbly sweet honey almond topping, and corned beef and cabbage, whose pungent odor permeated the air and could lure anybody into a trance.

The thought of this food made Oscar's mouth water, as he had not eaten much in the last few days. His mind wandered home. *Ah . . . à la maison . . . What I wouldn't give for a good old homemade bouillabaisse right now.*

Oscar envisioned himself to be comfortably seated at the dining table in his house, while he began to drift to sleep, his mind filled with the smell of seafood and dirty rice he would sup on after a wild night with Mahogany Montigny upon his return. But the sounds of cricket frogs and spring leapers quickly ruptured his peace, and Oscar sat up. There would be plenty of time for feasting and fucking once he returned to New Orleans, he determined. For now though, he was still here in the dead of night, exposed in the open plains.

An unease settled over Oscar. It was not just discomfort at not knowing what was watching him from just beyond the firelight. It was also the quiet niggling of death almost pulling at the newly purchased linen shirt that covered his arms beneath his fine kelly green suit. It begged for its due, for the attention that he had failed to give it.

Oscar had taken little time to consider Remy's passing beyond his initial fury. It was much easier to press forward with his plans of retribution than to stop and grieve. There were too many emotions unfaced, but the eerie calm of nature made these feelings suddenly surface. Oscar shuddered as if to shake them back beneath his skin. He knew that mourning now would not bring his brother back. Why spend time crying for someone who was already gone? Instead, he could lean into the anticipation of what awaited. While he could never repay Phreddie fully for her deeds, on this front, he aimed to try.

A rotation completed, Oscar's mind ran back to the beginning, with fresh fantasies of how he would deal with Phreddie when he at last took her into his hands. Over days and weeks, his mind had conjured up increasingly maniacal ways to abuse his captive once the chase was over. At the onset, it had simply been about revenge, but the realization that Phreddie was not a competitor's daughter, as he had at first suspected, or even a plaything sent in to spy on the Delaroux sugar empire, meant that Remy's death was a crime of passion. This thought made Oscar seethe. Only a special form of sadism could ultimately repay the thorny hand that Phreddie had dealt his family.

If only she *had* been the economic assassin he'd imagined, things would seem far less complicated and likely far less humiliating. But humiliation was something Phreddie had never experienced before—not in comparison to what Oscar planned to mete out tomorrow morning.

Oscar thought back to the relentless hunt for the truth that he had embarked on. At first he had found little record of the woman his brother had married before the time of their wedding vows, and this made discovering a motive incredibly complicated. At last, though, there was a breakthrough when Luke uncovered a thin trail of breadcrumbs that led to a small orphanage. It did not take much to convince the *religieuse* to divulge the story of the young woman she had reared since a small child.

Next came the paperwork, handed to him by the sister herself in the hotel lobby, and like a torrent of rain released from the heavens, Phreddie's history had flooded Oscar's mind to the point of obsession. The sister's information made clear why Phreddie had walked in the shadows until the day his brother Remy plucked her out of oblivion.

No! A rope is too good for that woman, or whatever the devil anyone wants to call her.

He stewed again on the sight of her disappearing onto the ship as it pulled from the dock in New Orleans.

"*Pétasse*," he cursed excitedly into the air.

The image of Phreddie leaping across rooftops made Oscar's manhood twitch, and it began to swell. The unexpected chase had brought forth an unknown stirring, an excitement down in Oscar's *la bite* that he had never experienced before. This was an illicit quest, and it rested just beyond his fingertips. His hand reached into his trousers, and he clasped his member the way one takes hold of a forbidden matter, clutching it tightly for safekeeping.

Oscar looked over toward the men he was traveling with. Convinced that they were all asleep, he began to tug. *No one . . . absolutely no one . . . tells me . . . no!*

But Phreddie's continued existence clawed at Oscar's sense of self-importance, and it left him incredibly aroused. This was no attraction or even duty to a levirate marriage, as in many ways Phreddie repulsed him. But the endless hunt stimulated his organ as much as the thought of revenge did.

"*Arrêt*," he growled at last into the night air, but it was too late to stop, as pleasure had already released itself. So Oscar pulled his hand out and wiped the residue onto a patch of dirt alongside the fire.

He sat there in silence for a moment, but it was not long before thoughts of Phreddie began to fill him again, and he shook his head with disgust. *I will capture* le monstre *for you, Rémy*. He spat at the fire.

The corners of Oscar's mouth turned slightly upward as he reflected on the final plan that he had arrived at. Oh, it was almost as delicious as a long night inside Mahogany's licorice strip. *Oui.* All of that time he had spent spiraling around and around in starts and stops had led him into the depths of his mind, where at long last there grew an idea that was almost as perfect as Oscar himself.

By this time tomorrow, Phreddie would be in his total control, and he would lead her from town to town all the way from Kansas to Louisiana, naked and on display in a box with bars. She would be immobilized for the entirety of the nine-hundred-mile journey to New Orleans so that her shame was on full view. She wouldn't be able to so much as piss or shit without the whole world watching, and this exposure meant that there would be no opportunity for her to beguile another victim. The truth would be laid bare.

When this brilliant notion raised itself, Oscar had immediately commanded Luke to create a cage just narrow enough to leave its victim suspended in the air. He'd practically shaken with delight when he arrived in Kansas City and found the box to be everything he had envisioned. How he'd salivated at the metal collar that had been soldered to the sides of the cage, where, once locked in at the neck, Phreddie would be unable to sit, lie down, or even move her arms to cover her shame. He was exhilarated by the thought that, in every town on the return trip from the Kansas Territories, he would encourage the masses to come out and gawp at and taunt his caged beast.

Once they reached New Orleans, Oscar would set Phreddie's cage up in the middle of Hermance Marie Broussard's brothel on Delphine Street, where he would charge people two bits to come from far and wide to see the captured killer. There he would endlessly bed Mahogany by night right under Phreddie's watchful eyes, and by day he would make a torrential stream of money from the curious visitors who all would want a chance to see *la créature* the devil himself must have spawned.

"Oh, Remy," Oscar moaned to himself. A slight chill blew past as guilt rested on his shoulder. "I don't know if it's enough, but it is all that I can do."

Had he not been so blinded by self-importance back in New Orleans, perhaps he could have sensed that something was not right with his brother's relationship. Maybe if he hadn't been so focused on frivolously humping half the trade in the city's brothels, he would have thought to caution Remy more on his decision to marry. Instead, Oscar had been so caught up in his own heady living, where power and pussy drove him the way honey drove a bear to the hive, that any thought of the sting had been completely boxed out by the taste on his tongue. But the sweetness proved fleeting, and what remained was the bitter aftertaste that selfishness had left behind.

Oscar pulled his arms around himself and stared into the fire. Remy had always been the better loved of the two brothers, and though he was jealous of his parents' preference for their younger son, Oscar loved his brother deeply, almost as much as he did himself.

He recalled how Remy would cling to his mother's skirts in childhood. "*Mon canton*," his mother would say as she rubbed the boy's head. It had seemed fitting that she called him her duckling, like the fowl Remy would chase into the pond at their chateau in Toulouse. He was as sweet as those babies in their soft downy feathers frolicking in the water. In fact, like those babes, Remy had been caring, kind, and all of the things that Oscar was not. He had also proved, up until his death, to be far more intelligent and disciplined. And while Remy spent most of his young life following behind his older brother, it was Oscar who envied his sibling—though he never told him so, as he'd never really admitted it to himself before now. But Oscar had admired how clear-headed Remy was, and how he operated with the best of intentions, putting good before bad in a way that Oscar was never able to do.

In the end though, Oscar was alive and Remy was not. He could spend his time being sentimental, but his brother was gone, and Oscar determined that it was anyone's fault but the man who was warming his body by this fire on the plains.

The clock struck the hour, and the blazing wood crackled and popped as Oscar scanned the horizon. The first faint light of dawn could be seen in the eastern sky. He would be glad to get back to the journey, not just because of his plans for Phreddie, but for the simple fact that he did not like to feel as if he was out of control. The eerie silence of the creeping twilight reminded him that sitting here in the open meant he was anything but the master of his own fate, as money and power had little sway over the wilds of the American West.

Prior to leaving Kansas City, Oscar had been warned repeatedly that he was a fool to lead a group of men on horseback through Indian territory.

"Why would you forgo the safety of the railroad?" one shopkeeper had asked.

"You've got a better chance of a war party descending on a wagon train than they would on a steel one with a steam engine," another person commented.

But Oscar figured that Phreddie would be keeping half an eye on the depot that ran through town, and coming in on horseback would offer more of an element of surprise. Plus, it gave him extra mobility if she did try to make a run for it. So he'd liberally spent his Delaroux funds to depart on wooden wheels and hooves, and with enough firepower to support a small US cavalry unit.

At last, the morning light grew, and it rang in his ears like an alarm clock. Oscar decided it was time to get on with things. He didn't want to remain idle another minute longer, so he stirred the others from their slumber and watched as they packed up their overnight gear and stored it away.

Before long, Oscar was on his horse. He allowed a smile to spread wide across his face the way the sunlight now spread across the prairie as he rode with his head high in the direction of the town called Newton.

•

The knife attack was never mentioned again. Hodges decided that he would ignore Phreddie's impertinence and actions this once, as their time together was almost at a close. Although the knife had come close enough to launching backdoor trots into his underclothes, she'd missed. Yet she had done what he had bargained her for, as his home had not looked this put together in over a year. Hell, this morning he'd actually had to fiddle through a neat pile of clothing to find a pair of socks. They didn't have so much as an ant hole, as she'd mended, cleaned, folded, and stored everything away so nicely that he felt halfway civilized again.

With one night left, Hodges decided to let bygones rest. He aimed to keep his promise on the morrow, even if it meant death by knife blade should she get her knickers all twisted again. Still, inside he simmered and stewed over what Lily's sister might have said to Phreddie. The more he thought on it, the angrier he became. "That goddamned woman," he suddenly yelled out, standing up from the table.

Phreddie was cleaning up from their lunch, and she near to jumped out of her skin from his words. "What?" she asked nervously.

"Never mind." Hodges pouted, then he made his way around the table and headed for the door. "Oh, speaking of women, I just remembered that it's the first Sunday of the month."

"Yes, I believe it is," Phreddie said.

"I'll be expecting you to fulfill your womanly duties then, before you go," he declared. He watched as her eyes widened with something akin to fear.

"Womanly duties?" she asked. "I'm afraid that is simply impossible. I—"

"Lady, whatever it is you aim to tell me, I don't give a hoot nor a holler. You're the woman, and it's the first Sunday. That's all there is to it."

"I—I can't," she stammered, shaking her head repeatedly.

"Of course you can," he asserted. "Lily insisted it happen on the first Sunday of every month. You know how organized you womenfolk can be. A man like me could happily do it any ole time."

"Any ole time?" Panic rose in Phreddie's voice. "That wasn't our agreement," she protested.

"Huh? Of course it was."

"If I wanted to do womanly duties, I could have just stayed at Miller's, lain on my back, and been out of this town already," she shrieked.

"Wait." Hodges took his hand from the doorknob he had just begun to twist. Then his shoulders started to heave up and down. At first it was a slow roll, but then it turned into a full fit of laughter. "Is that what you thought I meant by . . . by . . . womanly duties?" He let out a body-shaking guffaw.

"It's just that I'm modest," Phreddie replied.

Hodges turned back around and opened the door. He stepped outside briefly and put his hand on the large metal tub that sat just outside, then dragged it inside over the threshold.

"I meant that Lily always drew hot water for me—to bathe with—on the first Sunday of the month," he said between booming baritone laughter interspersed with gasps for air.

Tears formed in his eyes as he watched Phreddie's face pinch up in confusion, then her own frame began to shake with fits of giggles.

"Oh," was all she could manage to get out between tee-hees and titters.

Hodges could still hear her as he carried his limp body outside, having spent all of its power from tippy toe to hair root on hysterical hee-hawing for the first time in more than a year.

"She thought I meant—" he started to say to himself, but his body cut the words off with a howl of delight, and he gimped over to the barn to start his day of work.

•

Church bells sang out a thunderous call as Oscar rode into Newton. *It's as if they know I have arrived,* he thought.

As he led his party up the street, he noticed the small group of townsfolk exiting the Saint Mary's Parish Church, whose limestone sparkled bright in the Sunday sun. Approaching the congregants, he could hear a woman dressed from head to toe in black as she spoke to the priest.

"Thank you for your sermon, Father Milfken," the lady said as she shook the clergyman's hand. "I would be most happy to have you over for supper on Tuesday evening if . . ."

Her words faded when she noted that the father had turned his head away from her. Oscar watched as she turned to follow the priest's gaze, which was firmly set on Oscar and his small group of men on horseback.

"Would you look there, Ms. Ortiz," the priest said. "What a most peculiar metal box." He pointed up at the cart with the cage fastened with ropes atop its wooden frame.

The congregants, including the widow, cautiously made their way toward the strangers, their curiosity appearing to have edged out any fears. As they neared, they were joined by the town's nonworshippers, who had stepped out from their homes and places of business.

"Good day," Oscar called out to the people.

Ms. Ortiz stepped forward and returned the greeting. "Hello there, and welcome to Newton. What brings you folks to our town?"

The other onlookers stared at Oscar and his men with suspicion. Oscar chuckled seeing their uncertainty over whether they should relax their shoulders or run back inside for safety.

"We come in peace," he called out to them, and he put both hands in the air so as to allay their fears. "We are looking for a murderer who has come to reside in this town."

Whispers began to ripple through the crowd, but Ms. Ortiz stepped closer. "This town is no stranger to thieves and killers, so you will have to be more specific, Mr. . . . ?"

"Delaroux," Oscar purred as he removed his hat and leaned down from his horse. "Oscar Delaroux from New Orleans by way of Toulouse, France, *mademoiselle*."

Ms. Ortiz smiled back at him, but unlike most women, she seemed little moved by his accent or the way his thick lashes framed his blue eyes. *Interesting.* Oscar slid off of his horse and stepped toward her. *Even the nun couldn't resist me.* He considered the challenge that this frigid woman posed.

Moving in quickly so that she didn't have time to stop her face from flushing at his closeness, he leaned forward and whispered in her ear. Her body froze, and Oscar couldn't decide if it was from his breath on her neck or from the name that he had unleashed.

"Phreddie?" she said in disbelief. "You mean that poor vagrant woman who lost her ticket?"

"Don't be fooled by her meekness," Oscar growled.

"But that woman doesn't look like she could squash so much as a burying beetle," Ms. Ortiz protested.

"She ran a stake through the throat of my own brother once he had discovered her shame."

Ms. Ortiz cocked her head. "Her shame?"

Oscar leaned into her once again and whispered.

For a moment, the woman just stood there, her jaw as open as her eyes. "A . . . a . . . a . . . what?" she cried at last, shivering as if it were the dead of winter and not the end of June.

Quickly, Father Milfken came up alongside her and put a hand on her arm to steady her, as she appeared as if she might fall. Oscar looked on as she whispered into the priest's ear the same words he had just slipped into her own only a moment ago.

He saw Father Milfken register the same disgust at the word as Ms. Ortiz. "Is that even possible?" escaped from his pursed lips.

Soon the news had spread up and down the dusty street, from lips to lobes, and the townspeople gasped and gagged at the information.

"Unnatural," someone screamed from the crowd.

"And now you see why I must take hold of this dragon by the tail," Oscar called to the group of now riled-up onlookers, who nodded and cheered.

"I fear the man she is with is even worse," Ms. Ortiz, who appeared to recover from her shock, proclaimed.

"Ah yes. She is not alone. What can you tell me about this man?" Oscar pressed.

"Why, Charlie Hodges is an absolute madman," she exclaimed. "That slayer murdered his wife, my own sister, in cold blood."

"They sound like the perfect couple," Oscar declared.

Some of the townsfolk nodded and grunted in affirmation.

"From my own experience, he will certainly not allow you to simply ride in and take possession of someone he himself has taken possession of first," Ms. Ortiz said. "At least not very easily."

Oscar surveyed the scene for a moment, then responded as much to the crowd as to the woman dressed in widow clothing. "Then in this case, I will rid this town today of both of these fiends," he announced, noting how Ms. Ortiz could not help but clap and cheer like the rest of the residents of Newton.

She's not so cold anymore, he thought. *Perhaps I will bed this widowed woman as a reward to myself upon my return to this town. These types are always the most lusty, despite their outward appearances.*

"His homestead is that way," someone called out, and another shouted directions and the distance.

"Go with God," Father Milfken interjected, and he blessed "Our savior, Oscar Delaroux" with the sign of the cross.

Oscar remounted his horse, his chest puffed up with heaps more pride than he'd ridden into town with. Then he turned around and led the cart with his men past the small row of shops. More people fell in behind them to cheer and whistle. Men and women tipped their hats and shouted cries of "hallelujah" to this posse, which rode on in silence, their faces full of resolution.

"Bring down the murderers," someone yelled.

"Kill that Cain and his Jezabel," shouted another.

Ms. Ortiz called the loudest: "May God at last strike dead all of the sinners that flock to this forsaken town, and may you finally free me from the burden of my sister's memory."

Oscar stopped and turned back to face her as she lifted her rosary high in the air and passed its black beads between her fingers. He grinned. *My lips will be those beads come sunrise.*

"By this time tomorrow," he said, "I will lead the she-wolf back to New Orleans in this box of righteousness that we carry, and I will leave your own demon, Charlie Hodges, rendered impotent."

As their procession traveled on, the sound of hurrahs slowly diminished as the crowd faded from view. Long prairie grass lapped at the sides of the wagon train as it made its way out of town and into the infinity of the Kansas plains.

Oui, Oscar thought, *I will be back for that widow and her flower, which has likely not been pollinated in an age.*

He felt invigorated by the attention the people of Newton had given to him. He was used to deference in New Orleans, but it was born almost exclusively out of fear. Here, though, people seemed to worship him for the good he promised to bring rather than solely for the bad that the strength of his fist could unleash.

As he led his men away, he sucked in the clean air of the plains through his nostrils. *Mon Dieu, in l'Ouest, everything is possible.* He sat up in the saddle and rode into his future. *There is no one who can stop me*, he proclaimed in his mind, *least of all one lone man from Newton and his bitch.*

Oscar looked back at his apostles, who faithfully followed behind him. He nodded at Luke, who nodded right back. He had given them each more than thirty pieces of silver, and he knew not one of them would turn their back on him.

Finally, his eyes landed on the iron cage that rested on top of the wagon that Landy was steering. Oscar beamed inside. Then he turned his horse forward and rode on.

•

Landy watched through closing lids as Oscar rode up ahead. The sound of the wagon wheels turning over and over had lulled him into a trance, and his eyes were only half-open. It was not as if he needed to pay particularly close attention, as the team of horses that pulled the cart would just follow behind the solo horses ridden by Luke and Oscar. Even if he caught a few minutes of shuteye, who was to know or care?

One of the bearded twins pulled alongside the wagon and asked Luke up ahead, "What's up with whitey?"

Landy pretended not to notice.

"Hasn't spoken a word since childhood, far as I know, but I'd hate to face him in the dark just the same," Luke called back.

"Seems a bit weird," the other twin added.

"Not weird, quiet. Deadly quiet." Luke laughed, then rode his horse up far ahead.

Landy ignored their conversation the way he ignored most of the musings of speaking men. Instead, he contemplated the grass in Kansas, which seemed to go on forever—just like his own thoughts. The constant, never-changing scenery eased him as much as the spinning circles on the ground with their rolling and rolling and rolling.

They cleared his mind, which was a rare thing. Not being able to speak meant one had loads of time to think, and so he did. Every waking second, Landy was relegated to the turnings of his mind, with no way to vocalize them. It had been like that ever since he could remember.

Once while growing up, he'd heard one of his brothers tell a stranger that he used to talk incessantly as a youngun. In fact, he'd talked so much that their father, a mean drunk, supposedly screamed at him one day to shut up, and Landy did exactly that. After that, not a peep did pass his lips, though Landy himself remembered neither talking prior to this nor his father's reproach. In place of everyone else's idle conversation, his mind became like fatty cream being whipped into butter, the way his mother used to twist and turn the plunger in the churn.

It had gone on like this for so long that he'd simply forgotten how to make a sound, so he compensated with hand and body movements or looks, and occasionally by jotting something down on paper or etching right into the ground. He also found that, instead of speaking, he could listen better to the cries of others, and so he took delight in squeezing things real hard until they squealed. It was as if their noises broke his own silence.

It had started with the mouse he caught in his bedroom in his early teenage years. He kept it in a box for two days until his brother caught him with it. "Landy's got a rat in his room," he'd tattled.

His father roared between sips of coffin varnish for him to "take that shitting thing outside or I'll beat the Dickens out of you."

Landy skulked out back with the box and sat down in the dirt. Pulling back the lid, he lifted the mouse into his palm. He was delighted by its attention, as it didn't seem scared like most people were of this white-haired boy who couldn't speak. He stroked its fur gently, then placed the mouse on the ground between his legs with a smile.

But the mouse, once its feet were on the dirt, made a run for it, and this angered Landy. He reached out instinctively and snatched its body back up. *Why would you leave me?* he thundered inside. But all that sounded was the song of a robin in a nearby tree.

Then Landy did something unexpected even to himself. He squeezed. At first he was frightened of his own strength, but as his hand constricted tighter and tighter around the mouse's body, he watched with delight as its tiny brown eyes began to bulge. The faint mew it emitted before its tongue slipped from its mouth brought a sensation Landy had never felt before. There was a fiery feeling in his loins, a great excitement from the act of suffocating another being.

It wasn't two years later that his entire family was wiped out during the cholera epidemic of '58, rendering him a homeless mute with no one to depend on. It didn't matter if you were sixteen or sixty, or yapped constantly or never whispered a sound—you had to pay the bank note and put food on the table. Landy had no job and no income, so his meager home was seized.

He wandered into New Orleans proper one day and got caught pinching an apple from someone's larder. As he was being led out in irons, a rag-proper dandy happened to be passing by. He placed a coin in the policeman's pocket, and Landy was released into his care. While the man was only a few years older than Landy, he carried himself like someone of worth, and from that day on, Landy found a home beside Oscar Delaroux.

Most days, Oscar would have him run odd jobs for him and his family. At night, he would take Landy to the brothels, where he would pay for Landy to mount as many ladies as he wanted. For Landy, it seemed to be the only way he could attract female attention. Yet his fetish for choking extended beyond the occasional mouse. Whores looked best when your fingers were wrapped around their throats and their eyes looked to be coming out of their heads.

Over time, the pet rodent was forgotten, and his mind became filled with adult playthings, and feminine flesh and lust for death became inextricably one. Absolutely nothing urged him to want to crush the life out of a woman like the sight of their breasts and the blood-surging response they elicited in his genitals. Though Oscar would hoot and holler that Landy better stop his abuse, every night he would still shell out silver so that Landy could release his fury on both ends of a daughter of sin.

A jolt of the uneven earth caused Landy to open his eyes. He mused on how he would remain true to Oscar from here till death because the man gave him the unconditional love that no one else ever had. Then he licked his lips at the thought of what his leader had planned for Phreddie, who was perhaps more freak than he was, and he felt the familiar stirring in his loins once more.

•

One final bucket of heated water poured into the steel tub and Phreddie's task would be complete. She ran the back of her arm across her brow, then dumped it in. While it was getting toward sunset, the plains continued to bake from the heat that had cooked its earth during the hours of unabated sunshine.

Hodges came inside, dipped his finger into the water to test its temperature, then began to unbutton the top of his shirt. "I've missed this," he exhaled, sighing loudly.

She smiled. "I'll step outside for a bit so that you can have your alone time." She had barely placed a toe over the threshold when she spied a group of riders headed for the homestead. "Looks like you have visitors."

"Visitors?" Hodges stated with alarm in his voice. He stepped behind her in the doorway to see who it could be, then turned around abruptly. Phreddie followed, watching as he ran to his chest and threw it open. He pulled out the shotgun and began to load it with some shells.

"Why are you doing that?" she asked nervously.

"In my experience, a group of riders that large don't come at dark unless they're an Indian war party or a group of bandits." He cocked the gun and headed for the door. "And I'll be shitted if it makes a difference to me either way."

"But—"

"Stay inside," he ordered,

Phreddie walked to the window as the sound of hooves grew closer. "Oh, bobbing apples," she exclaimed when she peered out and saw a familiar silhouette sitting atop one of those horses. She quickly yanked her head out of the way to avoid being seen through the glass.

What will I do? she asked herself silently as she tiptoed over to the open door to listen.

"Good evening," she heard Remy's brother say politely.

"What do you want?" Hodges replied curtly.

"My name is Oscar Dela—"

"And?" Hodges barked.

Phreddie leaned over and gingerly snuck a peek with one eye. There he was. Oscar Delaroux himself sat self-righteously high on his horse, flanked by the mustached Luke and two more strange men with beards. Behind them was a wagon with an odd-looking cage tied to its bed. Steering the wagon was the terrifying pale-haired man who had chased her across the rooftops in New York City, and further on, two other mean-looking characters on their steeds.

Oscar slid down from his horse and began to reach into his pocket. That was enough to make Hodges lift his gun and point it at Oscar's groin. "Hands up, and don't step any further unless you want to be neutered," he ordered.

The men with Delaroux all reached for their weapons, but Oscar put his hands up in the air and chuckled. "Steady, boys. I'd be alarmed too if a pack of unknown men showed up on my doorstep." They all lowered their guns, and Oscar nodded in the direction of his pants pocket.

"I have a photograph in my pocket that I would like to show you. Perhaps if you saw it, you would see what kind of a person—"

"I don't need to see a dang thing," Hodges declared.

"Monsieur Hodges," Oscar said soothingly. "I was told by the people in town that you have a visitor, and that the person in the photo is the one I am looking for."

"I'm not sure why it would be their concern, or frankly yours, as to who I've got here."

"This person is of great interest to me, as I said. You see, this . . . woman," he said with some effort, "goes by the name of—"

"The only person I have here goes by the name of *my guest*, and I don't care by the Lord Harry what kind of business or interest you have with them," Hodges told him.

"I'm afraid you don't understand— "

"Mister, *you* need to be afraid, as it is *you* who clearly does not understand. Be afeared not of the person you seek, but of what I am capable of."

"I can offer money," Oscar stated. "No small sum for the return of your guest."

"I have more than enough money," Hodges replied. He stepped closer to Oscar with his gun. "Now, you have your answer, so I'll thank you to go to Jericho and get the hell off my land."

"*Oui, oui, Monsieur Hodges*," Oscar said slowly, and began to back up until he was once again near his horse. He reluctantly swung himself back into the saddle. "We are patient," he continued, "and can call you again when you have had some time to consider my offer. Perhaps in the morning?"

"No need." Hodges tone was curt. "I've given you my answer."

Oscar turned his horse to leave, but after only two or three steps, he wheeled it back around. "Phreddie!" he bellowed out. "You cannot hide! I will get you for what you have done!"

Hodges lifted his gun into the air and fired a warning shot.

Oscar's horse bucked up in fear. Once he regained control, he backed it away accordingly. "Okay, Monsieur Hodges, okay. You have until tomorrow morning to think about your choice. I tried money, but there is always force. Know this though: by money or by force, I will take Phreddie either way. Rest assured, we will be back."

"You would do wise not to return at all," Hodges declared, spitting on the ground.

At that, Delaroux and his men rode off.

After a minute, Phreddie tiptoed outside and watched as the men faded into the distance. A chill ran up her spine at sight of the cage that wobbled slightly from side to side until it was over the horizon.

"I . . . I think I ought to go ahead and explain everything now," she said softly.

Hodges lowered his gun, then turned back to her. "No need."

He walked to the house, and Phreddie followed behind. Once they were inside, she watched him place the loaded gun up under the window frame.

"But you see, I . . . well . . . I . . ." she stammered. "Maybe it's best I just leave here rather quickly. Where I come from, Oscar Delaroux is the last person one would want to mess with, and I don't want to cause you any more problems than you already seem to have in Newton."

"Lady, I feel like by now you should have gotten the sense that I don't give a goose's tit about what anybody, least of all some dandy with fancy words and offers of money, thinks about a goddamn thing. Now I said I would hire you for the week and pay for your train fare, and that'll be exactly what I do."

"I am not sure that is a good idea. I am not even sure how I would get out of town." Phreddie started to pace. "If I just leave tonight, maybe Oscar won't know which direction I've gone. I can—"

"Oscar ain't in France, and I will not let anyone tell me who I can have or what I can do on my own land. No," Hodges declared, "I will put you on the locomotive of your choice myself in the morning. But for now, I want my goddamn bath before that water gets any cooler."

Then he abruptly dropped his drawers and pulled his shirt right up and over his head.

Phreddie's eyes widened at the sight of the naked man, then nodded in dumbfounded agreement. She slowly backed out through the front door and sat down in deep thought on the lone wooden porch chair. Her eyes drifted off with the sunset, and her teeth nibbled her bottom lip.

Tomorrow . . .

Ride or Die

The train pulled into the Newton station at half past twelve in the morning and Grace Weaver gasped at her own reflection in the window. There was the familiar sight of a slight woman with raven hair speckled with irregular streaks of gray, but this one had an unfamiliar look of determination on her face. She nudged the sister out of the train with a gentle shove. "You've seen it through this far," she said to the nun. "If you want the full inheritance, I have to find my daughter alive."

Sister Adrienne turned around. "I've done all that I can with what little I now know," she snipped.

"A deal is a deal, or so they say, and I will not hand over so much as a copper penny if Nadine is not placed into these same arms from whence she was stolen. Only then are you welcome to all of Mr. Weaver's money, for I will have no further need of it."

Sister Adrienne smirked. "I will make sure that I've led you back into the arms of your child so that you can both rot in the fires—after you've given me all that you have promised, of course."

The recently widowed Grace Weaver sighed with near exasperation. It had been an eventful couple of days since her husband, the irritable George Weaver the Third, had up and died on her.

"I place one demand on you, woman: that you won't go lookin' backwards," he'd snarled at her from his deathbed before he forcefully exhaled and passed from this world to the next.

She'd stood over his body for a few seconds before she took the butt of her right hand and pushed him right onto the floor. When his body landed with a loud thump but no cusses, and no further remonstrations erupted from his insufferable tongue, she exhaled as loudly as he had, only her breath was laced with relief.

"You have been a horrible husband," she announced to the air, "and I regret not killing you my own self sooner, but your violent hands that tore my baby from mine, and bruised my body at whim, kept me hemmed in and dutiful for too many years."

With her chest lightened by the declaration, Grace Weaver didn't even stay to tend to George's body. Instead, she instructed the house staff to call for the mortician, then grabbed her coat and hat and slammed the door to the family mansion behind her.

It didn't take long before the hand that had pushed her dead husband from the bed was pounding on the doors of the Sisters of Children and Charity Orphanage.

"What is the meaning of this at such an hour of night?" an unfamiliar *religieux* had demanded to know when she opened the door with a lantern in one hand.

"Get me the head sister at once," Grace coolly demanded, and for the first time in decades, she heard her own voice and—dare she say it—she felt alive.

How could I have let George and that nun conspire against me and steal the fruit of my own womb? she wondered as she followed the sister's light up a flight of stairs.

Minutes later, she was sitting in Sister Adrienne's office, panting. She noticed a small box on the desk covered in lapis lazuli, the deep blue stones softly reflecting the light from the fireplace the other nun had stoked upon their entrance. A painting of the Madonna and child hung on the wall, and Grace noticed swirls of what appeared to be gold paint that spun around the head of the Mother of God.

"Why do you disturb our sleep, you silly woman?" the sister hissed when she entered.

"I know she's alive, as we have watched her from the gate every year since my husband gave my child to you as if she were a farm dog, free to be exchanged."

"Your child is no longer a child, and thus has not been a boarder at our orphanage for a few years," Sister Adrienne said to her with an air of disinterest. "But you already know this."

"My daughter, Sister, was forcibly removed from me against my will due to my husband's inability to deal with her particular issues, and you have been paid handsomely to look after her. You must keep some record somewhere of where your charges go once they have left your tutelage?" Grace insisted.

"Then you have not heard, have you, Mrs. Weaver?" There was delight on the nun's tongue, but Grace could only shrug her shoulders.

"No, I have not heard anything," she replied softly. "These past few years, I have heard nothing about my daughter, and surely even you must understand that I still love and long for my child?"

"I'm afraid your motherly desires have come too late, as even now there are people that hunt down your offspring." The sister smiled. "For all we know, she may already be taken."

"Hunt down? Taken?" Grace asked.

"Phreddie—for that is what we called her once she became this establishment's thing—is wanted for murder, Mrs. Weaver, and it appears that you will not be reunited after all. Therefore, might I suggest that you return to your husband and leave us all to retire to our beds."

"But . . . all of that money he gave you . . ." Grace stuttered.

"Your monies were well used over the years," the sister said as she took the box of precious blue stones from her desk and placed it into a drawer. "We did our best, but even still, one cannot treat with the devil, nor expect him to change his course."

"Where though, Sister? Where might people be after her?" Grace fell to her knees and sobbed before Sister Adrienne. "I have waited all of these years, and now that my husband has passed away, my chance to find my child is finally here. You must know something that can help me to be reunited with her?"

Sister Adrienne looked at the jade tiger that sat on her windowsill. Grace saw this as an opening.

"I will pay handsomely for information," she pressed, looking up from the floor.

"Oh?" Sister Adrienne remarked.

"In truth, should you help me reunite with my Nadine, I will sign over to you the entire Weaver inheritance that my husband has willed to me—and it is considerable."

Grace saw Sister Adrienne's eyes sparkle at the words. She could not understand why a woman who had renounced the world for poverty would make an exchange for treasure, but she was thankful for it.

"Well," the sister began, "I do know that she was in New York City—"

Grace leapt up. "Then we will depart for New York at first light," she excitedly broke in.

"Slow down. She was in New York, but escaped out west."

"Then where shall we go?" Grace cried. "The West is endless."

"I did hear talk of a small town in the Kansas territory as the last sighting."

Sister Adrienne had barely finished speaking before Grace had herded her toward the door, helped her gather some belongings from her room, and then marched her down to the train station, where they boarded a locomotive.

I will happily give up George's money just to hold my baby in my arms again, she thought, tears forming in her eyes as the train chugged along.

"It would have been best for you and your husband had you ceased to remember that you had given birth to a live child at all, Mrs. Weaver," Sister Adrienne said when she noticed her wet cheeks.

For twelve years, Grace had come to the gates of the orphanage to see her daughter. Every March 15, she'd stood on the corner of Camp Street and Aline as Sister Adrienne led Nadine outside to play. Grace had not dared call out to her, as George had threatened to cut off all funding to the home if she interfered in any way with the arrangement he had put in place for Nadine's care up until her sixteenth birthday.

"At least you know where she is," he'd said one March as Grace prepared to take her yearly sojourn. "If it had just been me, I would have taken that child out to the swamplands in a burlap sack and drowned it."

"She's turning into a beautiful young lady," Grace insisted, but George did not want to hear anything more. He had stopped going to see their child after the second year.

"I've done more than any man would dare, and I'll not hear another word about this unfortunate circumstance ever again," he growled at her.

Grace let it be, as George Weaver could be the surly sort. She did not want her ears boxed in, nor did she want to risk him abandoning his promised payments to the nun.

"No," Grace responded to Sister Adrienne at last. "Nadine may be different, but she is still my child."

The sister rolled her eyes and looked out the train window, muttering "sentimental fool" under her breath.

Finally, the train stopped and they were here at the place where her little Nadine had last been spotted. Grace knew in her heart that she would at last be fulfilled in that space deep within where only a mother could understand.

"We can take rooms at the inn," she told Sister Adrienne as they made their way into the small lobby section of Miller's Saloon and Hotel. Music and laughter filtered in through the side doorway, which opened to the bar, but Grace Weaver had no interest in merriment. "Be at the breakfast table at half past eight, and we will scour this town until our task is complete."

Sister Adrienne pursed her lips, then departed with a room key.

Grace made her way up to her own small room, removed her bonnet, and sat on the bed. There, her shoulders began to shake from silent sobs. She was so close to her daughter but so far from the years stolen from her. Yet in the morning, she hoped to make all things right.

Women are subject to men's whims until men mercifully pass away and leave us to our own paths, she thought.

Once her tears dried, Grace undressed and slipped under the covers, gripping them with the same force she'd tried to hold on to Nadine with before the child was taken from her frail fingers those many years ago.

•

Phreddie clung to the covers of the bed as a strong wind pressed up against the homestead. It was late at night, but she couldn't sleep knowing that everything she had run from these last months was about to come to a conclusion upon sunup. She knew that she would either be long gone on a train to who knew where, or be on her way back to New Orleans, presumably in that terrifying cage that Oscar Delaroux and his posse were carrying with them. That last thought made her shiver, so she pulled the blanket up over her chin.

Hodges was next to her, snoring. He had insisted that they share the bed for safety, though she couldn't see why this would be any safer than her sleeping on the floor. General Lee could have marched through the kitchen with the entire Army of Northern Virginia and Hodges would have rolled over and snuffled in slumber.

A loud crackle from the fireplace caused her to bolt upright in the bed.

"It's just the fire," she whispered to reassure herself as she pulled the covers back and placed her bare feet on the wooden floor.

Phreddie tiptoed over to the hearth, then grabbed the metal rod standing beside it and stoked the coals until they were red-hot. Pulling a log from the small stack under the window, she plopped it on top of the glowing embers.

"Calm down, silly." She half laughed as she made her way back to the bed, but as she sat down, she turned her head just in time to see a shadow move past the window.

"Charlie," she whispered, but he let out a snore. "Charlie," she pleaded again, only this time she leaned over and pushed him.

Suddenly, a piece of burning wood smashed through the window and landed on top of the dining table. With Hodges still unconscious, Phreddie lunged onto his side of the bed and shook him by the shoulders.

"What the—" he started to ask, but he was cut off when another firebomb flew through the glass. "Use the blankets," he barked at Phreddie, and she rushed at the now burning table and began to snuff it out while Hodges grabbed his gun and skulked over to the window.

The fire put out, Phreddie turned in time to see a bullet whiz past Hodges's ear.

"Wake snakes," he yelled out before using the barrel of the gun to clean some shards out of the shattered windowpane. He then pushed the gun through it and shot out into the Kansas darkness.

The second fire that had entered the house now raged, and the bed burst into flame.

"Shit," Hodges yelled. Then he bent down, shimmied over to a pile of clothes, and quickly pulled on some britches and shoes.

He tossed Phreddie her dress and shoes. "When I say so," he yelled over the now roaring flames, "you follow me!"

"What?" Phreddie's voice warbled.

"I said you follow me," he insisted even louder. "Got it?"

All Phreddie could do was nod. She wasn't sure how to make her feet move, but roasting alive did not seem pleasant, so when Hodges headed for the door, she followed quickly behind.

More flaming logs flew through the window, and the house began to burn from all sides.

"Now," Hodges yelled, and he flung the door open and stepped into the night.

Phreddie followed him outside, where she found Oscar and his men on horseback, their guns drawn.

"I told you, I made a promise to *mon frère* that you would burn one way or another, *salope*! Now you will—"

Before Oscar could finish his words, Hodges let another shot out from his lever-action Winchester. Phreddie screamed in shock as the man on the horse next to Oscar fell straight from his saddle and landed on the ground, dead.

Within seconds, Oscar rolled off his horse and behind a nearby hay bale. The other men scattered by hooves or by foot.

Hodges freed one hand from the gun and used it to tug on Phreddie's dress sleeve. "To the barn," he whispered sternly, and the two of them made a run for it while Hodges reloaded the gun along the way.

He kicked open the double doors and stepped inside, and in the moonlight that peeked in, he pressed the gun into Phreddie's hands.

"Wait," she said. "What am I supposed to do with this?"

"If anything moves, you shoot," he ordered, disappearing into the barn's darkness.

A crack sounded, followed by a bullet that slammed into the open barn door. When a fragment of wood landed at Phreddie's feet, she let out a small cry, then moved into the shadows.

"I never meant for it to go that far," she called out in a shaking timbre. "I wanted to stop it long before there was a wedding."

A shadow ran past the door, so she hoisted the gun into the air. When the figure passed again, she pulled the trigger and felt pain as the butt of the gun kicked against her shoulder.

The bullet hit the top of the door frame.

"Yet you saw it through," Oscar yelled out from somewhere just outside the barn. "And when the truth emerged—"

Phreddie lowered her head. "We loved each other," she cried into the moonlight.

A pair of black boots stepped out before her. "And now my promise comes true," Oscar said softly.

Phreddie dropped the gun and lifted her eyes. She was staring into pure blue hatred. Oscar's jaw was clenched, and his right arm was extended so that his pistol shook as much as the hand that gripped it.

"Did you think that you could escape me?" he asked between huffing breaths. "I would have followed you from New York to Sodom and Gomorrah, and perhaps I have."

"I really didn't mean to—" Phreddie started to say, but he cocked the pistol back, and his finger moved against the trigger.

Ready for her judgment, Phreddie dropped her shoulders and waited for Oscar to finish the job that Remy had been unable to complete. Suddenly, from the back of the barn, thundering hooves rang out as Hodges emerged on horseback, a revolver of his own in his hands.

Oscar turned quickly, and Phreddie inhaled loudly as two shots were exchanged. Next she knew, Oscar's gun was on the ground and he was pressing his left hand over his right arm as blood poured out. Hodges trotted forward, shoving the gun into his paint-waist.

Phreddie leaned down and picked the rifle back up. Then she stared uncomfortably as Hodges offered his hand to her. She looked up at the large beast before her and took a half step backward.

"It's ride or die, Phreddie," Hodges said sternly.

She looked at his hand again, then urged her own hand forward until she had grabbed his. She allowed him to help her swing up behind him onto the back of the horse.

Two bullets whizzed past them, and Hodges yanked his gun out once more and shot into the air. A man yelled out and rolled forward into the doorway, dead.

Hodges kicked the horse, which flew forward, and they emerged into the night. It was then that Phreddie realized all the light she had seen from inside the barn was not from the moon. Rather, it also came from the house, which was entirely engulfed in a raging yellow-orange fire.

"Damnit," Hodges thundered at the sight, then kicked Phreddie and the horse again with the same backward motion.

"I'll kill both you and that *putain de chienne* dead before this is over." Oscar's words faded as the horse bolted across the yard and out into the blackness.

As the wind shook the skin on Phreddie's face, she noted the tiny web of shaded blue on the eastern horizon. Morning had at last come, and she had somehow escaped Oscar yet again.

After a few minutes, the horse slowed, then stopped. "What are you doing?" Phreddie cried. "You think that he's just going to wait around and not follow us?"

She tracked Hodges's gaze, which ran off into the distance, where instead of one, two buildings were now ablaze.

"They'll lick the salt off my damn ass before I'm through with them," he declared as he turned his body in the saddle, then pushed hers straight off the horse and onto the ground.

She landed with a thud. "What?" Her voice quaked with shock and panic. "We need to get out of here!"

"*We* are not taking another step forward," Hodges declared.

"I should have known that you would leave me to suffer at his hands after all. All of you men are alike. You should have just turned me in before they burned your house and barn," Phreddie said icily.

In the distance, she could make out two forms riding their direction. *If only I'd snuck away last night like I planned to,* she admonished herself.

Hodges lifted his arm up and pointed. "You see that line of trees?"

Phreddie squinted in the dark. "I suppose so."

"Run for it."

"Run?" she asked. "That's got to be a mile off!"

"When you get there, find a place to hide."

"Where would I hide?" she asked. "I don't know anything about the woods or about hiding."

He ignored her. "If you don't see me after some time, head toward the path that's over yonder." He pointed again, then reached into his pocket and pulled out some folded bills. "Follow that trail up to the town of Briar about five miles up and buy yourself a ticket the hell out of here."

"But what about you?" Phreddie asked. "There are seven men back there, and you are only one."

"Five men," he returned.

"What?" she asked, exasperated.

"Five men. I already killed two," he said plainly, leaning down and yanking the Winchester out of her grasp.

Phreddie's empty hands shook with fear and fury. "Even five men are four more than you," she responded through a tight jaw.

"Don't you worry about me. I said I would get you to your train, and by hell's bells, I am doing just that. Now fuck off and run," he yelled. Then he turned the horse around and charged in the direction of the two men on horseback that were headed their way.

•

"*Putain de mère*," Oscar yelled as Luke tied a piece of cloth tightly over his wound.

"It only passed through the flesh," Luke informed him.

Oscar was seated and now leaned his head back against the single hay bale that still stood in the yard between the burning buildings.

Landy came around the side and nodded toward somewhere in the distance.

"Yeah I know they went that way," Oscar grunted as he tried to get up.

"Easy," Luke said. He leaned down and helped Oscar to his feet. "That Hodges fellow took Fred and Alvin out, but I sent the Bacon twins after them on horseback."

"Good thinking," Oscar said, letting out a little moan of pain. "Landy'll take me back to town to get sewn up. You join the guys."

"Sure thing." Luke started to walk away, but Oscar reached out his good arm and grabbed him.

"Kill Hodges," he commanded. "I want to see his body being dragged behind your horse when you get to town."

Luke nodded. He turned to leave again but was once more pulled back.

"And I want Phreddie alive," Oscar proclaimed. "Do you hear me?"

"I got no mind to kill a girl unless you tell me to," Luke said, and Oscar released him.

Something about the way Luke's eyes had shifted at the mention of Phreddie put Oscar ill at ease. "Luke, that ain't no girl," Oscar remonstrated through the pain. Then he followed behind Landy, who soon helped him onto his horse. Oscar moaned as he galloped toward the town of Newton with only his left hand on the reins.

•

Phreddie's lungs felt as if they were on fire by the time she made it to the trees Hodges had pointed out. She looked up and found that the horizon now looked as orange and red as the flames that smoldered in the distance behind her.

When she found a clump of eastern pine trees, she plopped down against one to rest. In between receding heaves, she heard a series of distant gunshots ring out, and each one caused her to jump up just a little more.

Then there was nothing but silence, save for the soft swaying of the evergreen branches. The minutes ticked by. After a while, the stacks of dead needles she was sitting on rustled slightly, and for a brief moment she caught a glimpse of a prairie vole peeking its brown face up through the forest floor. It paused briefly, disoriented as its large eyes were not fit for sunlight, then quickly dipped back into the darkness beneath the mulch.

When more than an hour seemed to have passed, Phreddie began to wonder whether she ought to finally get up and make the trek to Briar. Hodges had told her that if he didn't show up after a while, she should assume the worst, and the loneliness of the forest made her conjure up thoughts of him lying lifeless on the plains.

If Hodges is dead, she thought, *getting to Briar is going to be the easy part. Sneaking onto a train will take nothing short of a miracle.*

After a few more minutes, she at last stood up and dusted the pine droppings from her dress. Just as she was about to take her first step, she heard a lone gunshot and a man scream nearby.

Terrified, Phreddie ran the opposite direction from the noise until she came to the remnants of an old wall, where rocks had been stacked to create some sort of long-abandoned enclosure. Rustling leaves and approaching footsteps brought a shiver up her spine, so she crouched down low against the stones. She could hear her breathing again and hoped it would not betray her should it be Oscar who was approaching.

A twig broke loudly just beyond the wall, so Phreddie quietly crept over and peered out. What she saw made her gasp, and her shoulders jumped. This was no man. Instead, she found herself staring into the eyes of Hodges's faithful horse. "Oh, it's you," she said as she stood up and nervously approached the beast.

It was riderless.

Unsure of what to do, Phreddie tentatively extended a hand toward its nose. It gently moved its muzzle until she found herself unexpectedly nuzzling the giant, which had until this moment terribly frightened her.

"I guess he didn't make it?" she asked the horse, but it just snorted lightly and leaned down further to look for things to graze on along the ground.

Phreddie knew what she had to do, but her hands shook at the task. She pushed them down firmly and lifted her head in resolution. "You can!" she said defiantly. She then moved alongside the body of the steed. It stepped forward when it found a morsel of goodness on the forest floor, and Phreddie shivered and took a step back.

Her breast pulsated with the rapid racing of her heart.

"I have to do this," she said. Then she stepped forward and inhaled deeply. She lifted her left foot and put it in the stirrup, then attempted to pull her body up onto the horse. But the beast moved forward again, and Phreddie fell to the ground with a thud.

"I can't," she whimpered, and she lay her head back onto wet grass and stared up at the blue sky that peaked out between the treetops.

After a pause, she forced herself up again and started to slowly approach the horse. *If I can just get my foot in good, I think I can grab hold of that pointy thing on top of the saddle and swing my leg over hard,* she told herself.

She closed in and lifted her foot toward the strap just as a hand grasped her right shoulder.

Phreddie screamed.

With force, the hand spun her around and placed itself over her mouth. "Shhh," Hodges implored. "I took out the two with the beards that looked like kin, but there's still one more lurking. Okay?"

Her eyes were wide, but she nodded yes in reply. "Oh my goodness," she said through labored breaths once Hodges removed his palm. "It's you."

"I hope so," he grunted.

"No, it's just that I heard shots, many shots, and then someone screamed . . . and then your horse was here alone . . . and . . . "

"Yeah," he said. "Someone *was* shot , and it wasn't me, so let's get the hell out of here." He climbed up onto his horse. "Two wives and years of marriage, and neither one cost me my homestead. Meanwhile, you barely have been here but a minute . . ."

"I'm so sorry." Phreddie lowered her face. "I never thought that Oscar would burn down your entire place. I have so many regrets about the way things have played out since New Orleans. Maybe I should—"

"Lady," Hodges interrupted as he extended his hand toward her, "this is no time for camp stories, or for second thoughts."

Phreddie studied his strong palm, which was covered in calluses from hard work. Her eyes trailed up to the arm, which was riddled with pulsing veins that were all covered lightly in brown fuzz. *Oh my, it's firm,* she thought to herself as she grabbed it with all of her might and used its power to leap up into the saddle behind him.

"What do we do now?" she asked as the horse started to saunter. "Is this the way to Briar?"

"Those men aren't gonna stop till both of us are dead," he told her. "If we go to Briar, we are like to be met with the three that's left—and maybe a whole lot more."

"Then where do we go?" Alarm returned to her voice.

"For now, it's best to draw them further afield. There I'll have the advantage, as I can pick the terrain. And trust me, they will find out quick enough that the Kansas plains are no place for a handful of bayou boys and pretty boy Europeans," Hodges said, urging the horse deeper into the woods.

2 Corinthians 3:17

The smell of salty sizzling bacon woke Grace from her slumber. Her stomach grumbled at the thought of the crispy meat melting into her tongue, and she remembered she had not eaten so much as a bite since tending to George in his last hours.

Most passengers raced off to the Harvey houses whenever the train made a water stop, but Grace remained on board, anxiously chewing her lower lip and wondering when they would get back on the tracks.

Sister Adrienne had offered to bring her back a bite, but Grace refused as she didn't care a thing about food. She cared about getting to where she was going, but now that she was here, her stomach protested that enough was enough.

Grace decided to heed its call, so she dressed quickly and splashed a little flower water on her neck, then gathered herself and left the room.

The nun was already gnawing on a biscuit when Grace entered the small dining room.

Grace nodded and took the seat across from the sister. "Good to see you are early—it's only a quarter past."

Sister Adrienne paused midbite to glare up at Grace.

A young woman approached the table and set down a plate of scrambled eggs, bacon, biscuits, and corn cakes.

"Thank you," Grace said as the waitress turned Grace's empty cup over and began to pour some brown liquid into it.

"Oh, not coffee, darling." Grace put her hand up to signal a stop.

"It's Misty," the waitress snarked. "Bad enough the men call me names like darling and tap my bottom. I'd just as soon other women call me by my actual name."

"Oh. Okay, Misty." Grace considered her words. "In that case, I'd actually prefer tea, and thank you."

The waitress shot her a look and laughed. "You seem clueless." She chuckled.

Grace looked confused.

"Let me make this clearer: this isn't merry ole England, love," Misty declared in a terrible Cockney accent. "It's this weak coffee, or you can get a whiskey over at the saloon through those doors." She nodded in the opposite direction while she continued in her normal tongue.

"I'll take the coffee," Grace relented.

Once the girl was gone, she decided it was time to focus on the matter at hand. "Where do we begin today?"

"Let's start with the church," Sister Adrienne said, dabbing her mouth with a cloth napkin. "They usually tend to at least be aware of the vagabonds and unsavories that enter a town like this."

Grace frowned. "Why must you be so mean-spirited when it comes to my Nadine?"

"Because, Nadine is just a fantasy in your mind. Your child was a diabolical imp that I had to willingly suffer for fourteen long years. Do you think I take it lightly that I had to care for that thing in order to beg for funds?"

"Granted, Nadine has her peculiarities, but must you liken her to evil constantly? It seems to me that if she were all that bad, she would have caused real problems at the orphanage, but so far, I've yet to hear anything so terrible that she did while she was there other than exist. You even told me on the train that you were able to secure her a job as a laundress. How horrible could she have been if you suffered her as long as you say and yet found her gainful employment?"

"Phreddie made me skin crawl," Sister Adrienne spat out. "It's as simple as that. But Mrs. Guidry paid a good sum for new hires." She stood up from the table and tossed her napkin onto what was left of her breakfast. "Just that child's presence itself up until the day she left for the Guidry household was difficult to bear. You ought to thank me, because your husband told me of his plan had I not agreed to provide a spot at the orphanage. The same one a person uses to deal with a litter of kittens they care not to house and feed."

The porcelain of Grace's coffee cup landed on the saucer with a thud, and her mouth fell open. "And you call yourself a Christian. How could you—" she started to say, but the sister cut her off.

"I find you almost as insufferable as your child, so if you don't mind, I will wait outside on the hotel porch until you finish your breakfast. Then we can walk to the church to get some information and hopefully get this whole thing over with by lunch. I'd like to be back on the train to New Orleans with your bankbook by evening and say goodbye to the Weavers forever."

Sister Adrienne turned and left.

Grace didn't feel much like eating after that exchange, but she forced herself to nibble while her spirit drooped at the thought of the loveless life that her daughter must have had in that nun's care. Not that things had been much warmer in the Weaver household.

George had kept his distance from Nadine right from birth. The midwives had hardly left the bedroom, where an exhausted Grace had lain with her swaddled baby in her arms when her husband entered and glared at them both.

"It's a shame it was a stillbirth." He sighed before he turned away and left.

Grace was stunned, as she was quite certain that she was holding an infant girl who clung to her breast at that very moment.

Soon George's mood concerning his wife also began to shift noticeably, as he struck her for the first time not two weeks later when she spilled some oat porridge on the table.

"You cannot seem to do any wifely duty correctly," he yelled at her. When his anger caused the baby to cry, he screamed, "Shut that thing up," then walked out the front door with a slam, leaving both mother and child in tears.

Her husband never acknowledged Nadine again. As a baby, if she crawled toward him or cooed in his direction, George would look past her as if she wasn't even in the room. After a time, his infant daughter even stopped making attempts to engage with him. So Grace went out of her way to both love her child and to keep her away from her father as much as possible.

One day, out of nowhere, George announced that all three of them were going for a walk. Grace smiled brightly at his suggestion, thinking a thaw must have started in his heart. They chatted happily as they made their way down the sidewalks of the city, until their leisurely family stroll ended abruptly at the gates of the Sisters of Children and Charity Orphanage. There Grace's smile turned into hysterical tears as her child was removed from her hands and placed into those of the woman who now waited for her outside this hotel restaurant.

Grace could only imagine, based on her own interactions with Sister Adrienne, what Nadine's years with her must have been like.

"Best get on with it, as I cannot change the past," she whimpered to herself.

She stood up and walked to the doorway. As she exited, three men who were about to enter stepped aside to allow her to exit.

"*Bonjour, madame*," an attractive one with a bandage on his arm said, nodding and smiling.

"Thank you very much." Grace smiled back. Then she took a few steps and paused to look back at the men.

Imagine coming all the way to the Kansas Territories and finding a Frenchman like the ones you see on every street corner in New Orleans, she thought. Then she turned her head and walked outside.

•

"You mean all four of them are dead?" Oscar asked Luke in a strong whisper.

Luke lowered his eyes and nodded.

"I asked you to hire me the best men in Kansas City, and that man Hodges still managed to kill them all in less time than it took me to *pour chier* in the commode this morning," Oscar hissed.

The serving woman he heard other boarders call Misty arrived with plates, and he lifted his head and smiled.

"Any luck with the two you set out to capture?" she asked as she poured them all coffee. Oscar noticed her wink at Luke as if they already knew each other.

"*Oui*." Oscar turned and smiled. "It is all going according to plan. So much so that we can even stop for this lovely breakfast served up by the most beautiful of women." He picked up his fork and stabbed a sausage link, then smiled and gave it a theatrical chomp.

Misty giggled. "He's almost as charming as you." She winked again at Luke before turning back to Oscar. "I kinda liked that Phreddie one. When she came into town and rode off with Hodges that first day, I did think to myself how wild the West can be, but I never dreamed it was half as wild as the tales I've heard since you lot came to Newton!"

When she left, Oscar spit it into his napkin. "How long did you say you stayed in Newton when you came here first?" he teased Luke. "But enough of that. Now that the doctor has cleaned my wound, *il n'y a pas de temps pour les conneries*."

Luke and Landy looked to each other for understanding, but they were both wearing the same blank face.

"No time to fuck around," Oscar clarified. "Eat quickly, then we will see to this ourselves for good."

As they gobbled down their fare, Oscar stewed in his mind until he became as stewed as the tomatoes on his plate over what had happened at Hodges's. His wounded arm stung slightly, but his pride stung worse from the looks some of the townsfolk had been giving him since he was forced back to town to seek the doctor's attention.

Not very heroic. And this from the man they thought was their liberator only yesterday.

Had he not ridden out in such a show of confidence with everyone looking on, no one would have even noticed who he was, let alone that he had been shot. But those sour faces let him know that this Charlie Hodges had helped Phreddie one-up him, and it made Oscar hate Hodges with almost as much ferocity as he despised Phreddie. While his plans for her were borne out of familial vengeance, Hodges had injured Oscar's body, not just his pride. It had made Oscar look a complete fool to the people to whom he had projected strength and control. For that, he could stop at nothing short of a bullet placed right between Hodges's eyes.

The public loss of face was perhaps worse than the loss of his brother in Oscar's mind. He distinctly remembered a time when he was eleven years old, right before they had emigrated to the United States. He'd been tripped by an older boy named Lucien at École Le Caousou in front of all of the other school children. The fact that *les garçons* had laughed at him boiled his soul with the same fiery temperature he now felt on his face.

As he'd sat at home that evening, his puss had pushed into a pout, and his father inquired what was on his mind. Remy blurted out that Oscar was angry because everyone had laughed at him earlier in the day. Upon hearing the story, Aloïs chuckled along as well. Oscar's face turned crimson when Remy joined in too.

"If you are so weak as to allow someone to make an ass of you, just know that I will always laugh as well—only harder." His father's words added to his fury, and Oscar left the table to sit in his room, where he spent the night pickling in his anger.

By the next morning, he was more sour and more enraged than when the incident happened. He got up and left the house without stopping to eat the buttery breakfast rolls the cook had made especially for him.

For about thirty minutes, he sat crouched along the wall of the Cathédrale Saint-Etienne that was adjacent to the school. When his assailant arrived and was about to enter the schoolhouse, Oscar stood up and stepped out into the crowd of boys, who began to giggle at him.

It didn't take Oscar long to pull from his pocket the slingshot that his father had bought him for his birthday the prior year. Quite quickly, the boys' laughter turned into gasps of horror.

With one yank of the band, the rock sailed the two or three meters between him and Lucien, where it landed with a loud crack on the older boy's nose. Lucien screamed as blood shot out of his nostrils, and all of the other boys stepped back in fear as Oscar approached his humbled enemy. He lifted his finger in the air and stepped toward Lucien's face. It was now covered by the boy's bloody hands, which were trying to stop the red that streamed out from between his fingers and over his lips.

"Now *that* is funny," Oscar declared, then he turned to the other boys and howled and guffawed until one by one they all joined him in laughing at the greatly injured Lucien.

He never again let anyone get the better of him, and given that Lucien—who had only tripped Oscar—had suffered the way he did, Oscar considered what type of response would be appropriate for Charlie Hodges.

No one makes an ass of me lest I give them a hundredfold in return.

"Let's go," he said loudly, slamming his coffee cup onto the table. His two companions stood, shoveling up their final bits of eggs and downing the last drops of their coffee in order to follow their firm commander.

"Doctor told me that there's an Indian tracker for hire who lives just outside town. By sundown, I plan to return here for a hot bath and a hooker at the saloon. Maybe even your gal, Misty." He laughed in an attempt to show confidence and reaffirm his charges' support.

Plus, he knew nothing would motivate Landy to action quicker than the thought of being able to choke a trollop, as it was as strong as Oscar's own need to hurt Phreddie and Charlie Hodges. After all, he needed both Landy and Luke to come through for him, especially now. This was due payback for the way his money had come through for the both of them during the years of their friendship.

•

Hilaria Ortiz was headed into the church to meet with Father Milfken to discuss the church's booth for the July Fourth celebrations that would take place in six days' time. This year, she had spent months sewing 2 Corinthians 3:17 into Bible bookmarks that the church planned to sell.

Where the Spirit of the Lord is, there is freedom.

She had pushed and pulled her needle repeatedly until those fine words stood out in bright blue against a white background. They rang truer now on account of all that was happening in Newton. Ms. Ortiz felt this town was closer to this fine citation of God's scripture than it had ever been before.

Soon, Charlie Hodges would be punished, and the murderous creature he had taken into his home would be routed out as well. Yes, all of her hard work in sanctifying this small corner of America was paying off, and she could not wait to celebrate both the town and this nation's freedom at this year's Independence Day festivities.

True, the band would play as it had every year from the stage that was being erected in the town center this very minute. People would put out tables of food that everyone would load up their plates with and munch on. Local politicians would stand up and regale everyone with stories about the meaning of the day. Glasses of beer and firewater would be held up high, and toasts would call out all along Main Street. Though Ms. Ortiz was a supporter of temperance herself, even she might be persuaded to clink a glass or two in honor of Mr. Oscar Delaroux.

As she made her way to the front of the church, she could hear the sound of hammers hitting nails on wood from afar and laughter in the lead-up to the festivities, but these noises faded quickly when the most peculiar of sights did catch her eyes. Two women were approaching, and one wore a nun's habit. Ms. Ortiz hadn't seen a nun since she left the Texas border, as few, if any, ventured into the Kansas Territories unless they were in a large group headed to some outpost flanked by armed men the church had hired to ensure their safe transport.

"How do you do?" Ms. Ortiz approached the two women and extended her hand. "I am Ms. Hilaria Ortiz, and you are?"

"I am Grace Weaver," the dark-haired woman replied, "and this is . . ."

The nun stepped past her and extended her own hand. "Sister Adrienne of New Orleans," she answered for herself.

"My, my, my," Ms. Ortiz said with a trill of surprise. "We seem to have half of New Orleans in our town at present."

The woman called Grace clasped her hands together and let out a gasp of happiness. "Then you know of my daughter, Nadine, Ms. Ortiz?" she said with great hope. "She is from New Orleans too."

Ms. Ortiz furrowed her brows, then replied, "No, I have not heard of any Nadine, Mrs. Weaver," though she looked at Sister Adrienne instead when she answered. "Sister, it is so rare to have another woman of faith visit our town. I myself would have gone into the ministry, as you have, had I not been wedded off by my parents at such a young age. How I admire a life such as yours, devout and dedicated. I welcome you to this town, and if there's any assistance I can be of while you are here, please do not hesitate."

The sister's face stayed as stone, but she did reply. "Perhaps you know this Nadine by her other name—Phreddie?"

Ms. Ortiz sucked air into her lungs violently, and the sister and Grace took a step back.

"Why, what in heaven's name would a *religieux* want from such a sort as that?" she asked, and her face curled up as if she had seen a rat on her pillow.

"This sort"—Grace Weaver stepped forward again—"Nadine, known to some as Phreddie, is my child, as I said before. And I am told that she was last seen here in this town. By your reaction, I see it is the truth."

"It is as you say, Mrs. Weaver, but I don't know whether to hug you in mercy or shake your hand in admiration at your bravery for claiming parentage over that thing, or to run from you in fear. Not only did she kill another human, but there is the question of whether she is even a human herself." Ms. Ortiz shook her head with consternation.

Sister Adrienne came closer and put her hand on Ms. Ortiz's shoulder, which caused her to relax. "Now, now, Ms. Ortiz. I can only guess you have been told more about Phreddie than you cared to hear, but I am doing a heavenly service in trying to reunite this innocent mother with her child before that child is likely to perish at the hands of justice. I am sure you can see the kindness of such an act, even if you do not understand it."

Ms. Ortiz watched Grace's surprise at Sister Adrienne's words, and the tense muscles in the woman's face almost seemed to relax into a smile at the nun. This thawing in turn softened Ms. Ortiz's heart.

"Well." She sighed. "Even if I wished to help, she is on the run, and there in the distance rides the man who aims to kill your child, Mrs. Weaver." She pointed off yonder, where three men on horses were riding away onto the plains.

"We must ride after them," Grace insisted, her voice rising in panic. "I have to stop them. I have to get to my child. I must find Nadine," she shrieked.

"Mrs. Weaver. Mrs. Weaver!" Ms. Ortiz shouted over her until she'd calmed herself down. "This is not New Orleans. This is the wilds of Indian territory, and you would not last an hour out there on your own with only you and a nun before both of your bodies would be brought back into town scalpless," she explained sternly.

Sister Adrienne put her hand up to her head, and a look of fear came across her face.

"Instead, you should take shelter at the inn. I will be sure to update you of any information that I hear in regard to your child. Should you not hear it before me, that is."

"We must listen to this woman," Sister Adrienne pressed Grace. "In the meantime, I will meet with the leadership of this church—and you, Mrs. Weaver, should go lie down. The last thing this town, or I, needs is an unhinged woman."

Ms. Ortiz noted the look Grace shot at the sister.

"Perhaps the father here will have some additional ideas," the nun continued with firmness. "As I have made clear that I want this business to be over with as soon as possible." Then she looked at Ms. Ortiz and softened her tone. "As any good woman of faith would," she added sweetly.

"Of course," Ms. Ortiz replied.

"Might you lead me to the priest?" Sister Adrienne asked.

Ms. Ortiz smiled and opened the church door for the nun, and the two of them went inside.

"Good day, Mrs. Weaver," Ms. Ortiz said gently as she closed the door behind her. She looked over at Sister Adrienne. "Oh yes," she continued, "it is wonderful to have another woman who puts nothing before her devotion to the Lord here in Newton."

With that, they walked together through the church in search of Father Milfken.

Green Ocean

It had been several hours since Hodges and Phreddie exited the small eastern forest and rode out onto the Central Plains. Here, their horse had diligently pressed through the subtly changing flora that lapped at their kneecaps.

"I've never seen so much grass," Phreddie exclaimed in awe when they reached the top of a hill. They looked down and out over a vast expanse of green that rolled over endless acreage. "It feels like there is no other thing alive in the world but us," she whispered.

"And yet you are standing in the middle of a boodle of life," Hodges attested. "It is its own Garden of Eden." He slid off the horse. "Come on, let me show you." He beckoned with a hand.

Phreddie turned her head and looked behind them for followers.

"Oh, it will take many hours before they can catch up," he asserted.

"You don't know Oscar," she said matter-of-factly.

"That Frenchman was stoved up in the arm, and he didn't look the type to not get himself to a professional sawbones for stitchin' before he pursues us again. Plus, it's no good for the body or the horse to ride endlessly. We both need a break, him to relax and graze and us to stretch our legs for a spell."

"Okay, I guess," Phreddie said with some hesitation. Though she continued to glance backward, she let him help her down.

As they walked alongside the horse, Hodges scanned the ground around them. "You see, right where we are standing is the great mixing of two oceans," he explained.

"I don't see any water," Phreddie said with a shrug, "just straw."

"Well look here." He bent down and plucked a blade of grass that he held up in the sun. "This here's what you call tallgrass. It grows and feeds critters big and small, but most especially the mighty elk and great herds of thundering buffalo."

"I bet those are a sight to see," she remarked with wonder. "I've seen a buffalo hide once. It was above Mr. Guidry's library mantle, and it was huge."

"Yet even a full-grown bull is but a tiny speck of sand out here," Hodges remarked. He threw the grass up into the air, and it drifted off in the light wind. "You see, if it's not ate up, then this grass burns in great big patches from lightning storms that catch it aspark."

"Wait." She stopped walking. "Are you telling me that the grass randomly goes up in flames?'

"Sometimes for acres and miles at a time."

She held her hands up to her chest. "How terrifying."

"And then it's like Noah's ark, with all the animals two by two running to escape the danger."

"I still don't see any of those live things, though." She shrugged.

"Well, when you say we're alone, we're anything but. You're likely standing on, or next to, maybe dozens of critters—from lizards to snakes to who knows what—and you're just plain unaware."

"Lizards?" She looked down at her shoes. "Here?"

"This may seem lifeless to you, but everything is alive. It's all here if you only look and listen."

And Phreddie did listen. She listened intently to Hodges give masterful instruction on the Central Plains as if he'd been some kind of orator or professor in another life, a life she knew so little about. One where great learning took place, where her knuckles weren't rapped by the sisters and the skin on her hands didn't peel off from the boiling water she poured over Mr. Guidry's undergarments to clean them of their filth.

Hodges pointed to a smaller patch of grass as they approached on foot. "And that there's the shortgrass made up of blue gamma and purple grease grass," he explained as they bent down together to examine God's creation.

"That's actually quite pretty if you look at it up close, I suppose," she said as their kneecaps touched.

"In these shorter parts, there's birds aplenty, like that loggerhead shrike over there." He stood up and pointed. A gray-and-white large-headed bird let out a loud *schgra-a-a* as it flew away. "There's plenty of 'em, as well as small swarms of quail, each of whom pluck their way through everything from grasshoppers to rodents. Why, I reckon there's enough life near the two feet you are standing on to fill up the whole of New Orleans."

Phreddie chuckled, and he smiled at her in a way she had never seen before.

"I've never heard you so animated." She giggled. "Seems like all your anger fades away out here."

"How can it not?" he remarked. "Where the long and short grass meet, something almost magical happens, and you find yourself a part of something bigger. The worries of us people seem so . . . well . . . little."

As he mused, the horse kicked up a small kaleidoscope of large painted lady butterflies. Six or seven of those angels of the plains, with their mottled brown-yellow, white, brown, and black enormous wings, flitted up into the air. As they rode on the breeze, Phreddie marveled at their spots, which looked like great big eyes staring down into your soul, and she understood what Hodges was saying for perhaps the first time since they met.

At last, the butterflies fluttered overhead and then away to a nearby bushel of sagebrush.

"How did your wives die?" Phreddie asked bluntly as she stopped walking.

Hodges came to an abrupt stop and yanked on the lead of the horse, who did the same. "Time to ride again," he announced coldly, the muscles in his face now tight.

"But—" Phreddie started to reply, but Hodges was already back on the horse.

"Let's go." He offered his hand.

"Ugh," she exclaimed as she took hold and pulled herself up behind him.

"There's an abandoned hunting camp a few miles from here," he announced as he pushed the horse forward. "We can wait it out there for a spell."

The horse picked up speed.

"Either Oscar will give up and go home in a few days' time, or the camp is the place this will all come to a head," Hodges yelled over the wind that lapped at their faces in the horse's galloping wake.

"Okay," was all Phreddie could get out between the sound of pulsating hooves. But with their conversation ending so abruptly, she didn't feel like anything was actually okay right now.

All she could do was to hold on tight in order not to fall off. If she did, with the way Hodges had reacted, she wasn't sure if he'd come back to get her, leave her there alone to die on the plains, or turn back around and have the horse run her over.

She thought of Lily and winced at that last thought.

•

It didn't take long for Oscar to convince the Wichita man to track for him. Taakwic—or Four Lines, as he was known in English on account of the lines tattooed above and below each of his eyes—was one of the last members of his tribe to remain in the territory. He explained briefly to Oscar how after the smallpox, what was left of his kin had been picked off by rival tribes. A few had decided to stay in northern Texas during the last migration, but Taakwic had come back to the tribe's hunting grounds. The white men had renamed them "Kansas" after the Kansa Sioux, as if they alone had claim to everything around and no one else had existed in these parts for as far back as memory allowed.

While there were several other closely related tribes somewhat nearby that Taakwic could easily have joined, he'd decided to remain on his own, near the exact parts where he grew up, as it was all he'd known from infancy. This land was where he summered in the large grass lodges and grew crops, not the Tawakoni far away, where his family followed the buffalo down into in the winter. He wanted to die on the same prairies he had been born onto, so he remained behind here and worked for the white men doing odd jobs or tracking.

Oscar was all too eager to coat Taakwic's red hand with gold and told him there'd be more to come if he was successful in the hunt. He described whom he was looking for, though he left off much of the why.

This wild man wouldn't understand the complexities of all that has happened, he told himself. *Better to just get on with this than try to explain to a simpleton the whos and whats of civilization.*

Oscar was not here for anything more than to get what he wanted, and truth be told, in his mind this odd-looking creature made his skin crawl almost as much as Phreddie did. Yet he needed him, so Oscar did what he always did when he needed something: he paid out.

Ten minutes after they had struck their agreement, the four men rode off on horseback to what was left of Hodges's smoldering homestead, where

Taakwic had the three others walk him through everything that had happened. Oscar looked on with great interest at the way this aborigine bent down close to the ground and walked low. As he scooped up bits of charred hay and stared at prints where Oscar could see none, Oscar considered how peculiar these natives were now that he had actually seen one up close.

A bit like a dog smelling for the perfect place to piss. He laughed to himself.

Finally, the Indian man stood up and waved his arms in the air for them to approach. "They went east first?" he asked.

"Yes, I can show you where I last seen them," Luke said.

Taakwic nodded, then hopped up on his horse and waited for the rest of them.

Luke led the way while Taakwic trotted behind him closely, followed by Landy and Oscar, who took up the rear. *This native will be worth every coin if he does his job well,* he thought as they rode into the small forest.

It wasn't long at all before Taakwic found the tracks of a horse and the four of them were charging out of the forest and into the open plains.

As the wind flew across his face, Oscar inhaled deeply. *Now this is living.* The vastness of the vista and the freedom of powerful hooves made him forget his anger for a minute. He spent so much time on show and working to gratify his immediate needs, but never had any of those things been half as satisfying as this ride across an endless openness of both land and sky. It was so *enchanteur.*

Oscar almost forgot why he was here to begin with, but after hours of riding in silence, Taakwic drew to a stop, and the anger returned. As he watched the Indian slide off his horse, Oscar's mind was once again clouded by feelings of hatred and humiliation.

Even this landscape wouldn't be a sight prettier than Phreddie suffering at his hands, he at last determined. Then he smiled a toothy grin as the Wichita announced two people and a horse had walked in this very spot only a few hours ago.

Je vais t'avoir salope. Oscar sneered in his mind, as he did indeed plan to get that bitch, and oh, the things he would do to her caused the right side of his lips to part in a diagonal smile. Once more he stewed on the plan for Phreddie, now perfected after many weeks. But as they drew closer to Hodges, Oscar realized that his initial plan to put a bullet in the Kansan's brain was just too easy. It was like when a medieval king would hire a French swordsman to lob the head off a traitor that the king had once loved.

True, it got the job done, but there was mercy in the hiring. In Hodges's case, Oscar didn't want a smooth decapitation. No, he wanted a rough parting, where it took several painful whacks on flesh and bone before this man was separated from his cranium.

No, a bullet was too kind for Charlie Hodges. He too would suffer and beg for death to come quickly, but it would not relieve him any more than it would Phreddie.

•

Charlie Hodges was thundering inside. In fact, the noise in his head was louder than the hooves of his horse on the open plains.

After all that I have done for that deuce of a lady, he thought. *She came into Miller's looking like a half-drowned landloper. Destitute and not knowing a soul, Miller being all too ready to take advantage. But I stood up and offered her respite. By now she'd have just been another cheap lady of the line with years left on her contract. And in exchange, I've had a knife past my face, rude speak meaner than a moss head ready to be put out to pasture, and my dadgum house in flames. Now this peck of trouble asks me what I did?*

By the time they were approaching the small patch of honey locust and silver maples, Hodges was madder than a March hare. He pulled the horse to a stop near a tiny pool of water.

"What is this place?" Phreddie asked. "It's got a spooky feeling."

Hodges slid off and silently helped her down, then led the horse to drink. Afterward he walked over to the small decayed shack made of silver maple branches that lay semicamouflaged in the brush.

"One of the few places to hunker down," he said coldly. "If we headed a smidgeon further west, we would be more likely to attract Injun attention than here."

"There's Indians about?"

He watched as she crisscrossed her arms over her chest.

"Perhaps even close, but that's to our advantage, as Oscar and his men will perhaps be less likely to head this way when they hear there's red men afoot. Anyway, that's why we'll forgo a fire tonight," he answered frostily, sticking his head into the structure.

The wood on the ceiling and walls was old and dried out, but the floor was mainly dust, so the place would work fine once he added a few more sticks and some grass to the roof.

"The water here is potable enough. It seeps up from a spring underground," he said as he came back out. "That's why a few men use this place in the fall as a base camp for their elk hunts further afield. The Arkansas River isn't much further, about a quarter mile, and there's a good spot to hunt bucks there during the rut."

"I see," Phreddie said.

"The ground is gonna be hard and cold. Go yank some of the tall grasses just outside the tree line so that we can make some beds," he directed her. Then he turned his back on her and walked off to gather a few new branches to support this simple camping house.

An hour later, Hodges was sitting on the remnants of a tree near the small pond. He was wondering to himself why he was going to all this trouble for someone he hardly knew when Phreddie approached.

"Why are you helping me?" she asked as if she'd read his mind.

"I reckon I just don't like to see people pushed around," he said quietly. "Something about being cornered and accused that gets my back up."

"But you don't even know what it is they think that I have done. I could be anything. A thief who robbed a bank . . . I could have impersonated a housekeeper and stolen heirlooms from a dying woman . . . I could be a-a—"

"Murderer," they both said together.

Hodges stood up and faced her. "So what you're saying is really just another way to ask me what I've done to my wives?" he snarled.

"In truth, I'm just trying to reconcile what seems like two people," Phreddie told him. "The townsfolk all seem to think that you killed Lily. Heck, they believe you killed your first wife too. But watching you light up when you talked about the plains earlier . . ." She stepped closer. "Seeing myself how, though you can be cantankerous as all sorts, you've stood up for me, a veritable stranger, I'm just wondering—who are you really?" She squinted her green eyes and looked so deeply into Hodges that he thought she had reached down into his soul.

"And so do you think I'm a murderer?" he asked as he drew deeper into her gaze. They looked at one another for a moment, then discomfort and awkwardness reared their heads. Hodges broke the stare and turned away, sitting back down on the log.

"It's not often you hear of someone going through wives like water in a sieve, but I would much rather hear from you what happened," she said softly from behind him.

There was silence except for the slight swish of grass as Phreddie's feet pushed aside the blades along the fallen tree and took a seat next to Hodges.

"I met Alice in Missourah," he began at last. "My family was fixing to take the trail out west as fast as we could. You see, my parents came over from Ireland to escape the Great Famine—"

"Ireland?" Phreddie interrupted with surprise in her voice. "You don't sound even remotely Irish."

Hodges laughed. "That's on account of years of hard settling, and I was young enough to still be impressionable when we arrived. My brogue was broken in my youth in Chilhowee by the Post Oak Creek, both of which are a long way off now."

He looked over at her. "Anyways, as I said, we were waiting at St. Joseph to get ferried across the river like hundreds of other settlers when I saw her."

"Alice?"

Hodges's eyes glazed over. "She was wearing a large hat, bigger than the sun." He laughed loudly. "And the same color as it. Not practical at all for riding through hard country." Turning, he stared off at the water.

"She was trying to unhook the oxen from her family's cart and, needless to say, it weren't going very well." He laughed some more, and from the corner of his eye he could see Phreddie smile. "Anyway, she bent down to unhitch, and her hat flew off on the wind and landed right at my feet."

Phreddie chuckled. "Sounds like kismet."

"Long story cut short, my family went on westward minus one son, and Alice and I spent the next few years in St. Joseph. We lived on love and soup beans, until one day we decided we was gonna strike out on our own just like each of our parents had done."

"Oh, I was curious about what happened to them. Where did they settle?" Phreddie asked.

"Her folks made it all the way to Oregon City, but mine fell silent somewhere along the trail," he said, his eyes lowered toward his feet. "I half wonder, if I had been with them, if I might have saved them from whatever fate I assume they met." He fell silent again, and they sat there quietly together for a moment.

"Who's to say what could have happened to anyone if any of the choices we made had been different?" Phreddie wondered aloud at last.

Hodges shrugged. "Suppose we will never know. But half of my decision to head out from St. Joseph was to find out if they were alive, but we never made it very far."

"Why not?" she asked.

Hodges turned to face Phreddie. "Alice got pregnant."

"Wow," she remarked. "Now that I have had the experience of riding for only a single day, I can see that traveling across this land for weeks or months on end would be a hard journey for any woman, nevertheless a *pregnant* one!"

"Especially one as big as a mule." He laughed. "So we settled in a small cabin near Moundridge, just south of the Black Kettle Creek."

"Where is that?" Phreddie asked, "I really don't know much about geography, especially around Kansas."

"Oh, it's not too far from Newton," Hodges explained. "There, we put down roots. I'd work the land in the day, trying to get a few crops going, like Irish Murphys and Injun corn, and at night, Alice would practice on me how she was going to teach our baby its ABC's once it was birthed. By firelight, she would force me to learn my letters, since I never got to have too much schooling myself. And we would bust a gut at my poor skills. She was so excited to become a mother that she didn't mind my idiocy." He smiled at the memory.

"You mean to tell me that somewhere out there you have a literate grown child? There are two Charlie Hodges in the world?" Phreddie laughed.

"Afraid not." Hodges's face stiffened, and he narrowed his eyes.

"I'm so sorry if you took offense. I didn't know—" she stammered.

"I took our horses and went to town one morning for chicken feed. As I rode over the last hill back home, I saw the trail of smoke in the air, and I just knew." His voice faded.

"You knew what?" Phreddie pressed. "What happened?"

"Only thing left behind was Alice's scalp," he said softly.

Phreddie shivered. "Indians?"

They sat in silence for a moment, then Hodges continued. "I rode after them, but I couldn't find Alice or our baby she was carrying."

A light wind blew over the water, and its surface rippled gently.

"A few weeks later, I saw a flock of black vultures circling high over a patch of blackjack oak. There her corpse lay, and next to it, a single leather legging from a Kiowa hunter. The strap had been torn off, and I knew that

Alice must have put up a good fight with them till the end, even with part of her head missing."

"That's awful." Phreddie's voice quaked.

He turned to watch her as she scanned the small area they were currently taking refuge in, and he knew inside that it was no longer him that she was afraid of but the Injuns all around.

"I feel so frightfully exposed." She shuddered, and Hodges shrugged again.

"Best make a plan for what comes next, after we rest some tonight," he said as he stood up.

There was much more to Phreddie, and he had never thought to ask. All he knew was that she'd needed his help that first night, and he'd up and offered it. Again, he wondered to himself why.

The sky began to twist into shades of violet and orange.

"The day star is setting, and we had quite a long day," he continued as he took the lead on the horse and walked it in the direction of the dilapidated structure. It was now covered with fresh grass that Hodges had applied in hopes of slowing down the night winds that were bound to blow through it.

Phreddie got up and followed behind him as he tied the horse to the small lodge. Suddenly, she spoke up with some urgency. "Why did anyone think *you* killed Alice if she was scalped by Indians?"

"Easy," Hodges explained. "Each time I went to town, people would ask about her and the baby. I wouldn't . . . Well, really I just couldn't answer them. At first I would just stare at them all silent, like. The women would stop me, though, every few steps, each one wanting to know if it was a boy or a girl, as by then Alice would have had to have given birth."

Hodges put out his hand and motioned for Phreddie to go inside. After she did, he followed, and they both sat down on big mounds of tallgrass that she had heaped together like mattresses on each side of the door.

"Some would ask if Alice needed anything. Others wanted to know why I hadn't brought mother and child into town yet, and so on."

The inside of the shelter was growing dim, but Hodges could see the intense curiosity on Phreddie's face, so he continued. "You see, Alice, in the short time that we lived together near Newton, became beloved by the townsfolk. She was a tenderhearted and friendly woman, so it's no wonder that they all felt for her like I did."

"I still don't understand why you didn't just tell them what happened to her," Phreddie confessed loudly, some exasperation on her tongue.

"It wasn't that easy for me," Hodges rebutted. "I really am not all that comfortable talking about feelings, and besides, there was not nothing anyone could do for me to bring Alice back. I just wanted them all to leave me alone. Now I know they meant well, but eventually, my silence changed to anger. The more they asked, the more I started to fume. Finally, one day I grabbed the priest by the neck—and he was the last to ever ask about Alice."

Hodges lay back onto the grass and looked up at the roof. The peeling old sticks began to fade into shadow as it grew darker.

The silence of that darkness was pierced when Phreddie blurted out, "Well what about Lily, then?"

Hodges let out a great big sigh, closing his eyes tightly. "Real simple," he said into the air. "Lily had cancer in the stomach. It was slow at first, but then it began to grow rather quickly. She was in horrible pain, but she didn't want a soul to know."

"So wait . . . Her sister, Ms. Ortiz, the one that hates and despises you, didn't even know Lily was sick?"

"Not her sister, nor anyone else, as she didn't want them to worry or suffer her none. Lily was strong-minded and proud like that. Not soft like Alice. No, Lily was a mountain where Alice was the wind."

"So she just passed away slowly and silently?"

The shelter was now nearly pitch-black.

"One night it got to be too much for her, so she took herself out to the barn with my gun. I woke up to find a short note on the table that said *I'm sorry* and Lily's body on the hay pile."

"Oh my goodness." Phreddie exhaled loudly.

"That woman was tough as hardtack and as stubborn as a basset hound. She made sure to die where the hay would soak up her blood, on account of she didn't want me to have to clean up her mess," Hodges said softly. "No, she didn't want anyone to deal with her sickness—or her decisions."

He stopped speaking and listened to the gentle breeze that rustled the grass on top of the rotting structure. "You are the first person I've ever told what happened to my wives," he whispered aloud, but inside, once again all he could do was ask himself why.

Berdache

It was near midnight, but Sister Adrienne couldn't sleep. The melodies and mirth that drifted into her open window from the saloon below kept her awake for more reasons than the noise they made.

After tossing for what seemed like hours, she threw the covers off and got out of bed. She leaned on the ledge and looked out onto the street, where revelers threw arms around shoulders and entered or exited Miller's, happy to soon be—or happy to have already become—inebriated.

"Damn," she muttered aloud, "what I wouldn't give to paint the tonsils myself, or whatever these assholes call having a drink." She slammed her hands down on the sill, then went to the lone chair in the room and sat down.

Why in fuck's sake did Mrs. Weaver have to drag me to this shithole? There's that puritanical Ms. Ortiz who traipsed me around the church all day, as if I had any common interest with her or her insufferable piousness. I hate this place almost as much as I hate that damn orphanage and those brat-faced children. But at least in New Orleans, people have some respect for a woman of the cloth, especially one of my stature.

"Aside from that damn Ortiz, the rest of them would as soon step over my dead body as give me any kind of deference," she growled into the night air.

More importantly though, at home, Sister Adrienne knew that she was free to sip sherry in the confines of her room without anyone being any the wiser. After all, she hadn't willingly chosen to be a sober and chaste nun. It had been forced upon her by her father, who had caught a ginger-haired boy putting his hand up her skirt in back of the tenement houses they both lived in.

"You'll be a godly woman like your dead mum if it be my last act on this earth," he'd sworn. He had sentenced her to an abbey in the next breath.

That very afternoon, she had been abandoned to a world of rigidity so very far from the freedom she had felt when that boy had touched the sweet spot under her knickers.

She fondly recalled the excitement of his fingers and moved her own down her legs, lifting the sleeping shift she had worn to bed. An image of Oscar Delaroux filled her mind, and she wondered what a man of his experience might do to a woman like her. She remembered the smile on his lips when she'd brought him the envelope, and she imagined him opening her up like he had the package, and it made her moan with abandon.

A few minutes later, she sat there satiated. *At least I got some money from him.*

She chuckled to herself. Sister Adrienne had been convincing people to give her funds for as long as she could remember.

It was through her immaculate accounting that she had moved up the ranks to become a subprioress and then been placed as the leader at the Sisters of Children and Charity Orphanage. There, she kept the books in order, as well as the other sisters. She was strict, especially with the most devout of followers, as she herself thought it was all a bunch of poppycock. Mostly though, she was tough, even brutal, on those damn fellow nuns because she didn't want any other sisters meddling into her decisions. For Sister Adrienne had a plan, and it involved skimming funds from the home and saving them up for a dream of her own.

That was why she had accepted George Weaver's offer. Not out of benevolence, or a deep-seated belief in Christian generosity. Her kindness was transactional. For all of the vice that boiled beneath her outer layers, Sister Adrienne was not particularly progressive when it came to others. Sure, following the teachings of Christ was her vocation, and true, these were something that the others around her believed deeply in. Yet for Sister Adrienne, the tenets of God were almost exclusively to be adhered to by those around her. Why should those who chose this life be anything less than torturously pious? She had no alignment with them, beyond small snippets of course, like no sodomites or perversions. That was the extent of her support for godliness. Why did she have to embrace all of Catholicism just because she wore the black cloth?

After her period of discernment, she'd been invited to choose a new name. While the bishop had approved her selection on the assumption that it had been chosen in honor of Saint Adrian of Nicomedia, the patron saint of peacekeeping missions, in truth, it was an homage to the hard-drinking harlot named Adrienne who lived back home in the flat next door. So what if, like that trollop, this sister also dreamed day and night of mounting men? That didn't mean that she was a deviant, just deprived.

Sister Adrienne was more open to the old-world superstitions that her lusty neighbor had spoken about between shags: Celtic tales of Balor and Morrigan. They seemed captivating compared to the rites like sacraments and mass that her strict father clung to. But every belief system had dark forces that inhabited the bodies of the weak and depraved, and that was how Sister Adrienne had seen the Weaver child from the moment Mr. Weaver explained the toddler to her fifteen or some-odd years earlier. Maybe it had been longer? She'd lost track. Either way, the father's initial description had made the bile in her stomach rise to her throat, and it never settled back down. *No wonder he wants to foist it on me*, she thought at the time. But the money was hard to say no to, so she shook hands with the devil's father and took Lucifer in.

There was more than one thing about the child that Sister Adrienne hated. There was the obvious failing that had caused its own parents to abandon it. But also when placed in her arms, the toddler had been yet another person forced by their father into the halls of Catholic doctrine without free choice. In that, Phreddie came to represent everything Sister Adrienne loathed about what her own father had done to her, which made her despise herself and this god-awful life that had been foisted upon her. So she punished Phreddie for not just the child's sins, but her own as well.

It had taken her nearly two decades, between the Weavers' payments and peeling a little from the orphanage's books here and there and hiding it away, to be close to ready. When Oscar Delaroux offered to lubricate her hand in exchange for some information that she cared not a shit what he did with, she had met her full goal ahead of schedule. She'd left New York with more than enough to run off and leave the religious life behind, and she was still just shy of forty years old. Plenty of time to feast and fraternize.

She had at last been prepared to disappear from every drop of Catholicism she had ever feigned belief in when Mrs. Weaver pounded on the door to the orphanage a few days ago. Sure, Sister Adrienne could live quite comfortably with what she had already saved, but damn if she couldn't really make up for lost time with all of that Weaver money at her fingertips.

I just need to find that nasty thing that I had to endure for all those years. Then I can shed this habit and just be Eleanora again, not this fucking Sister Adrienne bitch whose name I loathe.

She planned at first to take her bags of gold and head for Italy, as all the drawings and tales she had heard over the years made it seem like paradise. Then she realized she did not want to live in a place where anything papal or sanctified would remind her of her wasted youth. Instead, she was considering something remote, like China or Japan, places she had only heard tantalizing tales about. *I wonder what it would be like to lie with a Chinaman?* she thought.

Then again, with the size of the Weaver fortune, there was no reason why she couldn't choose to dance the nights away in Paris under a new name. Perhaps she would take a new ginger-headed lover, or maybe even many lovers, ones that looked like that Oscar Delaroux with those moist lips that were perfect for sucking on.

Yes, she could feel herself flushing anew at the thought. She would lift her skirt high over the heads of men like Oscar, and never again would she be bitter over the years that she had been forced to forfeit her life to the church, all because of a teenage finger fuck.

Sister Adrienne crawled back into the bed and smiled.

•

A series of yips and whines startled Phreddie awake. The silhouette of a man framed in moonlight in the doorway caused her to shoot upright on the bedding, and her throat seized up in fear.

"It's just coyotes," Hodges said from the door.

Phreddie fell back down onto the grass.

"They have no interest in us, as they're content supping on cottontails." He entered and sat down on his own pile. "But that didn't stop them from quenching their curiosity, which was wet with the smell of horse droppings on the wind."

"Oh." Phreddie sighed with relief. "What time is it?" Her eyes now adjusted, she could almost make out Hodges's facial features with the bright silver orb casting its light into the shelter.

"Not long till sunrise, but with the moon as full as it is tonight, it may as well be high noon." Hodges lay down fully on his straw.

"I don't mean to sound ungrateful," Phreddie said through a yawn, "but what is our plan?" Stretching her feet downward, she lifted her arms into the air. She groaned, then pulled her body back to normal.

"What do you mean?" Hodges grunted.

"I mean, I don't suppose we are going to sit in this for days on end. There's no food, and it's hardly protected."

"No," Hodges replied. "You are right there. Yesterday I was just thinking about getting ahead of them, but I realized during the night that we need to think some things through."

They stayed there in silence for a minute.

Hodges sat up. "Come sunup, we will double back to the cabin Alice and I shared. No one has lived there since back then, and it will provide better protection than this."

"Is there food there?" Phreddie sat straight up as well, and her stomach growled.

"Might be some preserved things in the larder beneath the house—if nothing else got to them in these years."

She salivated at the thought of pickled vegetables or even jarred jams.

"If not, there's catfish and bass in the creek that will be easy pickings for you."

"Sounds like heaven," she said aloud as her eyes rolled up at the thought of frying filets.

"I'll drop you off, then double back myself toward Newton."

His words broke through her hunger pangs. "Wait," she said. "What? You're not going to stay at this cabin with me?"

"Nah," he replied bluntly. "It's time I have the final showdown with Delaroux."

Phreddie shook her head from side to side. "Absolutely not. Oscar is after *me*, and you are only involved on my account, so—"

"You're too mild natured and feminine to handle what's coming. No, this is something a man needs to tend to, and I refuse to let a woman who has come under the protection of my house face something like this," he informed her sternly.

"Mild natured?" Her voice began to rise. "And under your protection? It's not like I asked Oscar to come to Kansas. And by the way, we are not married or something that you can refuse me anything."

"Of all the ungrateful things to say . . . " He started to argue back, and they spat at each other, neither one hearing a word that the other person said until a shrill *peent* from a nighthawk diving for a late-night snack of insects broke the air and the horse snorted outside.

The two stopped their arguing, and Phreddie folded her hands into her lap and hung her head. After a few minutes, she looked at Hodges.

"I really appreciate how you opened up to me last night, about Alice and Lily," she said, gingerly adding, "but why did you never tell anyone about Lily at least?"

Hodges ignored the question and stood up. "You may as well look at the world known as the Kansas Territory under the light of the moon, as it's even more spectacular than it is in the daytime." He extended his hand.

Phreddie grabbed hold of it, and he yanked her to her feet. She followed him out the door and into a world draped in silver that glimmered off the watering hole. Past their small set of trees, she could see stars beyond measure in the sky, whose brethren faded into the light as they moved closer to the enormous orb that hung suspended high above the world.

"My god." She gasped at the sight. In the distance, the undulating hills of daytime green were now covered in swaying shades of dark blue and purple.

"It's beautiful, isn't it?" he asked as he came closer to her.

"No wonder you're enamored with this land," she stated in awe, and they stood silently for a few minutes.

At last Phreddie turned back to Hodges. "I just still can't reconcile the two people," she began. "There's the bitter, crusty man who everyone thinks is a wife killer, and then there's this one before me."

She watched him shuffle his feet for a minute, then he said, "To be frank, the reaper plagued me so closely for a period of time that I can hardly blame anyone for their suspicions that I am Pale Death himself." He shrugged.

"Hmm," she said. *Perhaps he has a point.*

"Enough about me, though," Hodges countered as the two of them walked back to the fallen tree log that they'd sat on at sunset the night before. "What's *your* story?"

Phreddie was glad that though it was bright out, Hodges still could not see the way her hands began to shake at his question. She tucked them under her legs and answered simply, "It's complicated."

Why did he have to ask me that? But then fair is fair, and don't I owe this man at least some version of the truth for all that he has done for me?

Hodges guffawed. "I figured that. Why else would a man come halfway across the country for you?"

She smiled. "You're a lot nicer than I expected when we first met." She was laughing as well now.

They looked each other in the eyes for a second, and then Hodges looked away. "Now, tell me about what happened with Oscar Delaroux."

"Well, nothing with him exactly," she said softly.

Hodges lifted his hands in confusion. "That man is on you like a feather on an arrow. He's fit to be tied about something."

She paused, then let out a sigh. "It was his brother, Remy."

Hodges shrugged. "Why wouldn't his brother be out here looking for you if he was so bothered by your actions?"

Phreddie's body stiffened. "Um . . . well . . ." she stuttered.

What do I do? she thought to herself in panic.

Her mind hadn't even begun to answer the question, but somehow she found that her mouth was already speaking. "Our courtship was unexpected." She looked off toward the reflection in the water. "Most of all to me. It was the kind of thing they write dime novel romances about."

She shifted her bottom on the hard wood and continued, "Remy Delaroux, like his brother, was breathtaking, but in a different kind of way."

Phreddie recalled the man of her dreams and his perfect face. Those deep eyes framed by the lushest of lashes that had melted her heart from the first moment she stared into them at Mrs. Guidry's.

She shared with Hodges how she had been a laundress, having only recently left the orphanage, and how Remy had swept her off her feet with roses and romance. Phreddie recounted the ways that he'd wooed and adored her until she had found herself swept away by his love.

"Only not all stories have happy endings." She paused. "Mine didn't."

How much more do I want to share? she wondered to herself.

"It's okay," Hodges said softly, "You can trust me. I think I've proven that much."

"I wanted to break it off," she told him, shouting from the nerves. "In fact, I planned to."

His face wrinkled. "Why though?"

"Sometimes the things you love are better left unspoiled by the truth. I had experienced such little joy that I wanted to remember it in its perfection, as I knew that things could never get any better than they already were."

Phreddie turned her head away from Hodges again and continued. "I prepared myself that this one night would be the last. I would tell him the truth, and that would end it. Oh, I knew it would end it," she cried.

"It's okay, you are safe here," Hodges consoled her. "You tried to end it?"

"Only Remy begged me to go to this party his brother was having. I couldn't tell him then, not before the party. He was too excited, and I didn't want to ruin his night, especially knowing that he would then be off to the party brokenhearted. I . . . I had seen the brother do a terrible thing to an immigrant man on the street, and I didn't want him to do the same, or worse, to me!" She sat in silence.

"Go on," Hodges encouraged her.

"Remy had bought me a dress in pink silk trimmed with tiny pink flowers along the bust and hemlines. Oh it was magnificent, and I had never worn something so beautiful before. So I told myself it was fine to play along just for this one more night. Then, after that, I would tell him it was over.

"So, I pinned my hair up like I had seen in a French drawing of a woman of high Paris fashion from a postcard in Sister Adrienne's room once when I was made to clean the baseboards. When I arrived at the address Remy had provided, I felt like I had entered another world. The house was huge, and it had candles in every window, and they felt welcoming and mesmerizing at the same time.

"Inside, it was filled with the most stunning of people—men and women dressed so that Mrs. Guidry herself looked to be a common piece of street trash. The dresses, their hair filled with feathers and ribbons. Oh, and the jewelry that sparkled almost as bright as this moonlight." She pointed up at the sky.

Lowering her hands, Phreddie continued, "A quartet of strings began to play, and Remy came out of the sea of flesh and taffeta with glasses of champagne. So I drank, and laughed, and let him twirl me around many times on the dance floor, until suddenly . . . suddenly the strings stopped playing." A tear formed in the corner of Phreddie's eye.

"Everyone in the room moved toward the sides, and I found myself alone in the center with Remy down on his knee and Oscar just behind him, beaming."

Her shoulders began to shake, and a sob came out of her throat as she relived that moment for perhaps the first time.

"'Yes,' my mouth answered, but inside I knew that it could never be," she cried into the ebbing night, as far off in the east, the skies began to lighten.

"But why?" Hodges asked with some urgency.

Phreddie turned back to face him, their knees touching. "Because I was not meant to be loved," she said softly through tears. She could feel the wetness against her cheeks as she looked up at this man who had selflessly saved her.

"I don't know that I've ever met anyone more desirable or deserving of love in all my life than you at this moment." Hodges gently leaned in to kiss her.

Their lips touched, and Phreddie felt that same excitement and fear that she had when Remy kissed her the first time, and it terrified her. She pulled away quickly.

"No," she began to cry. "I cannot do this again. No!"

"Why not?" He looked confused.

"I—I'm modest," she stammered.

He smiled. "I can appreciate that, but it was just a peck."

"We can never do that again," she insisted.

Hodges face crumpled up in confusion. "I didn't think the kiss was *that* bad," he said as he stood up.

Phreddie also stood and began to pace frantically in front of the log. "This cannot happen. I thank you again for all that you have done, but I've got to get out of here!" She threw her arms in the air and wept openly.

"Okay, it's okay. Calm down," Hodges said sternly. "No one is going to touch you again—believe me," he whispered bitterly as he turned and marched away.

She stood there shaking while he untied the horse from the side of the shelter.

"It's time to go now anyway," he informed her coldly.

Phreddie shook her head. "This is pointless. He's going to keep chasing me. Oscar is going to find me, and I feel like . . . like I'm suffocating!" She pulled at her neck.

All of this talk of Remy, the reliving of their romance, the realization of what she had done, and what had transpired since—it all came crashing in. Hodges's kiss and that same look Remy had given to her when he helped her pick the linen up off Mrs. Guidry's floor. Though she was in a space of endless openness, Phreddie felt as if the world were closing in on her and as if the breath in her lungs was being pushed out, with no new air entering.

She was near to hysteria when a loud crack shocked her back to her senses. A bullet ricocheted off a slender branch that stuck out from the back of the fallen tree.

"Shit," Hodges yelled, mounting the horse in a flash.

Phreddie bent down and placed her hands over the top of her skull to protect herself from more gunfire.

Approaching from the south was a small group on horseback. She could just make out Oscar's blond hair blowing in the wind that was created from the quick pace of the running hooves. Next to him were Luke and Landy, alongside what looked to be someone darker in complexion wearing buckskin.

"Get on," Hodges yelled at her. She turned her head and found he had closed the distance between them and was already pulling her up onto the back of the horse.

"Hold on to the back of me like your life depends on it," he shouted, and she did just that.

Phreddie sunk her fingers into Hodges's sides and pressed her arms up closely to his body and prayed. *If you are there, please don't let me die by the hands of Oscar Delaroux. Please . . .*

The horse galloped like the steam engine she had ridden into Newton. Out they bolted from the honey locusts and into the mixing of long and short grasses. Up and down over rolling hills and flatlands they rode. Once, she turned her head and saw that the four men were closer than she had hoped. When she turned forward again, she could see off in the distance a trail of rocky crags and lines of trees that ran along a winding river.

Thunder came from all sides as both the click-clack of the horses and gunfire pierced the morning air.

They were near to the top of the river basin when Phreddie's grip began to loosen. "Ah," she yelled into Hodges's left ear, and he slowed the horse down as they reached some trees just in time to blunt the fall. Phreddie slid off and landed on the ground.

"Quick," Hodges shouted at her. "Get back on." He extended his hand, but she was not quick enough for the firing of a rifle that cracked and hit nearby with a loud whack.

The horse whinnied and threw its front legs into the air, and Hodges came right off and landed near to Phreddie. Then he shoved her and rolled his body out of the way just in time for the horse to land dead on the ground next to him with a thud.

The men were closing in on them.

"Run!" Hodges barked as he shot up and grabbed his gun from alongside the horse's lifeless body.

Phreddie leapt to her feet, and the pair of them headed full force for the river basin.

As she bolted, Phreddie's ankle twisted, and she fell in a lump. She stood up and half limped, half ran behind Hodges as he dashed behind a tree, but it was too late for her. The lanky man was already upon her, and he grabbed her violently and tore at her dress.

"I want her alive," Oscar yelled out from several paces back, but Landy did not seem to hear. Her neck and the exposed weight of her ample bosom made his eyes bulge, and he licked his lips as if she were a Sunday roast. Slowly he moved his hands up and around her neck where he began to choke her.

Phreddie could feel the life being crushed out of her. Her eyes landed on the now swollen member that protruded from his trousers. He squeezed harder upon her glance. Then Landy's tongue wagged as if he were a dog with a bone.

"Uh," he moaned unexpectedly, and his eyes lit up at the surprising sound that came out of his mouth. Excitement spread across his face as well as the front of his britches. He heaved, and his tongue, which hung outside his mouth, went still. Then he slumped over and fell at her feet.

Phreddie turned to see the remnants of smoke escaping from the barrel of Oscar's gun several feet away. "I said I wanted her alive, *espèce de fou pervers*," Oscar said to his man's body from horseback.

"Over here," Hodges motioned wildly.

Crying out in pain, Phreddie stood up, gritted her teeth, and forced her body to move toward Hodges. She was almost to him when an Indian popped up behind Hodges and held a gun to the back of his head.

"Dammit," she could hear him say when she stopped running.

The man pushed Hodges out into the open, and within seconds, he was behind Luke's and Oscar's horses. With Phreddie alone and cornered, Oscar slid off his horse and approached her.

"Well look what we have here," he said coolly. "It appears that justice has finally caught up with you, Phreddie Weaver-Smith-Delaroux." Oscar's eyes then went to Landy. "Though at more expense to me, it seems."

Phreddie slowly backed away from Oscar. Luke climbed down from his horse, sighing as he passed Landy's body.

Oscar nodded. "I want this *chienne* tied up."

Luke came toward her with something of a sad grimace on his face.

"Presbyterian minister, huh?" Phreddie said to him under her breath.

Luke was holding a rope in his hands. "You see what happens when you don't follow the boss's orders?" he muttered to Phreddie, still looking back at Landy.

Phreddie sighed and knew that fate had found her. There was nothing left in her. She was as defeated now as she had been for most of her life at the orphanage. There was no escape, no place to run. There never had been. She would end like she'd begun—alone. The only thing in front of her now was whatever darkness Oscar decided.

She was about to turn her body away from the men so that Luke could tie her hands behind her back when she saw Hodges hook his leg around the back of the Indian man. In a flash, the native was on the ground.

Before Oscar could turn to look or to even draw his weapon, Hodges flew past him and Luke. As he rushed by, he grabbed hold of Phreddie's arm.

"No!" Oscar yelled.

But Hodges pulled her with such great force and speed forward several feet until there was no ground left to run across. They had reached the end of an outcrop, high above the Arkansas River, and there was nothing but air between the ledge and the water below.

Before she had time to think, they were over the ridge and falling.

"Berdache!" Oscar's voice echoed off the canyon rocks, but it was too late, as it was soon drowned out by her own.

She screamed as her arms and legs flew madly in the air, until several seconds and a hundred feet later, she crashed into the water, which hit her extended toes hard. Down, down, down, she sank as river swallowed her whole.

When she stopped descending, she hung there suspended and still in the depths and wondered if this was not the peace that she had always longed for. It was as if the water was hugging her like a lost mother and she was no longer the fractured and abandoned being she had been on the surface.

Here, she was wanted. She was safe. She was secure.

•

How did it happen? Oscar raged on the inside, but on the outside he cursed Taakwic, calling him names like "redskin" and "savage."

"I hired you to find the *les déviants*, not to lose them!" he screamed at the hired tracker.

Taakwic did not respond, which infuriated him more.

"You are no longer needed, *crétin*," he barked, and he threw some coins to the ground and ordered Taakwic to collect them on his knees and then depart. "We will find our own way back to town. Surely there has to be a white man who can better serve us than you."

Taakwic stood there and stared at him.

"These primitives are easily fooled," Oscar stated plainly to Luke, who nodded. Oscar walked back and stood over Landy's body. "*C'était stupide*," he said to the dead man.

Luke came up alongside him with hunched shoulders. "He worked hard for you," he said quietly.

"Maybe, but he was *un homme dépravé*." Oscar chuckled as he nudged the dead man's body with his still shined boot. "At least the *les putes* at Melancon Manor will be happy."

"Hmm," Luke murmured.

Oscar looked at his last standing man. "Well, his choking *did* cost me plenty of gold bullion."

"I suppose." Luke shrugged. "He may have been strange, but he was loyal."

"He's dead now," Oscar clipped. "So get back on your horse."

Luke did as instructed, even if Oscar did note the sideways glance the man gave him. The two of them rode fast out of the winding river basin, leaving behind the staring Taakwic.

•

After a few seconds submerged in the darkness, Phreddie opened her eyes and kicked. Up she went, until she at last broke through to the surface.

The river was slow moving, but off in the distance she could see that it sloped over an edge. She let it carry her for a moment while she looked up at the lone Indian man far above, staring out over the rocks and distance.

Hodges laughed as he swam up next to her. "I thought you were dead."

"Still here," she replied as she broke her gaze with the native. The distant sound of a roar began to grow louder in her ears.

"Best get to the shore," Hodges instructed. "By the pace of this current and that sound, I reckon this river spills out onto a waterfall not too far off."

More swiftly now, they rode along in the current, paddling ever more strongly at an angle toward the opposite shore. This went on for a minute or two, until at last they entered a deep pool of gently swirling water hemmed in from the current by some large boulders. At last Phreddie could feel small river rocks beneath her feet.

There along the shore, Hodges walked up close to her, his hair dripping down his square jaw and onto his broad shoulders, which had started to emerge from the water.

As he got closer, he looked into her eyes. "God, you are beautiful," he said, then he reached his hands out and cupped her head in them and pulled her in.

She didn't have time to react as his lips were on hers, his tongue plunging between them and into her mouth. For a second, not even the roaring sound of the waterfall cascading nearby could break her from the moment.

When he finished, he pulled back and released her head from his grasp and smiled. They looked at each other. She stood there happy and in silence, her arms submerged in the water as they brushed up against her sides.

Suddenly, a look of panic spread across Phreddie's face. "Oh my god!" she yelled out.

Hodges's eyes widened. "What is it?" He looked around, but there was no one else there. Turning back to her, he grinned. "Surely after all of this morning's excitement, a kiss wasn't too presumptuous."

Frantically, she pressed her hands all over her body under the water, but all she could feel was her undergarments. "It's my dress," she cried, "My dress is gone!"

Hodges smiled at her. "It's alright. It's just a dress, and maybe after that kiss, we won't need our clothes that badly," he joked.

"You don't understand," she exclaimed as she shook her head. "I can't—" Then she looked at Hodges closely. "You will have to give me your clothes."

"My clothes?" he gasped. "But you have knickers on. I can see that from here. Those will dry out quickly and will be protection enough until we get to the cabin. I'm sure there are plenty of Alice's rags and threads there still."

"Now!" she shouted.

Hodges took a step back.

"Oh, please don't ask me to explain," she implored him. "Just get out and pass them to me, even if you just give me your trousers."

"Wow," he said, stepping closer to the shore, "you weren't joking when you said you were modest."

As he walked up onto dry land, he lifted his shirt over his head, and Phreddie nervously eyed his ripped torso, hardened from manual labor and lined with fur along his chest. Her eyes started to follow the trail down his stomach and toward what lay hidden beneath as he pulled his shoes off one at a time.

"By the way," he called out, and his tone conveyed some annoyance at the fact that he needed to undress for her, "what in the heck was that word that Delaroux called you back there?"

He started to unbutton his trousers.

"Was it a bear—bearda— "

His mouth was moving, but Phreddie heard nothing as her lips parted with longing. She held her breath as he bent over and began to lower his trousers slowly. "Beardash—"

Just before his pants were over his hips, he suddenly froze. She looked up and saw an arrow pressed against Hodges's neck. An uncontrollable scream came from her throat as all of the nightmarish tales she had heard rushed into her mind.

At Hodges's back stood a Native American with his bow drawn. Behind him were four other males. One who was slightly older than the rest, his hair somehow shaped like one of the buffalo horns from the mounted head in Mr. Guidry's library, nodded firmly to two of the men by his side.

Phreddie trembled. *He must be their chief.*

"*Cápaat*," he commanded, and two of the three closest dropped their bows onto the ground beside him and rushed into the water.

Phreddie turned to swim away, but it was too late. She thrashed as they grabbed hold of her arms and began to drag her out.

"Stop," she cried out, but as much as she protested, she was no match for their muscled forms.

As they pulled her forward, the water line fell beneath her knees. The chief's eyes widened, and he gasped loudly and extended his arm in the air directly toward her. "Berdache!" he yelled out in amazement.

The man behind Hodges lowered his bow. The two men at Phreddie's side looked down as they dropped her arms. Everyone took a step back, their mouths wide open. "Oohs" and "aahs" escaped their lips.

Phreddie was frozen in terror as her eyes moved to Hodges, who was looking at the men with puzzlement on his face. "What in the hell?" he sputtered.

His head turned back to Phreddie, and their eyes met. He shrugged his shoulders. His face was full of joyous wonder that the natives were no longer threatening them, but then she saw him look downward. His smile broke, and his eyes became as large as last night's moon.

"Fuck . . . me." He gasped each word slowly.

Phreddie looked down at her body. Her cotton chemise was soaked and pressed against her skin. It revealed her full and voluptuous breasts, her nipples erect from the cold dampness.

Her eyes fell further, down past her belly and below, where a small, flaccid penis-like appendage appeared to press against the wet cloth just above her fully formed, exposed vulva.

My secret is revealed, she thought with immense sadness. *He will never look at me the way same again.*

She heard Hodges retch loudly and saw him use the back of his hand to wipe at the lips that had kissed her only moments ago. "I do not know this creature," he suddenly spit out in anger, addressing the men. Then he paced back and forth. "Do none of you know English?" he threw his hands in the air.

"I speak white man's language," the chief answered.

Hodges pointed at Phreddie. "I am told she's . . . he's . . . they're wanted . . . for murdering . . . her . . . husband," he hyperventilated. "She's running from a group of men right now, in fact." He paced some more. "I—I can bring you to them, as I am certain that they are close by." He retched again.

The chief stood silent and looked on.

"Oh, God," Hodges cried out.

The chief put his hand up to silence Hodges.

"I'm sorry that your eyes have seen this," Hodges blurted out as he ignored the chief. "I am sorry *my* eyes have seen this— "

The chief turned to Phreddie. "Apu. Apu," he said. "It is me, Dark Tree, and we chahiksichahiks . . . Pawnee . . . who say sorry."

Then Dark Tree said something to his men, and the two nearest to Phreddie gently escorted her ashore with smiles. Two others pulled animal skins from their backs and came forward reverently. They began to wrap Phreddie in them so that her genitalia was no longer exposed.

Phreddie was confused. *Aren't they going to scalp me?*

Instead, the men all nodded and backed away with grins.

"You come us," Dark Tree said plainly, pointing west.

The Pawnee men started to walk off, and they turned and motioned for Phreddie and Hodges to follow. Phreddie looked over at Hodges, who stared back at her in disgust, then she dropped her head.

A grunt emerged from Hodges's throat, followed by the sound of movement from his feet in the direction of the natives.

Phreddie sighed sadly and followed behind.

Chahiksichahiks

The sun was high in the sky when Oscar rode back into Newton with Luke at his side. Leading their horses to Miller's Saloon, they tied them to a post, and Oscar hopped down and looked around at all the hoopla in the town center.

The final touches were being made on the stage, with bunting in red, white, and blue being tacked to the edges. As Oscar stepped closer, a flood of people came from all directions with looks of hope on their faces. Among them were Ms. Ortiz, flanked by some woman and a nun who looked oddly familiar.

"Who's he?" A raven-haired woman asked over the crowd while Oscar stepped up onto the platform.

"He's the one hunting for your child," Ms. Ortiz said plainly.

"Then you've seen her?" Grace called out to Oscar. "You've seen my daughter, Nadine—I mean Phreddie?"

Oscar looked down as the crowd quieted.

"Who are you?" Oscar asked.

"My name is Grace Weaver," she replied, "the mother of the woman you seek to harm."

Amusement and consternation pulled at the skin around Oscar's eyes. "Can this be *la mère* who gave birth to Satan?" He looked down upon her and sneered.

"She's no devil," Grace insisted to both him and the growling crowd.

"I've got five men and a brother dead who say otherwise," he said in a patronizing tone. He squinted as he finally recognized the woman standing next to Phreddie's mother.

"You followed me?" he asked with great confusion. *Why, that minx*, he thought as he shook his head.

"You two know each other?" Grace Weaver asked with surprise.

"That's how I knew of Newton," Sister Adrienne sniped to Phreddie's mother.

"What about Hodges?" Ms. Ortiz interrupted with gleeful anticipation. "Did you kill him?"

Oscar scowled at her and lifted both his head and his voice to the crowd. "That is why I am here, good people of Newton," he called out.

The crowd silenced.

"Charlie Hodges and his disgusting *hémaphrodite* remain free."

People began to shake their heads and murmur to each other.

"Right now, evil roams these plains, and we, as good people, have a choice to make." Oscar paused and waited for complete silence. "We can either stand here, preparing ourselves for a day of empty celebrations, or we can take hold of our lives and stand up to say no more. No more to murderers in Newton!"

"No more!" a man to Oscar's right shouted back.

"No more to lawlessness," he continued.

"No more!" There were several more shouts this time.

Oscar looked down on the puckered, sad face of the woman who purported to have given birth to his brother's killer.

"No more to gross deviance and perversion."

"No more!" Most of the town was shouting now.

Oscar pointed to a father, mother, and their young child, who were standing in front of him watching. "We have to clean this town up for our children!" he yelled, pumping his fist in the air.

The father put his arms around his family.

"While there may be danger, I need a strong group of men to go home, grab their weapons, and meet me back here in an hour. We will go out and take back this town for the children of Newton once and for all. Only then will we have true independence!" he finished loudly, and was met with thunderous applause and shouts of commitment from many men.

Satisfied with his performance, Oscar smiled broadly and nodded to the crowd. Then he climbed down from the stage and headed for Miller's, where the three women rushed to catch up with him. As he stepped up and began to push the swinging doors open, he was met with a shout from behind.

"And what exactly do you plan to do to my child?" Grace Weaver cried out.

Oscar turned and let the door hit his backside. "Exactly what she did to my brother—humiliate her," he spat, then turned and pushed the doors again and walked through.

A few feet later, he was sitting on a stool. "Pour me a drink," he ordered Miller, who plopped down a glass and pulled out a bottle.

"I heard your little speech," Miller said while he poured.

"Good," Oscar grunted, then swallowed the warm liquid.

"I'd reconsider going after that Hodges," Miller said as Oscar tapped his glass for another round.

"I didn't ask," Oscar retorted.

"That Hodges is a mean motherfucker," the bartender continued anyway. "Your five men and his two dead wives can attest to the fact that no one here in Newton is strong enough to rein him in."

Oscar stared at him, again lifting his glass and swallowing. "Lucky for you all," he said as he stood up and plopped a couple of coins down onto the bar top, "I'm not from Newton."

Then he turned and marched over to Misty, who today had a plume of feathers in her hair. He hooked his arm in hers. "I have one hour with nothing to do, *jolie fille*," he said. "How about a little fun?"

She giggled and led him up the rickety stairs that overlooked the entire bar.

"I'm sure you are no Mahogany Montigny," he told Misty as she stopped and pushed a bedroom door open.

"Who?" she cooed.

Oscar laughed. "Hmm . . . maybe you can convince me that not all of the best girls live on Delphine Street." He narrowed his eyes seductively.

The waitress-turned-showgirl-turned-pleasurer cooed again and pushed him inside toward the bed. He kicked the door shut loudly with his boot.

•

They had been walking for several hours. During this time, Hodges had stewed on the sight of Phreddie's body back at the river. Hell, it was burned into his eyeballs, like when you looked up at the sun but still saw it after you turned away.

How is it possible? he asked himself. *How can she be so much a woman? Yet I know what my eyes saw, and that part was as if it was my own.* If he could have washed his pupils and his lips with lye, he would have done so on the spot.

Is this witchcraft? he wondered.

At last, he sped his steps to catch up with Dark Tree. "Where are you taking me?" he asked brusquely.

"You share my *taruuc*, my fire," Dark Tree said firmly.

"Then you will kill us?" Hodges pressed.

"You share my pipe, too," Dark Tree said with a smile.

"Huh?" Hodges lifted his hands in the air.

Dark Tree only looked at him with more kindness.

"Why?" Hodges pushed him. "Why would you have us share your fire?"

Dark Tree stopped walking, which meant that the others did as well. He looked up to the sky and pointed. "For the *Páh*, we dance," the chief replied. Then he looked into Hodges eyes and said firmly, "*Berdache* is sacred." He began to walk again.

Hodges stood there a second, then rushed forward again to walk alongside the chief. "What *exactly* does 'berdache' mean?"

Dark Tree stopped yet again and looked confused. "This white-man word, berdache," he said. "You should know. Pawnee say different word, *chúsaat*, but this word not for white man's mouth."

"Well, we have another word in our white tongue too—evil," Hodges barked back.

Dark Tree shook his head and moved forward again.

They all walked on in silence.

Maybe they are going to sell us instead, or give us away as a peace offering to some of those Kiowa-Apaches they say are constantly raiding Pawnee villages out here.

After another thirty minutes or so, they emerged over a hill to find a small village against a backdrop of trees that ran along a high embankment of the same river Hodges and Phreddie had emerged from hours ago. It consisted of a dozen or so earthen lodges covered in dirt and thatch. Scantily clad children played on top of these lodges, and now they jumped down and ran to greet the chief and his men.

People of all ages began to emerge from their shelters, each calling out to others in their native tongue. Old and young walked briskly, alone or with the help of others, toward Dark Tree, all smiling and chattering to each other and to their returned kinsmen.

The men that traveled with Dark Tree whispered to some people, who in turn looked at Phreddie and gasped. They then turned to others, and the whispers and their wide eyes spread throughout the small community.

"*Chúsaat,*" Hodges heard repeated over and over as fingers pointed and people nodded at Phreddie and smiled brightly.

Finally, Dark Tree addressed his tribe. "*Hiirisu,*" he exclaimed. "At night, we dance!"

The crowd cheered, and one of the native men slapped Hodges on the shoulder and smiled at him with gleaming teeth. Then men, women, and children rushed forward gently and patted Phreddie all over her body. They spoke to her in their language, though Phreddie just stood there with a look of surprise on her face and nodded.

"*Nowa, nowa,*" they said, and Hodges understood that for some strange reason, Phreddie's presence had made them welcome in a place where he assumed the tops of their heads would otherwise already have been removed.

Dark Tree motioned for Hodges and Phreddie to follow him, and this was also seen as a command to his people, who departed in different directions toward their lodgings and duties. Hodges could feel Phreddie's eyes on the back of his neck as he entered one of the lodges behind the chief. Inside, his eyes adjusted to find a large, dim structure with numerous erect wooden poles holding the roof up. Large buffalo hides separated sections as if they were rooms, and there was thatch along the walls.

Dark Tree led them into a subsection of the structure where a small fire burned brightly beside a bed made of branches and dried grass. "I return with more clothes," he announced.

"You cannot leave me with—" Hodges started to protest, but the man was already gone. He watched cautiously while Phreddie leaned down, then sat on the bedding.

"Damn," Hodges said aloud.

"We really should talk," she said softly.

"I have nothing to say to you," he barked. He seated himself on the ground by the fire and fumed.

•

A group of eight men rode out with Oscar from Newton. Oscar was happy with the success of his recruitment, as he and Luke could not capture both

Hodges and Phreddie alone. However, there was one problem with his newly formed posse—or rather, three.

Pourquoi diable . . . Why the hell would they want to come with us? he asked himself bitterly.

Alongside the group of men, replete with shotguns, rifles, and revolvers, rode Ms. Ortiz, Phreddie's mother, and the nun whom Oscar had paid handsomely to divulge her ward's secrets.

Didn't I give the church more than enough silver for the information? Yes, it was the sister's presence that was perhaps the most confusing of all. Sister Adrienne's lustful glances made Oscar uneasy as while he was used to having an effect on women, a woman of the cloth undressing him with her eyes was both unexpected and unnerving.

The way she had nearly salivated at the sum she had squeezed out of him had not concerned him too much, though. After all, all churches wanted money, like everyone else. *But did she come all this way looking for more gold from me, or perhaps something else?* he wondered as she sent a coquettish glance in his direction. He chuckled. *Surely not.*

"Monsieur Delaroux," Ms. Ortiz grated in his ear from the other side. "I told you that man would be no easy pickings for you, didn't I?" There was a smugness in her tone.

Damn, I'm going to bed this frigid woman after all of this. Oscar sneered, then kicked his heels into his horse's sides and ran up ahead.

When he reached the crest of a large hill, he stopped and looked back at his group. The sun was beginning to set, and while he still planned to ride some hours further, with three women now in his care, he would do the chivalrous thing and stop to make a fire . . . eventually.

"Why did *ces maudites femmes* have to come along?" he muttered to himself again.

He turned and rode off toward the part of the Arkansas River where he had last seen Phreddie and Hodges before they'd jumped into the abyss below. There on the ledge, he stood for a few minutes and looked down.

Grace Weaver came up beside him and gasped. "Oh my."

Oscar sucked in his teeth. "The fall didn't kill them," he said impatiently, "but I will."

Turning on his heels, he went back to the group and led them on horseback down the ravine. When they reached flat land about a mile or so past the thundering waterfall, the river split. Here, two streams flowed gently, separated by a small island covered in fruit trees.

"We will cross here," Oscar informed the group. He was as anxious to find his prey as he was to get away from Sister Adrienne, who was riding close behind him and batting her eyes.

Either I will swim across and leave this woman in the dust or I'll be swept away, but her constant looks are unnerving me, he thought as he charged his horse into the water. Within seconds, he was on dry land, and he waited as the others swam their horses across one at a time onto the little island halfway between one shore and the other.

Fifteen minutes later, everyone had come to the other side, and Oscar led the group back upstream in hopes of finding where Phreddie and Hodges had exited the river once they'd swum ashore.

"Over here," said one of the townsfolk. "Looks to be . . . four, five, six . . . I count seven sets of prints that walked off in this direction." The man pointed north.

Oscar rubbed his chin. "Seven people?"

"Reckon they were taken by Injuns," the same man answered.

Grace Weaver gulped. "Indians!"

Luke pulled his horse up alongside Oscar. "Sounds like we might not be needed."

"I don't care if *Jésus Christ* himself walked off with them," Oscar growled. "I will not be denied justice at my own hands."

"But we are not prepared to take on an entire Indian tribe," Luke protested.

"These kind are on foot, so I'm guessing Pawnee," the townsman said.

"What does that mean?" Oscar asked him.

"Means they ain't Sioux."

"Speak plain, man," Oscar pressed.

"Pawnee on foot are likely to be more amenable to trade. If it was the Kiowa-Apaches, they would be dead. If it was Lakota-Sioux, *we all* would be dead by now," he explained.

"Well this is just great," the nun huffed from several feet away.

"It's like they say: feathers on the head, you know you are dead, when it comes to the Sioux on these parts of the plains. So if they had to be taken alive by any group of reds, the Pawnee are your best bet that they remain alive. They might even be open to a bargain," the townsman finished.

"That settles it, then," Oscar said. "If we move swiftly, maybe we can cut them off before they make it to wherever they are taking them."

He did not wait for a response from Luke or anyone else who might be inclined to offer their opinion. Instead, he whipped his horse around by the reins and rode hard in the direction of the flattened grass that showed where a group of humans had recently walked through.

I'll fight the Pawnee, Apaches, and even the Lakota-Sioux all at once before I will let anyone take away the moment I've spent many weeks in pursuit of, he thought.

Then he rode forward with all of his horse's might.

•

Hodges and Phreddie had been sitting in an uncomfortable silence since Dark Tree left them.

"Did you hope to lure me the way you lured Oscar's brother, Remy?" Hodges asked bitterly at last. "To trick my mind and then my body?"

The words stung, and Phreddie sat there in her shame, chewing her lip and herself up for her recklessness. "I told you," she said, her voice just barely loud enough to be heard over the crackling of logs on the fire. "I had planned to break it off with Remy, but things just got out of hand. Like they seem to have done again . . ." She trailed off.

"Next thing you know, you'll tell me that you didn't just humiliate Remy, so much so that his big brother chased you across the United States because of how you turned his little brother into a broken man, but that you killed him too," Hodges spat.

She stared at him, her eyes filled with fear and sadness.

"Wait." His jaw fell open. "No way. I was just saying that to hurt you, but . . . no. Is that why Oscar's the one following you and not Remy?"

She gave no answer.

"Well that's just great." Hodges began to pace. "I thought he was just too embarrassed. But, jumpin' Jehoshaphat! You've been giving me shit for days about killing my wives, and here you are the one who actually killed their old man."

"No . . . no, it was an accident," Phreddie stammered.

"I bet," he said bitterly. "A man marries a woman, finds out she has a pecker, maybe even one bigger than his own, and it's an accident when he winds up dead? Yeah, right."

His words poured like ice water over Phreddie's head, and they sent a shiver down her spine.

Silence returned again as Hodges began to pace to and fro on the other side of the divided space. Then he suddenly stopped moving and turned toward her. "That's the thing I don't get," he growled. "If you meant to end it with Remy,"—he began to move toward her—"if it was an accident, as you say . . ." The gap was closed in three steps, and he reached down and grabbed her shoulders. "Why didn't you just stop it all before it got that far?" he bellowed, shaking her violently.

Phreddie felt her neck swing back and forth with the force of his grip. He flung her around with ease, and she allowed it. There was no fight left in her, so back and forth her limp frame went. She let his violence punish her, and she accepted his sentence, hoping the end would be quick and that he would snap her neck. Hither and thither, Phreddie surrendered.

At least until the fifth or sixth time that he jostled her.

Then at last something did snap, but it wasn't her spine. It was something inside. Her mouth opened, and she released a slight moan of wakening that grew into a piercing roar, almost like one heard during a pang of birth. It was as if the veracity of Hodges's anger had cracked a rib in her chest, and that through that one small opening, a piece of Phreddie, unknown to her until that moment, had broken free.

Her body stiffened and her shoulders squared. This feeling of him on her like this chafed like sandpaper on silk, and it forced a furious scream to rise up in her throat. "Because I never felt loved before!" she bellowed back as she threw him off her with great fury.

The tall man fell two steps backward.

"All of my life, I have been alone," she began to rail. "My own mother placed me in the hands of that horrible head sister at the orphanage!"

Now she was the one pacing back and forth, and her eyes could no longer see the man who looked on in terror just outside of her line of vision. All Phreddie could see were shades of yellow and red, like the fire that glowed nearby or the one that had burnt down Hodges's homestead. Yet neither of these carried the force or the heat that had been building up inside of her for as long as she could remember.

"I spent years being bullied and abused by Sister Adrienne, who made me into her personal slave," she continued to rant. "That woman would have the other children call me names, and once she even had them pin me down and pull up my skirts to point and laugh."

She stopped and turned to him. "Do you know what that feels like for a child? Or what it's like to be alone—always and forever?" Punctuating her words with accusation, she let the question hang in the air. "Any clue how you might act when you are finally shown even the tiniest speck of love?" She pointed at him.

He stared back at her, his mouth open, but no response came forth.

"I wouldn't expect you to," she spat. Phreddie began to wag her finger in his face. "You see, men like you, they look at my face. They look at my figure, and they find it comely—beautiful even."

Spittle shot from the sides of her mouth, and at that Hodges took another step back, but Phreddie took one forward.

"It's true." She nodded. "And when they look at my heart"—she lowered her voice—"they find it sweet and appealing."

Hodges looked uncomfortable as she stepped forward yet again.

"And when they look upon my body," she said, her voice now seductive, "my entire body . . ." She moved her hands over her hips and swayed. Then she leaned her head in closer to his face and screamed, "They find it appalling!

"All women want to be loved—and I *am* a woman!" Phreddie declared loudly. Her chest heaved up and down, and she stepped back to catch her breath. She was warm now, so she lifted the back of her arm and ran it across her forehead.

After a few seconds, Hodges responded matter-of-factly, "Well, deception is often a demon worse feared than the truth."

She shrugged. "Says the man who everyone thinks killed both of his wives."

Hodges inhaled a gulp of air. Phreddie turned away and started to walk back to the other side of the enclosed space.

From behind her, she heard him let out a guffaw. "I suppose that comment was fair play," he said, laughing nervously.

Phreddie released a loud sigh, and they both went back to silence. When she reached the bed platform, she sat back down and placed her head in her hands.

"One last question," Hodges said, voice softer now, as she heard his feet shuffle closer.

She sighed again. "Go ahead."

"How exactly did Remy die, then?"

Phreddie pulled her hands from her face and looked at the fire. Her gaze followed a patch of smoke that wafted up and traveled through the small hole at the top of the lodge. *Freedom,* she thought to herself. *The ability to rise and escape, unchallenged, into the air and out into the universe.* She wished she were like that smoke, as she recognized in that moment that no matter what she did or how far she went, she would never be free of herself.

"He died from the truth," she said softly at last. "My truth."

•

Phreddie had just finished. For the last hour or so, Hodges had sat silently and listened while she told him everything. She began with the orphanage, her life at the hands of the vicious nun who had brought her up. Then she'd moved on to Mrs. Guidry's, her first encounter with Remy, and the courtship. After some time, she spoke about their wedding, followed by the somewhat remarkable nature of Remy's death. At last she shared all that had transpired in the nearly two months since she first fled New Orleans. She didn't leave a thing out, from the moment she pulled the wooden stake out of Remy's throat until the very second that she was sitting here with him now, somewhere in the Kansas Territories, in a Pawnee village.

Her physical nature might have made him uncomfortable, and it confused him to no end, but damn it to hell if Hodges didn't have some kind of admiration deep in his gut for this woman. *Is she a woman?* he wondered for a second. *I guess fuck if it matters at all.* He shrugged. *Phreddie Weaver, Smith, Delaroux, or whatever name she used, is one tough person.*

For all the lip chewing, wide-eyed glances, and cries of frailty she'd claimed came down to modesty, few could have survived what Phreddie had been through, and for that Hodges felt she'd earned at least some more respect than what he had shown her.

"All I wanted was to feel like any other woman," Phreddie said, "and for a brief moment, I did."

Her tale now over, Hodges contemplated what to say next. Just as he opened his mouth to speak, two Pawnee women entered carrying stacks of clothing.

"*Tii*," the older of the two said as she placed her pile next to Hodges. "*Tii*," she said again, pointing to the clothes.

Hodges nodded as she left.

"I think we are meant to put these on," he grunted. He laughed as he lifted a leather breechcloth off the pile and held it in the air. "What the hell?"

Phreddie started to giggle. "Sorry," she said, putting her arm over her mouth to stop herself from laughing.

Hodges used his foot to push through the rest of the pile, which included some leather leggings. "Ain't fuck all here for me," he complained.

Phreddie lifted up a long buckskin dress. "Wow," she said as she admired the garment.

"You'll be well covered, though." He chuckled, then shrugged. No point offending his hosts, as they could have easily slit his throat hours ago. If wearing next to nothing meant staying alive, he might just as well get to it.

So Hodges turned his back on Phreddie and stripped his clothes off, then redressed in the loincloth and leggings. When he turned back around, Phreddie was almost breathtaking in the dress, whose skin had been bleached white. All across the chest was intricate beadwork in white, red, and yellow.

She smiled at Hodges, and they both chuckled at what they were wearing.

"Ah," said the woman who had brought them their clothes, leaning her body into the void. She waved her arm for them to come with her.

Hodges motioned for Phreddie to go first, and as he followed behind, he noticed how the dress hugged her curvy bottom. When they stepped outside the lodge, he was surprised to see that the sun had already set and a large moon hung in the evening air.

"*Páh,*" the woman whispered, pointing up at the bright disc.

Another woman tiptoed behind Phreddie and placed a necklace made of large blue beads around her neck. She backed away, and Dark Tree exited the lodge that they had left seconds earlier.

The chief was wearing a large feathered headdress, and he held his head up high. "You come," he said proudly, motioning them toward a large fire.

Around the flames that danced up high above their heads, Hodges saw many men with feathers in their hair, sitting in a circle. Behind them, women and children were seated on logs or standing around, and everyone started to sing in low hums.

Just beyond these people sat a trio of men each playing a drum, hitting them rhythmically with large sticks or their hands. Their instruments were all different sizes and covered with tight animal hides.

The native people smiled at Hodges and Phreddie as they were led forward and the drums crescendoed, then ended with one loud final gong all at once. A man who Hodges presumed to be some sort of shaman stepped forward. He was dressed in only a loincloth, exposing his old and wrinkled skin, which was painted red with some white markings on his face.

What seemed to be two acolytes stepped forward and placed over him the fur of a buffalo that had been skinned in one piece, situating on his head the head and horns of this animal that had once lived and walked the plains. The shaman then stepped closer and placed a small bundle wrapped in leather at Phreddie's feet.

"This our sacred bundle," Dark Tree explained.

Hodges watched as Dark Tree nodded to the shaman, who bent down and unwrapped its bindings to reveal a red clay pipe that had been intricately carved. On one end there was a small red bowl, and on the other a bear through whose mouth one could inhale the bowl's contents.

Dark Tree motioned to one of the acolytes, who brought forward a small pouch, which he handed to the shaman. The native priest then opened its clasp and reached in to pull out a pinch of dried leaves, which he placed in the red bowl.

Another acolyte stepped to the shaman with a lighted stick, which the shaman then pressed against the leaves as he held up the pipe and placed the bear into his mouth. He inhaled, and as he sucked in, the herbs lit up brightly and smoke began to puff out of his mouth.

"We make smoke," Dark Tree commanded. The shaman handed him the pipe, and all three religious men backed away from the fire.

The chief lifted the pipe to his mouth and inhaled deeply. He waited for a moment, then lowered it and exhaled a giant plume of smoke that wafted into the air.

Slowly, the drummers began to play again. Voices began to hum and chirp intermittently as Dark Tree passed the pipe to Phreddie and Hodges watched on in awe. He had heard many tales of Injun rites and rituals, but never once had he seen one. Here he was, so close to something that would have terrified him only a few hours ago, but all he could feel now was amazement at being let into their world.

Phreddie took the pipe from Dark Tree and hesitantly lifted it to her mouth. "I'm not sure," she said as it closed in on her lips.

"Truth-teller smoke," Dark Tree said firmly. "Then we dance to *Páh*, for she alone created *Ckússat*, or *Berdache*."

Dark Tree stared resolutely at Phreddie, so she acquiesced and took a puff, then bent over coughing as trails of smoke escaped her mouth. Dark Tree smiled, taking the pipe from her hands and passing it to Hodges.

Hodges lifted it toward his face and caught a whiff of the smoking herbs.

The singing stopped, and everyone stared.

"Whoo-wee, that is pungent," he cried out, but the faces around him made it clear that to do anything other than smoke the pipe would be an unforgivable insult. "Here goes caution in the wind," he murmured to himself, then clasped his mouth around the bear's maw and inhaled deeply.

Dark Tree's grin widened, and the shaman rushed forward to collect the pipe, while the two other acolytes each brought forward treated logs for the guests to sit on. The singers began to chant, and Dark Tree lifted his arms up into the night sky.

"All life start in the heavens, and all life to the heavens return," he proclaimed.

The shaman began to undulate. Next he started to move his body to and fro in crisp jerking motions, lifting his hands up and down as if he were telling the tribe an ancient tale.

Dark Tree whispered to translate. "Our ancestors told it . . ."

The drums beat in staccato bursts.

"When we were in our mother's womb, the moon came, holding out two hands . . ."

The people began to chant in between the beats.

"In one, the tools of man."

More sounds erupted.

"The bow, the war-ax— warrior's weapons," Dark Moon said firmly.

Hodges looked over at Phreddie and saw that she was staring with great interest at the chief as he told the tale.

"In the other, the tools of woman," he said with great emphasis. "The quill, beads, a mortar."

The drums began to increase in speed, and the shaman's movements became wilder.

"Each person chose their wares, but one chose both . . ."

There was a loud sound, and in unison, the drums, singers, and shaman stopped, leaving only silence.

"Not all were man . . . or woman." Dark Tree continued to speak as the beats and chanting renewed, but this time low and slow.

The men who were seated around the fire got up and each grabbed the hands of a woman, who they pulled with them closer to the fire. Then they and the others clasped arms with the shaman and began to move in a circle around the fire.

Dark Tree started to speak again. "Only white man say this bad, but we *chahiksichahiks* know truth!" he testified into the air.

A woman and the shaman broke free from the circle and rushed at Phreddie and Hodges. The woman grabbed Hodges hands and lifted him to his feet, while the shaman did the same to Phreddie.

"That two spirits means one is blessed from heaven—twice!" Dark Tree shouted, and the people around the fire cried out to the moon.

Hodges and Phreddie were pulled into the circle, where they were dragged along. Round and round they went, and Hodges felt like he was going to faint as all seemed to blur, but instead he threw his head back and smiled up at *Páh*.

Each pass around the fire he slammed his feet into the dirt harder. The noise, and the colors, and the drums, they all seemed to shake his body, pulsing further and deeper into his soul. Before he knew it, he was holding hands with a woman on his right and Phreddie on his left, and he clutched Phreddie more tightly, for he found safety in her palm.

The drums became faster and the voices grew more frenetic, until it all exploded with one last sound. All movement ceased, and they stood there in silence for a few seconds. Then a group of giggling women rushed forward and pulled and pushed at Hodges and Phreddie, herding them toward one of the small earthen lodges off to the side.

"What's happening?" Hodges tried to protest, but he found himself laughing as much as they were, until at last he was shoved one final time into the void.

There he found himself in a small lodge, a fire burning in its center. Nearby was an earthen jug and skins laid out all around like bedding. He rubbed his head and looked over at Phreddie.

"What was in that pipe?" He chuckled, then stepped forward and fell down on the furs closest to the flames.

"I think he called it 'truth teller.'" Phreddie smiled back and sat down nearby.

Hodges watched as she picked up the jug and lifted its to her lips. She wrinkled her face and passed it to Hodges, who sat up and smelled it, then declared, "That's firewater." He considered for a moment, then continued,

"The Pawnee don't drink much, so they must have traded this with a white man and assumed this is what we would want most."

"Oh," Phreddie said. "I wonder why?"

"They think most of us are drunks." He chuckled again.

"Maybe they've been to Miller's," Phreddie retorted, and the two of them laughed.

Once the laughter faded, Hodges couldn't hold his question any longer. It was the one thing he had been bursting to know for hours now, ever since Phreddie's form had been revealed.

"When I saw . . ." he began with hesitation.

She looked at him with great big eyes.

"I mean, when you said, you know . . . you said earlier that you were . . . a-a woman. What did you mean exactly?" He had finally freed the words from within.

"Oh," Phreddie whispered, lowering her eyes.

Hodges looked on, as he did not wish to let the question go unanswered. He had to know, perhaps even understand something that he currently couldn't begin to grasp.

"Well, same as any other woman I guess," she finally responded.

"How can that be, though?" Hodges pressed gently. "When you say the same?"

She finally shrugged. "I have all the parts, just a little something extra."

Hodges sat there, unsure of himself. *I don't understand,* he thought. But he had seen it with his own eyes.

"How did it happen?" He shook his head as he asked this.

Phreddie threw her head back and laughed. "Same way yours did—in your mother's belly, I suppose."

When her laughter ended, she said matter-of-factly, "It's just how I was made."

There was silence for a few moments, and Hodges stared into the fire.

"Look." Phreddie stood up. "I could have been more honest about things, but—"

Hodges leapt to his feet and interrupted her. "Don't. I might have done the same thing if I had been in your position."

"Still," she continued. "These people, you, everyone has been more than generous with me, but I'll ask Dark Tree to lead me to the next town in the morning, and after that, you can return home and you will never have to see me again."

As she turned to walk to the door, she stumbled, and Hodges was there in a flash, catching her in his arms. He looked into her eyes and allowed the truth-teller smoke to release his feelings from his soul with abandon.

"I don't think I could live with that," he said, and he leaned in and pressed his lips against Phreddie's.

When they came up for air, she began to protest, but it was too late. Hodges knew that her words were futile.

They fell onto the hides and furs in a fit of smoldering passion, where lips and limbs were locked and bodies and spirits became one. There, they explored each other and discovered the power of *Páh*.

Nadine

The final embers of the fire in the small lodge glowed. Phreddie wrapped an animal fur around her neck. She looked over at the man who was snoring gently next to her. His naked shoulders peeked up from above the hides, but below them she could feel the warmth of his leg against her own.

A rush of adrenaline surged through her body as she remembered the way he had touched her in the hours after the Pawnee ceremony. There was a mix of fright and freedom in her being.

On the one hand, she had waited her entire life for someone to make love to her. There had been physical and emotional exhilaration in its realization. Yet she worried that now that Hodges had not only seen but felt her body, he would despise it. When he awoke and rubbed his eyes, would he hope to scratch away the memory of last night's sweet encounter? She felt she was once again standing on the precipice overlooking the river. Only this time, she did not expect that she would survive the fall.

As she began to fiddle her fingers, Hodges's eyes opened. Phreddie sat up and looked down at his face. She held her breath and pursed her lips in fearful anticipation.

"Ah." He smiled at her. "Good morning." Then he grabbed her neck and gently pulled her toward him and kissed her deeply.

Is this a dream? she wondered, but his hands moved lower, and his fingers pinched her nipples. Suddenly she did not care whether or not this was the waking world. His touch felt too good. So she relaxed her shoulders and threw her head back in a thrill as he slid on top of her and entered.

"I don't . . . care . . . what anyone . . . says," he moaned between gentle movements. "You are . . . all woman."

Phreddie didn't know if it was his words or the way his member hit up against her womanhood, but she moved her hands around to his bottom and squeezed. A thunderous rush gathered her waters, and they burst forth as release poured out from her urethra. Her thighs trembled again, and she yelled out a groan of pleasure that caused Hodges to erupt inside her.

Then he fell on top of her and they both gasped for air, and he kissed her on her lips and laughed. "I can feel it pressed against my belly," he said casually.

The weight of his body on top of hers meant that Phreddie could not wriggle away, though his comment made her uneasy.

"It's not big like mine"—she saw his cheeks redden—"but it's there alright."

Beads of sweat began to form at her hairline.

"I'm going to reach under and touch it," he informed her.

"No," she protested as his left hand slid down between them. Phreddie turned her head away from his gaze, but he took her chin in his right hand and stared into her eyes.

"Alright," she relented. She could feel the tips of his fingers as they made contact and then rolled her flesh in his hand.

He cocked his head to one side in thought. "And yet it has no function?"

"No," she whispered. A tear formed in the corner of her eye.

"I see no need to cry," he said as he released it.

"I am just surprised you are so understanding," she whispered, mist releasing from both ducts now.

Hodges shrugged. "My father had six toes on one of his feet." He leaned down and kissed her again. "Besides, the shock has worn off, and it just doesn't really seem to matter much at all now."

His head fell down on her shoulder, and Phreddie lay there beneath him. He felt warm, safe even.

"I saw a doctor once, after I had left the orphanage," she said. "He told me that he had seen one other person like me in his years. They had something resembling a man's egg purse without the shelled berries."

"Interesting." Hodges sighed and began to kiss the side of her neck. She could feel his member awakening again.

"The doctor said . . . oh . . ." He nibbled on her ear. ". . . that there are 'many forms and variations' . . . oooh . . . Well, that's how he put it."

"Oh yeah?" Hodges voice was husky now, and he moved his hand between their love nests once again, only this time he grabbed hold of his own attachment and guided it back into her warm spot.

"He said, well, he said that doctors . . . are . . . learning . . ." Her voice started to rise. " . . . that sex . . . and gender too, well they are just . . . not . . . just . . . not . . ."

"Phreddie," he said with great passion.

"Uh . . . yes?" she gasped.

"Shut up," he growled playfully.

And she did.

Not long after they had finished, a few of the women who'd escorted them to the lodge last night giggled their way back inside, bringing with them Hodges's now clean pants and pairs of moccasins for both of them

Phreddie's cheeks flushed when one of the younger women came up alongside her while she was still beneath the hides and smiled. *Clearly they know what we have done,* she thought to herself. The image of Sister Adrienne shaking her head and slapping a stick against her palm shouting about the evils of sin came to her mind and made her tremble. But the only person there was the sweet-faced Pawnee. Phreddie nodded shyly at the woman, who grinned and exited quickly.

Uncomfortable and even embarrassed by the realization that the entire tribe would soon know that she and Hodges had copulated, she quickly got up and pulled the dress she'd worn the night before over her head.

"Hey," Hodges teased. "What did you go and do that for?"

"We better . . . um . . ." She began to pace.

He jumped up out of the furs and walked over to her, putting his hands on her shoulders. "It's okay," he said softly.

Phreddie looked into his eyes. "It's just that I never . . ." Her voice faded.

"And now we have," he answered gently. "And I'm still here." He rubbed her back in reassurance. "Hell, if anything, I'm the one that should be amazed that *you're* still here!" he laughed.

"But don't I terrify you?" Her brow furrowed, and she held her breath for fear of his response.

"Yes," he said with a guffaw. "But not because of your body."

"Then how?"

"You terrify me because frankly I never know what you are going to say or do next." He laughed again, and this time his whole body shook. "But you excite me too, and to no end." Then he pulled his hands from her shoulders and grabbed ahold of both of her palms.

"Why do I feel so ashamed?" she whispered.

Hodges squeezed her hands. "Because all of your life you have been told that there's something wrong with you, when in fact there's more right with you than most folks." He wrapped his arms around her and drew her close against his body. "I'm just glad I wasn't damn fool enough to not let myself see it."

Phreddie released her fear and let herself fall into his embrace.

Finally, someone loves me, she told herself. And it felt beautiful.

•

The crack of what sounded like dozen or more rifles tore the peace right out of the morning air.

"You are surrounded," Hodges heard the voice of Oscar Delaroux call out from beyond the lodge. His body stiffened, and he released Phreddie from his grasp.

"Oh no," she cried as he quickly pulled his pants on and shoved his feet into one of the pairs of the moccasins the Pawnee women had delivered.

"Get dressed," Hodges ordered her as he skulked to the lodge door and peeked outside.

"There are many of us, and we will not rest until we take possession of that woman!" Oscar's voice broke through earth and sticks until they penetrated not just the lodge, but Hodges's soul.

Phreddie began to tremble. "What do we do?"

"Shh," he scolded her, trying to think.

"I want Phreddie!" Oscar's yell reverberated again.

Hodges peered outside. It was midmorning now. The sun was already halfway through its ascent, casting its light down on what looked to be half a dozen or so gleaming rifles and shotguns from Hodges vantage point.

The voice of Dark Tree called, "We have no Fr-e-dd-ee in village," but more gunfire erupted at these words.

"We know you have two white people with you, and we will not leave until you give us both!"

"Nadine?" A woman's voice sounded from near where Oscar's had.

Hodges turned to Phreddie, who tilted her head to one side. They shrugged at each other in confusion, as neither of them were named Nadine.

"Quiet," Oscar reprimanded the lady loudly. "Take that woman away from here!" he yelled to someone else.

Hodges poked his head back out and surveyed the scene again. From where he was standing, they did indeed look surrounded.

"We will burn this entire village to the ground in only a minute unless you give us the white man and the woman you harbor inside."

Hodges turned back to Phreddie. He grabbed her shoulders and squeezed. "I never thought I would feel this way again. Goddamn if I ever felt quite *this* way at all, if truth be told, and I truly loved both Alice and Lily."

Phreddie squinted. "Why are you saying this to me like that right now?" she asked, pulling her head back with suspicion.

"You have your whole life ahead of you," he continued.

"Wait . . . what are you doing?" Her voice began to rise.

"Now you just stay here," he ordered. "Once I'm gone with them, you get Dark Tree to take you to a different white town, not Newton. Someplace from where you will be able to make a run for it." He released her and began to slowly back away.

"No," she protested frantically. "Don't you even think of going out there alone!"

Hodges put his hands up to stop her from following. "Now you do as I say. I had the chance to experience this not once or twice, but apparently three times. I only hope that you get every bit of the love you have coming to you still in this life."

He turned on his heels to go. From the corner of his eye, he saw her lurch forward, but he wheeled back around once more and whispered, more firmly this time, "Stay!" Then he left.

Once out in the morning air, he stepped into the center of the village, right where he had danced around the fire under last night's full moon.

"Phreddie ran away," he shouted, his hands up in the air.

Many Pawnee women were standing around holding onto their children closely, fear in their eyes. Oscar approached from up on the hill and rode toward them with his gun pointed at Hodges's chest.

Hodges looked around and noticed that none of the Pawnee men were present. Except for the approaching figure of Dark Tree, he saw no evidence of protection against the white mob that surrounded this village.

"We are peaceful people," Dark Tree stated firmly. "Do not want war."

"Nor do I," Oscar sneered from atop his horse. "So tell me where's that damn woman, and we will be on our way."

"I told you," Hodges barked. "She ran off."

Oscar guffawed. "You think me an *idiote*?"

"Well," Hodges started to say, then thought better of it and closed his mouth.

One of the men with Oscar yelled out, "There's a group of warriors coming on horseback about half a mile east."

"*Merde*," Oscar huffed. He moved his gun over until it pointed at Dark Tree's chest. "I'll blow your red head off, *putain d'indien*!"

Hodges stepped forward quickly, positioning his body between the barrel of Oscar's gun and Dark Tree. "Look, she's gone," he said plainly, his hands in the air. "And right now for all I care, that damn Phreddie can die on the plains. She's a deceitful liar, just like you warned me."

"Hmm." Oscar studied Hodges's face.

"Hey," Hodges challenged him, "you wanted someone, so take me. I have had it with women, period."

"They're getting closer," Luke called out.

Hodges watched as Oscar's eyes seethed with fury. "*Baise-moi*!" Oscar screamed into the air, and Hodges could only imagine what that meant.

"Fine," he barked at Hodges, then lifted his head and shouted so that if Phreddie was still there, she would be able to hear him. "But know this, Phreddie—I will take this man, Monsieur Hodges, prisoner, but I will execute him tomorrow at noon exactly if you do not turn yourself in to me in Newton."

One of his men rode up and got down from his horse.

"I will let him go, though, if you hand yourself over to me to be taken as a prisoner back to New Orleans," Oscar yelled.

The voice of Ms. Ortiz from on top of the hill began to carry on the wind. "What do you mean let him go? That man killed my sister!" she screamed, but Oscar ignored her.

The man pulled Hodges's arms behind his back and tied him up. Hodges caught Dark Tree's eyes and nodded toward the small lodge. Dark Tree nodded back gently, and Hodges sighed, knowing that whatever happened, these Pawnee would see to Phreddie's safety. It was all that he could do for her for now.

Then Oscar's man shoved him up on a horse and got on its back behind him. As they started to ride away, he heard Oscar shout back to the village, "How many men must die because of your lies, Phreddie? Because of your deformities? You already killed my brother. My man Landy and men with families who rode out from Kansas City are in the dirt on your account. Will you have this man Hodges's blood on your hands too?"

With that, a small group of other men on horseback converged on Oscar as protection, and together they rode off south.

"I'll finally see you hang," Hodges heard Ms. Ortiz growl from his flank.

As they rode away, he turned his head slightly until he could see that, off in the near distance, half of the returning warrior group were riding into the Pawnee village. The other half turned and rode hard after Oscar and this group that were taking Hodges back to his death in Newton.

•

Grace Weaver walked up from a small ravine as she saw Oscar and his group of men go thundering by. Her mouth was open, but no sound came out.

"Fuck me!" she heard from behind her, and she turned her head to find Sister Adrienne trying to pull her robe down over her hips as she ran out from some trees.

Grace didn't know which shocked her more, the fact that Oscar appeared to be riding away or the foul language that came from the sister, who had insisted she follow her into the woods to urinate rather than stand by and watch Oscar shoot up the entire Pawnee village.

"He left us," Sister Adrienne yelled frantically. "And he took our god damn horses too!"

"But you insisted we go on this break to urinate," Grace said in disbelief.

"Yeah, but it was not me who pissed," she replied in anger. "It was that damn Frenchman, and he showered it all over us."

"Even Ms. Ortiz has left us," Grace continued.

"Never trust anyone who is that religious," Sister Adrienne retorted, then stomped her feet on the ground. "Now what do we do? We don't have a way to get back."

Grace shook her head.

"Well, fuck me twice," Sister Adrienne shouted anew.

"Your language, Sister," Grace shrieked.

"Oh, the hell with this," the nun snapped back.

"Women of the cloth do not speak like this!"

Grace looked on in shock as the sister pulled the habit off her head and released a wild mane of brown locks. "I am through pretending, and

I'm through with this shit," she screamed as she tossed it into the ground, where she stepped on it over and over again. "All because my father caught me with him. I never wanted to be a damn nun, and I certainly never wanted to be here with you!"

Then Sister Adrienne looked past Grace, and her jaw fell open. Grace followed her eyes across the open plains and saw that the Pawnee warriors who had made chase after Oscar had slowed down and instead turned their horses. The group now charged at the two women with breakneck speed.

Grace raised her voice at Sister Adrienne. "Do something."

"Like what?" she said, fear in her voice.

"I don't know—pray!"

"Jesus Christ," the nun cursed, but it was too late for prayers. The warriors had them surrounded in less than two blinks.

Grace trembled with fear as the natives marched them at arrow point back to the village a few stones' throws away. As they came over the hill, she saw a great many Pawnee, who were gathered around their chief. Grace started to faint for fear of what was to happen to them, but Sister Adrienne grabbed hold of her and slapped her face hard.

"You brought me to this native hell, and you will not take the easy way out through unconsciousness," she scolded before she shoved Grace back to her feet. "At least not until you have given me my money and I have found a way out of here."

They were moved near a circle of rocks that surrounded ash and bits of char from a large fire that had now grown cold.

Grace's lip began to quiver in fear as the tall chief stepped forward. "Oh please," she started to beg. "Don't kill me . . ."

The chief's hand went up to silence her, then he turned to one of the tribesmen and gave some sort of command. Grace's knees began to shake uncontrollably as her mind raced with all of the terrible ways she imagined the final moments of her life were going to feel like.

They are going to peel the skin off the top of my head! she thought to herself.

But the man walked away from the chief, and as he returned, Grace could swear he was smiling at her. Then he stepped aside, and from behind him came a sight Grace had longed for but had hardly imagined would be granted to her in a moment such as this.

"Nadine?" she asked tentatively as a white woman in a long, beaded dress, who looked remarkably like her own mother, stepped out from an earthen lodge.

•

The woman with raven hair fell onto the ground. "Nadine." The stranger sobbed, and Phreddie looked down at her with great confusion.

"Do I know you?" she asked tentatively. It was like looking through white bed sheets that were wet and thin after you had boiled, scrubbed, and hung them out to dry. Vague shapes were visible, but their forms were not fully identifiable.

Something is there, but what? Phreddie's mind asked her.

"I have waited more than fifteen years." The woman was crying hysterically, crawling on her knees toward Phreddie's moccasined feet.

"Who are you?" Phreddie's mouth twisted at the corners.

"It's me, Grace. Grace Weaver—your mother. Oh, please forgive me," she begged.

Phreddie looked in confusion from the woman on the ground up to the Pawnees, who had moved in closer to watch.

"Please, Nadine . . ."

"Why do you keep calling me that?" she asked.

"It's your God-given name," the woman who claimed to be her mother replied.

"Ha," spat a voice in the crowd. "Anything *but* God-given."

That's when Phreddie saw her. In between two warriors was the face of the one person she had hoped to never see again.

"You!" she lifted her finger in accusation and bellowed.

All of the native people turned their heads in the direction of the nun. Sister Adrienne's eyes spread open, looking as wild as her freed hair, when she saw the Indians' faces change from curiosity to anger as they realized that Phreddie was not happy at this meeting.

"What are *you* doing here?" Phreddie's voice rang out.

The sister's feet shuffled. "I . . . I brought you your mother," the nun said sheepishly.

Phreddie's finger fell to her side. "But why?" she asked. "And how did you even find me?" She looked back down to the woman on the ground.

"It was my fault," Grace sobbed. "I made this horrible woman take me to where you might be. I was desperate."

"Desperate?" Phreddie's head hurt from the lack of understanding. "Why would you wish to find me after throwing me away for all of these years?"

"Oh, Nadine." Grace's tears stained her slippers. "He took you from me. He told me he that he would have you killed if I tried to contact you. And now . . . he's dead!"

As this stranger fell over weeping, Phreddie knelt down next to her. "You mean you didn't want to give me away?" Her voice could barely be heard over the woman's cries.

"Never," her mother wailed, then she grabbed Phreddie by the neck and squeezed. "Oh god . . . I just want you back!"

Phreddie hesitated for a moment, then put her own arms around the woman who claimed to be her mother. Deep wails and tears broke forth from mother and child alike, and they squatted on the ground for a moment, rocking back and forth. All around them were smiles as the Pawnee women held their own children closer. While Phreddie knew they did not understand the words that were exchanged, the sentiment was obvious. A family reunion had just occurred.

At last, Phreddie regained her composure and got back on her feet. She then helped her mother up as well.

"But how did Sister Adrienne know that I was in Kansas, nevertheless a Pawnee village deep in the central plains? This is, well, remarkable!"

She stared hard at the nun, who had taken the distraction of the reunion as an opportunity to back away some from the warriors. Sister Adrienne suddenly turned as if to run, but an arrow shot out and landed directly in front of her feet, and this appeared change her mind.

"I . . ." she began to stutter. "He, that Frenchman, he made me tell him—"

"Tell him what?" Phreddie pressed as she stepped forward. "What exactly did you tell Oscar Delaroux? I should have known that you would have had some kind of hand in all of this."

"I only provided him with background knowledge."

"You mean you outed my personal business to him, obviously for some kind of selfish gain. Or was it just the joy of knowing that you could hurt me once again?" Phreddie spat.

"You are and have always been despicable." The nun's shouts were cut off by Phreddie slapping her across the face with her open palm.

The crowd gasped. Then there was silence as Phreddie glared at Sister Adrienne, who rubbed her cheek.

"I have never done a thing to you, yet you have the nerve to call me evil. Me? Evil? The poor child who you made sit on my knees holding both palms up for hours at a time, lest you beat me? The quiet one who you forced to make all of the other children's beds while you had them kick me? The small girl whose hair you would pull whenever I walked past you for no reason other than for sport? No. It's not me who is evil, Sister Adrienne."

"My poor Nadine." Her mother started to sob again. "If only I could have protected you!"

Phreddie turned back to her and smiled. "Knowing that you wanted me is more than enough to erase everything that has happened." She walked over and placed her mother's hands in her own.

"That's why I agreed to give her everything," Grace confessed.

Phreddie could feel the tension grip at her neck. "Give her everything of what?"

"If only she could lead me to you, I told her she could have all of the money I've inherited from your father's passing. I gave it all away just to have you near me."

The tightness fell off her nape first, then across her shoulder blades and down her spine. "You mean, you loved me enough to lose an entire fortune?" Phreddie couldn't believe what Grace was saying, but in her belly, she felt warmth. At last she knew her mother's love.

Dark Tree approached them. "What you do?" he asked Phreddie.

She released Grace's hands and looked at the chief. "There's only one thing I can do," she said plainly. "I will turn myself over to Oscar tomorrow so that he will release Hodges."

Her mother gasped loudly. "No!"

"I have to," Phreddie said calmly.

"Oh you can't, Nadine. I only just found you." She sobbed, but her protests did not move Phreddie.

"In one day, I have known the greatest of love not once but twice. Impossible odds, but somehow they have appeared. Remy died at my hand because I pulled the stake out of his neck, though I only tried to save him. And for that, I will give myself over to Oscar and die content with my mother at my side." She smiled. "Really, I could not ask for any more than I have gotten today."

Dark Tree nodded that he understood. "*Chúsaat* brave. *Chúsaat* have honor. I give you horse to ride when the sun return on the morning sky."

"Thank you." Phreddie nodded. "Until then, let me enjoy every minute I can with the mother I have been denied all of these years." She put an arm around Grace's shoulder. "Even just one night is more than either of us ever thought that we would have together. So no tears," she said as she wiped her mother's eyes with her free hand.

"Well, what the fuck about me?" Sister Adrienne shouted.

Phreddie turned back to her in great surprise. "Oh, I thought I was the only one you let hear how you really speak," she mused. "If only the church leadership was aware of your tongue—or of the silver and gold that you have hidden beneath the floorboards you had me mop each day."

"Yes, that's right, you horrible creature. And I demand to be taken away from you and this heathen village so that I can enjoy the spoils of my years with you and be rid of all of you Weavers at long last!" the nun spat.

"I can't help you," Phreddie said. "It's up to these Pawnee if they want to give you a horse to ride back to town on."

Suddenly, Sister Adrienne lunged at one of the native children, grabbing them away from their mother and putting her arm around their neck.

"What are you doing?" Phreddie asked with alarm.

"Guaranteeing myself safe passage," she hissed. Then she turned to the tribe and shrieked, "I will kill this child if you do not take me back to town."

Phreddie looked at Dark Tree and raised an eyebrow in question. "She wants to leave," she stated.

"Take me back to Newton—now," Sister Adrienne demanded. "Only first, your mother over there is going to sign the paper that gives me what I am due!"

Grace took a folded sheet out of the pocket in her dress and marched over to the nun. "Here, you—you—you . . . bitch!" she said as she slapped the document giving up the Weaver fortune right into the nun's free hand.

"We ride woman to where she belong," Dark Tree told Phreddie.

"See?" She sighed at the sister. "They are taking you, so you can let the child go free."

Sister Adrienne smiled, then released her grip and pushed the youth away from her with a laugh. "I guess these fools can be negotiated with after all." She chuckled.

Phreddie turned to Dark Tree. "I guess if I've got only one night left, I certainly don't want to spend it with her."

Then she took her mother and guided her into the small lodge where she had made sweet love to Hodges only a short time earlier.

•

Sister Adrienne held on to the mane of the horse with one hand while she clutched the signed paper that Grace Weaver had given her even tighter with the other. *At last I can leave this life behind!* She laughed with abandon. *I will depart on the next train out of Newton and head to New Orleans to collect my belongings.*

She was filled with glee and thoughts of the rich life that she was about to live. She could almost taste the French champagne and feel the lips of her lover, who would be even more attractive than the lusty Oscar Delaroux, whom she'd longed to bed but had failed to.

Surely we must be getting close by now, she mused as the small group of warrior men led her over yet another rolling hill. When they reached the top of this one, though, she could see another band of Indians about half a mile away across something of a valley.

The horses stopped, and Sister Adrienne looked on as the chief began to talk in his native tongue.

"What's he saying?" She turned to the man nearest to her, but he did not answer.

A few more words were exchanged and then grunts of approval.

"We leave you here," Dark Tree announced as two of his warriors got down from their horses and began to pull Sister Adrienne off hers.

Her eyes bulged. "What do you mean leave me here?" Panic rose in her voice. "You told me you would take me back to Newton!"

Dark Horse shot her a sinister smile. "I say we ride woman to where she belong."

The two warriors leapt back onto their horses.

"But I don't know where this is," Sister Adrienne lamented. "Is the town close? And who are those men riding at us with all of those feathers on their heads?"

The Pawnee turned their horses away from her.

"Lakota-Sioux," Dark Horse called back as the warrior's steeds bucked and fled away.

A shiver ran down Sister Adrienne's spine. It was the dreaded name the townsman had warned Oscar about. *Feathers on the head, you know you are dead,* he had said.

"Wait," she yelled as she gripped her Weaver letter with all her might and ran after the Pawnee, but they were gone.

All she could do now was wait as the hooves she heard thundering in her direction grew louder.

•

They were like strangers. Phreddie held no memory of Grace Weaver beyond the tragic day she had been left behind as a small child. Well over fifteen years had passed, but somehow she knew this woman was exactly who she claimed to be. Maybe it was the way Grace nibbled the fleshy edges of her mouth, just as Phreddie did when she was nervous or in deep thought. Or perhaps it was just a feeling that existed only between mother and child.

"Tell me a memory of my childhood," she asked Grace at last. "I have none beyond the orphanage, and I would love to know if I was ever happy."

Her mother smiled at her. "You were the most curious of children." Phreddie cocked her head to one side, and Grace looked at her and chirped quickly, "Oh, by curious I don't mean strange. I mean you were inquisitive."

Phreddie relaxed her face. "Oh."

"Wherever I went in our home, you would follow after me, waddling on your chubby little legs." Her mother giggled. "And it wasn't just on account of you wanting to be close to your momma. No, you were always watching what I was doing and then trying to do the same. Like the time you saw me dab some perfume on my neck. I turned my back for not but two blinks of my eyes, and you had pulled the entire bottle down from up above and doused yourself head to toe. Oh, if the whole house didn't stink of clove and cinnamon sticks for a week."

Phreddie laughed along as Grace's shoulders heaved from a giggle fit.

Then her mother's face became serious. "Of course, your father refused to acknowledge your presence, so that night he had all to do not to sneeze from the strong smell. He sat with a wrinkled nose and a rag that he would pull up each time he was about to blow, and I was glad that he was made to be in discomfort. After all, he made the two of us uncomfortable with his loveless spite."

The lodge darkened, so Phreddie placed another log onto the small fire. "Why did you decide to name me Nadine?" she asked.

"On account of it means hope," Grace replied. "You see, at first George was a wonderful husband. He was doting, and our home was full of love. When I got pregnant, it seemed as if the world was smiling on us, and everything about our futures screamed that all was possible. I had asked my own momma to help me pick the name, and she told me about her grandmother and how, back in her time, they all believed that the name you picked told of the life you would have. Well, I just knew that life had so much in store for you, and I was full of hope. And there, but a few months later, you were laid across my breast, my little Nadine. Though your daddy turned his back, I knew that you had something worth believing in."

Phreddie wiped her cheeks. "I don't know what to say," she cried through a smile.

"I know exactly what you will do." Her mother grabbed her by the hand. "You will say your real name from now on. You are not now, nor ever have you been, a Phreddie. You are Nadine, and you still bring me hope—and I still believe in you."

The declaration filled the part of Phreddie's soul that had bled dry the day Sister Adrienne rechristened her Phreddie. "I am so happy that you found me," she blubbered.

"Me too, Nadine," her mother said, then she hugged her neck tightly. "Me too."

Independence Day

The smell of eggs cooking in pork grease carried on the wind. Hodges salivated from the small cell he had been placed in at the abandoned sheriff's station that sat in the center of Newton. From behind the rusty bars, he could see out of the glass-paned front door to a world of red, white, and blue.

". . . and at noon they're fixing to tie him to a horse pole and shoot 'im," someone said, their voice fading as they passed by.

". . . the fiddler came all the way from Memphis," said a woman.

"Wonder if he knows how to play a funeral dirge?" a man replied, laughing.

Hodges looked around for any chance of escape but couldn't find a one. So he lowered his head. "Snake's balls," he muttered.

He could hear more footsteps nearing, but these were not accompanied by the sounds of whispering voices. A key rattled in the door, and he looked up to find Ms. Ortiz, a plate of food in her hand and a smug look on her face.

"Eat up, Charlie Hodges," she said in a patronizing tone. "By this time tomorrow, you will be in an unmarked ditch, unlike my sister, who was beloved."

Hodges rolled his eyes, then grabbed the plate through the bars. He looked down, tore a piece off the toast, and used it to sop up some of the brown beans.

"And I bet that makes your rosary wet," he retorted.

"You bastard." Ms. Ortiz pounded on the bars. "I brought you this food out of Christian charity, but don't you think for one minute I cannot wait to see the eyes bulge out of your head when Oscar Delaroux spatters your blood all over Newton's Main Street!"

"At least I'll be reunited with your sister," he said between bites.

"How dare you," she hissed. "Where Lily is now is sweet reprieve, unlike the fires you are going to burn in, you cheap, murderous villain."

"See, that's what I always liked about you," Hodges teased. "You are shy and prone to hold your tongue."

Ms. Ortiz spun around and stormed to the door. "Oh," she said, pausing long enough to look back, "and you will die with the whole world knowing that your last act was to lay with a dirty berdache who is long gone from here by now."

The door slammed shut, and Hodges stopped chewing. *At least my sacrifice wasn't in vain.* He shrugged. *Dark Tree will have her halfway to the Dakota Territory by now.*

•

"Nadine," Grace whispered.

"I know that's what you call me, but I have been Phreddie for so long that I am afraid that I cannot think of myself as anyone else," Phreddie responded.

"And I cannot think of you as anything but."

Phreddie and Grace sat knee to knee on the lodge floor, having not moved a single step away from the village since last night. When the last of the blue corn mush was gone from their hardened hide bowls, Grace started to weep once more.

"If you had only listened to me, we would be far away this morning," she lamented. "I only just found you, and I am going to lose you all over again."

"I know." Phreddie patted her mother's leg. "But I can't allow another man to die on my account."

"But that man went willingly," her mother protested.

Phreddie smiled. "And I am willingly going to surrender."

"Why? If you didn't kill Remy on purpose, why would you give yourself in for a murder you didn't even commit?"

"Ki'sáawiš!" There was a shout from outside. "Ki'sáawiš!" The cry grew louder.

"I guess that's what they call love," Phreddie reflected aloud. Then she stood and helped Grace to her feet.

Once outside, they saw the entire tribe was excitedly gathered. Dark Tree turned to Phreddie and explained, "A warrior say buffalo there." He pointed over the hill. "We send warriors now to see. This mean we cannot take you to white man village. You must go on own."

A warrior came up to them with a single horse. "All others need for buffalo hunt," he explained as the animal was led to Phreddie's side. "You go now, two on one."

Phreddie was saddened that she had to make the journey without the company of the Pawnee, as they had come to mean so much to her in such a short amount of time.

"Thank you, Dark Tree," she said with deep urgency. "You and all of your Pawnee are family to me." She looked around at the villagers and smiled. "My brothers, my sisters, my children, mothers, and fathers." Her eyes settled back on the chief.

Dark Tree's mouth spread open, and he smiled brightly. "And you, Phred-ee," he said slowly, "you family."

"Oh no, Dark Tree," she corrected him with kindness in her eyes. "My name is not Phreddie." She looked at her mother and smiled. "My name is Nadine."

Grace radiated back at her.

"Nay-dee-nuh. Nay-dee-nuh," Dark Tree repeated. "May *Sakuru* give you warmth, may *Páh* give you sight, and may the *Huupírit* give you happiness, Naydeenuh."

"My oh my, this is wondrous." Grace slapped her palms together with joyous approval.

The chief pointed south. "Ride with river until you find five lakes. Then run to yellow fire, and keep it above your head. There, after many hours, you find Newton."

Phreddie looked on wistfully as Dark Tree walked away and joined the rest of the Pawnee warriors, who mounted their horses and rode off from the village. She climbed up on her own steed, then reached down and pulled her mother up behind her. The Pawnee villagers that had stayed behind surrounded the two of them, and many hands rubbed Phreddie's legs.

"*Kuutiriksibi. Kuutiriksibi*," the women, children, and elderly repeated over and over.

"Thank you and goodbye," Phreddie told them fondly, before the horse began to trot away from the village.

"I never knew the world was full of such interesting people," her mother said as they made their way out of the basin and into the wide-open plains that ran alongside the river.

After some time in silence, they saw a large black form laid out on the ground. As the horse neared, Phreddie could see a few thin, wild wisps of brown hair that remained along the brow line of a bloodied body that had been separated from its scalp.

She sighed. "I almost feel sorry for her."

Her mother hugged her from behind. "You're a better woman than me, Nadine Weaver."

Phreddie warmed at both the touch and the name. "I don't suppose she will have any need of that," she said plainly, pointing down at the crumpled paper that was still tightly clutched in Sister Adrienne's dead hand.

Grace Weaver inhaled a loud gulp of air. "Well I'll be."

"I can die knowing you won't be penniless in your old age at least," Phreddie continued.

"Small solace, though I am glad that horrible woman won't make use of your daddy's fortune, no matter how tainted his memory is to me."

"Ashes to ashes, dust to dust," Phreddie began to recite as they rode away.

Not long after that, they at last reached the five rivers and turned east.

•

The band had just finished playing "Lincoln and Liberty" when Oscar left Miller's Saloon. "Ahhh," he said as he closed his eyes to soak in the warm sun that beamed down on Newton from high above.

When he opened them again, he took in the scene. He discovered that overnight, the townspeople had set up chairs and tables all along dusty Main Street. There they now sat and stood. People of all ages and sexes partook in the merriment of food, drink, and conversation, surrounded by flags, bunting, and jubilant anticipation at what was to come in less than an hour.

A mother smiled at Oscar as she walked past him, her son happily chewing on a corn dodger. "Thank you for making our town safe, Mister," the tyke said, beaming as bits of fried cornmeal cake shot out of his mouth. Oscar smiled back and nodded to the boy, then turned and headed over to Luke, who was standing just outside the small sheriff's jailhouse. As he approached, his New Orleans man barely looked up.

He is really saddened by Landy's death. Probably even a little angry at Landy for behaving as he did, Oscar told himself.

"Morning," he greeted Luke gently.

"Uh-huh," was all he received in reply.

That is a bit icy. He considered things for a moment.

"I didn't want to kill him." Oscar felt compelled to explain, which was something he rarely did. "But I couldn't let him choke the life out of her."

"I suppose not," Luke answered weakly.

"I did warn him, and you know how Landy was when it came to women," Oscar attested, but this time curtly.

He decided this was to be the end to all conversation about Landy. There were things to worry about this midday that were of significantly more importance than one lecherous fledgling who'd disobeyed Oscar Delaroux at his own peril.

Not waiting for any response, he pushed past Luke and through the door. Inside, Hodges was standing in his cell, leaning against the bars.

"Maybe you were not that important to her," Oscar teased the imprisoned man. "It's okay, Monsieur Hodges. If Phreddie does not come at noon, I will kill you as promised, and then go out and find that berdache again all the same." Then he pressed his fingertips to his chin. "And if she does come, I still plan to kill you. Both of you, in fact."

"I expected as much," Hodges replied coolly.

"You have really pissed off the people here, Hodges," Oscar explained in a sing-song manner.

"Uh huh."

Hodges seemed disinterested, but Oscar was enjoying making sport of his prey. "Especially Ms. Ortiz. My oh my, what I've had to promise that woman was nothing less than your head on a silver platter to shut her up. So, you see, you have not saved either yourself or Phreddie with your noble sacrifice." He narrowed his eyes and grinned. "You only made things more . . . interesting."

Oscar ended with a laugh, realizing that he felt better today than he had in many weeks. *I always get what I want!* he thought to himself. Then he inhaled and filled his lungs up with the good Kansas air that was wafting in through the open door.

As children ran by the jailhouse, Oscar looked out, his eyes landing on the delightful iron cage that sat atop a wagon hitched just outside of the sheriff's office. "*Quelle journée glorieuse*," he exclaimed aloud, as today was indeed as glorious of a day as he could have hoped for.

It would not be long now. His contraption would sit empty only a little while longer, then the real fun would begin.

"*Quelle journée glorieuse*," he called out again.

•

Phreddie's skin crawled at the memory of the iron cage that had rattled behind Oscar and his posse when he'd first appeared at Hodges's homestead several days ago.

I wonder what he means to do with it. She bit her lip.

As the town of Newton appeared on the horizon, she stopped the horse and considered.

"Not too late to turn 'round," her newfound mother teased.

"The thought had entered my mind, I do admit it." Phreddie sighed and kicked at the horse, which trotted onward.

"It'd be best if I let you get off close to town and walk from there," she told her mother. "I don't think it would be wise for you to witness whatever is about to happen."

"Oh no," Grace protested. "I'll be right where my child needs me—there by your side."

Phreddie warmed at the thought of her mother being there at the end, no matter how terrible it might be. "I will ask Hodges to take care of you once I'm gone," she said. Then her mind wandered back to the narrow box and its suspended metal collar, and she shivered once more.

"Take care of me?" Her mother sounded surprised. "I'm the one with money. Maybe I should take care of him, seeing as he will be all I have left of you in this world."

Phreddie smiled in her heart at the thought of the two of them together.

It wasn't long before the horse's hooves crossed the town line, and Phreddie could hear hoots and hollers run up and down Main Street when her presence was noticed.

"She's here!" was the cry.

By the time she was at the center of the town, straight in front of the band stage, not even "Yankee Doodle" could drown out the chatter.

"You came!" Oscar shouted with glee as he walked out of a building to her right. A hush broke out at his words, and all eyes now turned to the two enemies.

"That's right. I'm here now," Phreddie announced. "So you can go ahead and let Hodges go."

A small trickle of laughter came out of Oscar's mouth. It grew until it was a roaring wave that bounced off all of the buildings. "Oh, no, no, no, *no*!" He tittered.

A man led Hodges outside, his hands tied behind his back. Ms. Ortiz walked up alongside of him, dressed in bright purple as if this were a wedding and she mother of the bride. She smiled at Oscar as Hodges was pushed out into the street.

"This is the day that the Lord hath made," she exclaimed to all.

Behind Phreddie's horse, Luke appeared, along with several of the townsmen she had seen from the safety of the Pawnee lodge yesterday morning.

"But you promised," she protested.

"I knew it," Grace Weaver lamented. "I just knew we were walking into a trap. Now you will both be dead, and I will have no one."

"You don't even know him though, Momma," Phreddie turned her head and said to Grace compassionately.

"I know that he was good to you, and that is enough for me to love him as if he were my own son," her mother answered, and all that Phreddie could do was beam sweetly at this kind woman whom she hadn't known existed until yesterday.

I wish I had gotten to know her.

"Did you think that you would come here like some kind of hero, Phreddie?" Oscar called out to her as he stepped closer. "That I would allow you to set the terms of this negotiation? Or that there would be any negotiation at all?"

"I thought you would at least be a man of your word," she responded.

He nodded at two men, who were upon her instantly, and they pulled her down from the horse by force.

"Let her go," screamed Grace as she kicked one in the back, but to no avail.

The two men dragged Phreddie toward Oscar, and they held her arms to her sides as she struggled to get free. Oscar took another step to close the gap and then grabbed her face in his right hand.

Phreddie could taste the salt on his palm as she looked through his fingers, which went up until they curved over the top of her head. He pulled his hand down and squeezed tightly on her jaw, then spit forcefully onto her forehead.

As his gob slid over her brows, she lifted her head up in defiance. "I did not murder your brother," she growled. "But sometimes I wish I had fought back, even hit him, for the way he reacted that night. Who could really blame me even if I had killed him after what he did to me?"

There were gasps across the crowd at her admission of motive. People started to run up and spit on her the way Oscar had done.

"Stop it," her mother yelled in anguish. "Leave my child alone!" She slid down from the horse and stretched her arms out between Phreddie and the mob as if to warm them off.

"And you," she looked to her daughter and implored her, "don't you dare say anything more!"

Phreddie would not be silenced anymore, though. "He turned violent on me, threatened to gut me with a stick just because my body looked a little different than what he expected," she tried to explain. "But my heart, my soul even, they were the same."

But the crowd gnashed back at her. "Murderer," one person yelled out.

"No," she begged at them. "It wasn't like you imagine. When Remy found out I had been made different, not on account of my own doing, but by birth, he tried to kill *me*. I did not try to kill *him*. I loved him."

"Liar," Oscar yelled. "You killed him because he refused to stay married to you once he knew what you were! You knew that if you could make it seem like an accident, you could keep not only his name, but the Delaroux money as his widow."

"That's not true, though," Phreddie cried. "How could I have taken any inheritance when I left him there—on the floor, dead—of my own free will? It's not like you say. I wanted nothing from him. I loved Remy."

"Loved? How can you love?" Oscar spit at her.

Phreddie sobbed quietly, more to herself now. "Why couldn't Remy just love me for me?"

"Enough of your attempt to elicit sympathy," Oscar screamed. "What I have prepared for you is too good for your wickedness." Then he pointed to the wagon. "Strip her bare and lock her inside!" he ordered his men.

Gulps and sounds of choking rang out from the crowd.

"Nekkid?" Grace worried aloud, with great panic in her voice.

But one of the two men tore at Phreddie's leather dress until Luke rushed closer. "Wait." He put his hand up to the men and turned to Oscar. "Why must she be removed of all clothing?"

Ms. Ortiz stepped up behind him in solidarity. "We must bring what is dark into the light."

"*Exactament*!" Oscar beamed at her. "It is because of the secret that Phreddie holds tucked away beneath her skirts that many men have died, including my own brother. Now, I want to put her where all can see so that no man can be lured by her falsehoods ever again."

Some in the crowd nodded, but others looked confused, even shocked. One mother grabbed her child by the arm and marched him away from the scene, exhorting him to "look away."

"It's okay, folks," Oscar said, trying to soothe the roiled waters. "If you prefer, first we can all watch Charlie Hodges's death, and by all I mean Phreddie, too! That is what most of you patiently waited for all of these years anyways, was it not?" Ms. Ortiz linked her arm in Oscar's. "Someone to come in and deal with the wife killer?"

"Yes," Ms. Ortiz excitedly answered.

"Well, I can give you that now, but afterwards? Afterwards I am going to dance around that naked devil all night to shouts of 'hip-hip' for our nation's birthright until the last firework explodes high over her shackled head."

People turned to look at each other, and light murmurs spread.

"I never knew this was your plan," Luke protested. "Why can't we just bring her back to New Orleans like she is now? Why must we do something so vulgar?"

"How can you do something vulgar to someone who is vulgarity itself?" Oscar preached, and while some around him nodded, there had been a noticeable change of atmosphere in the Newton air.

Yet as long as there was that twinkle in Oscar's eye, Phreddie knew he was incredibly dangerous. She didn't know if that gleam was a reflection of his happiness or the fires of hell themselves, but the spreading disapproval encouraged her to act, and as she could stomach Remy's fearsome brother no more, she pushed her neck out further in his direction.

"I challenge you to a one-on-one duel," she dared him defiantly.

Oohs and aahs echoed off the bunting.

"If I win, you'll leave Hodges and me alone, but if I lose, as all are witness to my vow here, I will go with Oscar. I will do whatever he says," she told everyone within earshot.

The people began to whisper and nod to each other in support of the plan.

"But you promised me that Hodges would be killed!" Ms. Ortiz yelled.

"For what?" Phreddie shouted.

"For Lily," Ms. Ortiz bit back.

"Charlie Hodges did not murder your sister, Ms. Ortiz. Cancer did."

More gasps were heard, and all heads turned to Lily's sister.

"But she was shot," Ms. Ortiz retorted.

"That is because she shot herself from the pain. She decided that she would rather take her own life than let you, or any of you"—Phreddie looked around at the townsfolk—"know how she was suffering."

"What?" people began to ask each other, but Ms. Ortiz stood frozen.

"How can that be true?" Her face scrunched up.

"And this man, the one that you want to kill so badly"—Phreddie lifted her chin to Hodges, who stood there in shock—"he didn't have the heart to tell you about the way Lily died. He would rather sully your opinion of himself than of your sister's memory, so he let you think whatever you wanted."

Ms. Ortiz looked back and forth from Phreddie to Hodges.

"It's true." The town doctor stepped out from the crowd. "At least it's true that your sister did have the cancer. Now, I don't know anything about how she took the bullet, be it by Hodges's hands or her own, but she made me swear never to tell anyone, especially you, Ms. Ortiz, about what was eating her up inside."

Ms. Ortiz's legs began to shake.

"And Alice?" a woman from the throng called out. "What about her?"

"No, don't," Hodges interjected, with sadness on his tongue.

Phreddie looked at him. "I have to. They have to know what happened to Alice and your baby, even if the retelling brings you pain."

Hodges hung his head, his hands still tied behind his back.

"Go on," someone pressed. "What happened?"

"Scalped," Phreddie said plainly. "Only this stubborn fool was too saddened to explain what had happened. So he let you all think whatever you wanted rather than risk crying in front of you when you asked about Alice and the baby's whereabouts."

There were loud gasps throughout the crowd.

"He even grabbed up on the priest, Father Milfken, as he couldn't share his pain—not even with him."

"Strange behavior," the old shopkeeper busybody said.

"Show me a man who's not prideful," Phreddie responded, and all of the women's heads began to nod in assent.

"True, true," she heard them mumble.

"Besides, if you think this man is an actual killer, do you suppose your sister would have married him so willingly?" Phreddie asked Ms. Ortiz.

The woman again looked back at Hodges, whose cheeks were wet. "I suppose not," she mumbled. "Lily was stubborn as an ox, but she wasn't near as dumb as one."

"Let the man go, then," someone shouted.

"But—" Oscar started to reply.

"No buts," a man said. "Hodges is innocent."

"That man didn't kill anyone," said another.

"Let him go!" The calls began to rise.

Tears welled up in Ms. Ortiz's eyes, and Phreddie watched as she walked behind Hodges and untied the ropes that held his hands together herself. "I suppose I was so white-hot with anger that I became the very sinner I claimed loudly to all that you were," she meekly told him.

Then she reached over and hugged him tightly. Hodges arms hung for a moment before he lifted them up and hugged his wife's sister back.

"I guess she had a wonderful husband all along." Ms. Ortiz smiled as she released him from her grasp. "By the sounds of it, Alice did as well."

"*Assez de cette merde*," Oscar screamed wildly at the townspeople. "My bloodlust will not be abated because you all have shown mercy to Hodges. This man shot me. This woman killed my brother. I want my vengeance," he howled into the air.

"Then take up my offer and fight me alone," Phreddie implored. "Let us end this madness once and for all."

"Do it," came the chants.

Oscar scoffed. "I am a man," he declared. "How can I duel a woman?"

"You have followed me across the United States and back on account of your claim that I am anything but a woman. Why would you not to accept this challenge now?" she countered.

Oscar sneered at her in silence.

"No," Hodges interjected. "Don't do this!"

Oscar pulled his gun out of its holster to dissuade Hodges from rushing forth to save his captive.

"You don't know tunk and tarnation about guns." Hodges stared at Oscar's revolver while he tried to reason with Phreddie. He turned back to her in panic. "Remember my barn? You couldn't hit Hodges by an acre!"

But she shook her head firmly, as she had made up her mind. "Doesn't that tip the odds ever more in your favor?" she looked at Oscar. "The chances of your success seem clear, or are you too afraid to risk it?"

I may not know how to shoot, she thought, *but when Oscar kills me with his bullet, it will remove all chances of my being taken back to New Orleans in that.* She looked past the man and placed her eyes on the wagon. *This time, I know that Hodges will be safe, as the whole town has heard my offer and pushed for his clemency.*

Oscar furrowed his brow, then declared, "I accept."

Phreddie felt relief flood her body, but then the terrifying realization that she was about to die registered in her mind.

The men who had been holding on to her let go.

"Alright," Luke called. "If this is what must happen, let's set the rules." He came forward and pulled his own gun out of its holster. "Fifty yards at a count of ten, then both open fire.

"Here," he said kindly to Phreddie. "You can use mine. I guess it's the least I can do after lying to you." Then he walked with her down the dusty roadway until close to fifty yards stood between her and Oscar.

Luke's cheeks reddened as they walked. "You know, you're not half bad. Oscar's my friend, but I don't know if you deserve all of this."

"Thanks," Phreddie replied. "That means a lot. Even though you aren't going to care for immigrant children." They chuckled softly together.

The people of the town parted until there was nothing but an open dirt-covered street between Oscar and Phreddie.

"You pull back the lever," Luke demonstrated for her, placing his hands over hers and helping her lift the gun. "Aim just like so"—he tilted it up—"and pull with your second finger here. Got it?"

"I guess." Phreddie nodded nervously, though she had no intention whatsoever of firing the weapon.

Then Luke left her and walked to the side of the road like the others, and she was all alone.

"Let us count to ten," Oscar shouted. "Then when you miss, know that I am going to shoot you right where your proper womanhood should have been had you not been born a freak!"

One last insult, Phreddie thought.

"Please don't do this," Hodges begged. "We could send for a magistrate or some kind of official to have a trial."

"Oh my baby." Grace Weaver wept and came to stand besides Hodges, gripping his arm.

Phreddie lifted her head up high. *I'm leaving them in the best situation that I can.*

"Let's go already, berdache." Oscar laughed.

"Guns lowered now, and the count begins," Luke called out.

"Ten," she said meekly as Oscar too bellowed the number across the void.

"Nine." Phreddie closed her eyes and mouthed along.

Images began to pass through her mind. There was Sister Adrienne, cackling while she beat ten-year-old Phreddie across the back with a broom handle. Landy now chased her across the New York City rooftops. There appeared the drunk men who harassed her in the night, followed by the look of disgust on Hodges's face when she was dragged from the water by the Pawnee. And last, she saw Remy's wild eyes as he ran across the bridal suite with a wooden stake in his hands.

"Four." Phreddie's mind turned to Oscar. She thought about the time he had placed his boot on the immigrant's head and how she'd shuddered when she heard the loud crack.

"Two." Finally, she remembered the day that he had arrived at Hodges's homestead.

"Phreddie!" Oscar had yelled after Hodges had turned him away. *"You cannot hide! I will get you for what you have done . . . I will get you for what you have . . . I will get . . . you . . ."* His words echoed inside her head as she opened her eyes and saw him standing across from her.

"One," the entirety of Newton shouted.

Shaking, Phreddie quickly pulled the pistol into the air, though her hands bounced around from both weight and nerves.

"I will get you," she heard Oscar whisper in her mind one last time. Then she gritted her teeth. "Like hell you will," she roared, and she unexpectedly pulled the trigger back with all of her might.

The gun kicked alive, and she was thrown back into the air. She wondered if she had been hit, but she didn't feel any pain in her body. There was a short whistle followed by a loud thud as her own bullet landed. Then Oscar dropped his unfired weapon onto the dirt and crumpled to ground in a heap.

"*Va te faire foutre*," he cursed the dust. "Fuck you!" He clasped his right arm in the same exact spot that Hodges had shot him only a few days back.

Phreddie watched Oscar struggle to sit up, and as it became clear that he would not be able to return fire, he lay back down in the dirt and screamed up to the sky.

"By rights, Phreddie has won," someone declared, and the town erupted into cheers.

Phreddie was stunned and did not move. Her mother ran over and hugged her frozen body and kissed her repeatedly on the cheeks.

In shock, Phreddie slowly walked over to Oscar and stood over him as the crowd closed in around them. "I'll say it again," she at last said softly. "I never meant any harm to your brother, and I would have been a dutiful wife for all of my days had he just given me the chance."

Oscar growled and looked up at Luke, who was standing alongside Phreddie. "I declare you my second so that you can take the shot for me since my gun never went off," he commanded him sternly. "And you kill this bitch!"

Grace's face fell. "But you can't . . ." she started to say, but her words faded.

Phreddie looked over at Luke, who stared back at her.

Then he looked down at Oscar. "Nah," he said plainly, "I don't think so."

"What?" Oscar railed with great surprise. "After everything I have done for you? You were nothing before I saved you!"

"It's like you said." Luke shrugged. "Two against one is not fair. Now one against one? Especially when one has already sent close to a dozen other men to kill her? Now that just seems like a fun time." Then he stepped right over Oscar's body and headed over to the band stage.

"I thank you to abide by the agreement," Phreddie said to Oscar, her hand extended, ready to shake his in gentlemanly sport. Oscar just glared at her palm.

She pulled it back and continued, "I hope now that you will return to New Orleans and leave me alone forever."

"I think that is quite a good idea," Ms. Ortiz declared, and stepped up next to Phreddie and locked her own arm into hers.

"So do I," said another woman, who stepped up and took Phreddie's other arm.

Then a cacophony of voices called out in support, and Phreddie found herself surrounded by the entire force of Newton, all standing behind and beside her. Her eyes at last landed on Hodges, who was next to the wagon in which they had meant to transport her away. He held a small torch that he must have found during the aftermath of the duel.

Hodges released a chuckle, leaned down, and lit the edges of the wagon on fire. "Anyone for a barbecue dinner tonight to celebrate?" he called out, and everyone laughed with merriment.

"Strike up the band." Luke lifted his fist in the air, and the fiddle led off a rousing rendition of "The Battle Hymn of the Republic."

Phreddie looked around at everyone talking and laughing with one another. She even spotted a few who were singing, and she thought to herself, *I belong somewhere at last.*

•

The next day, she watched from the window of Miller's hotel as Oscar walked up the steps and onto the train platform all alone. Then she saw steam on the horizon, and it wasn't but a minute before the squeak of brakes cried out into the morning.

Oscar turned his head and looked up at Phreddie. At that moment, Hodges came up behind her and put his hands on her shoulder. Phreddie lifted her own hand and placed it on top of one of Hodges's.

"That'll be the last of him," Hodges said as Oscar turned back and boarded the train.

"Now, what to do with the rest of my life?" She giggled, then spun her body around and looked up into Hodges's eyes and winked.

A whistle screamed, and the sounds of wheels rolling on the tracks behind her brought a smile across Phreddie's face.

"I have a couple of ideas . . . Nadine," Hodges said seductively.

Phreddie closed her eyes and let the feel of his lips against her own carry her away like gossamer across the plains on a light summer breeze.

Epilogue

Newton, Kansas

July 4, 1876

"He has syrup all over his face," tattled a nine-year-old girl in pigtails who was wearing a rust-colored dress.

"It's alright, darling," said her mother, who was wearing a light pink hat and was seated on a chair that had been placed in the dirt along Main Street. "Take him to your daddy—he's over by the saloon," she instructed as she bounced a little girl in a matching light pink baby bonnet on her knee.

"I guess you like corn mush. Well, at least your chin does," the girl admonished her four-year-old brother, taking hold of his hand as she marched him away toward Miller's.

Grace Weaver came up from behind the woman with two glasses in her hands. She handed a lemonade to her daughter, who thanked her and then took a large sip.

"You want some too?" she cooed as the toddler on her knee reached for the glass. Then Nadine Hodges chirped and tipped the drink to the little girl's lips and smiled as her daughter giggled at the sour taste.

"You really are an excellent mother," Grace attested as she took the empty seat next to her daughter. "The Lord only knows how, given that you didn't have me to model your parenting after."

The two women looked at each other and laughed.

Nadine glanced down the road to where Hodges had scooped up their young boy, and she admired from afar the way he wiped the child's face down with a wet cloth while their daughter hugged her daddy's leg.

Behind him stood a restaurant with the word *Nadine's* etched into the glass. To the right of it was the sheriff's office, with Luke standing just outside. He now wore a golden star, having been elected Newton's sheriff for ten years straight.

Hodges looked up from minding his son and caught his wife's eyes. In the back of Nadine's mind, she could hear Sister Adrienne admonish her with a scripture. "*You evil child,*" the nun had said. "*One day you will see the truth of your wickedness, and the truth will set you free.*"

She hadn't known what Sister Adrienne had meant at the time, but . . . *I suppose I do now,* she thought, *and Sister Adrienne was right. The truth did set me free.* Her mouth widened, and she became lost in Hodges's eyes, even from this distance. She pressed her lips together and she blew him a kiss.

I am home, she said to herself, and her heart overflowed with love.

Intersex people have existed since the dawn of time. There are many variations, and their traits can vary. One thing, however, remains constant: they are all human beings deserving of respect. Let us give thanks for the wonders and complexities of creation.

This book is by no means meant to be an authoritative description of intersex people, as it is a work of creative fiction. Instead, it aims to highlight the plight of anyone considered to be outside our limited accepted norms and to open us up to the reality of life across a spectrum.

Further, the language directed at or used to describe individuals and groups of people in this story are at times strong, racially charged, full of phobias, and may seem especially inappropriate in the twenty-first century. Please note, though, that any offensive words are meant to reflect the era in which this story takes place. They are also a tool used to highlight the ways in which we use both actions and language to harm each other.

I urge us all to love one another and celebrate the magnificence of humanity in all its forms, for it is truly glorious.

www.ingramcontent.com/pod-product-compliance
Lightning Source LLC
LaVergne TN
LVHW050641100826
845148LV00011B/1930